POLYGAMY

NORTH AFRICA

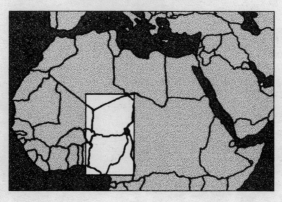

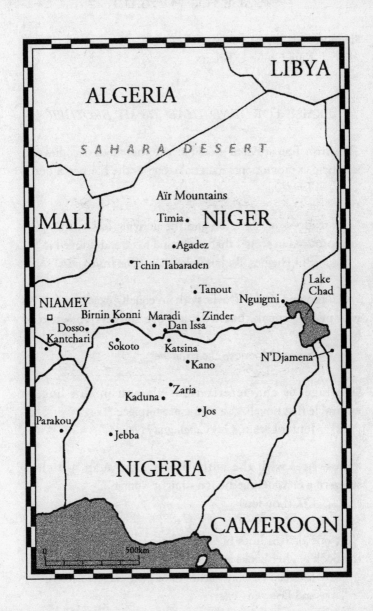

LIBYA

ALGERIA

SAHARA DESERT

Aïr Mountains

Timia•   NIGER

•Agadez

•Tchin Tabaraden

MALI

•Tanout   Nguigmi•   Lake
                             Chad

NIAMEY
□   Birnin Konni   Maradi   •Zinder
Dosso•   •Dan Issa
Kantchari
         Sokoto   •Katsina   N'Djamena•
                  •Kano

                  •Zaria
         Kaduna•
Parakou   •Jos

      •Jebba

         NIGERIA

                                    CAMEROON

0   500km

"If she continues in the same rich vein Shortland could well become to Cork what Maupin is to San Francisco."

Tony Lennard, *Thud* (London)

"New implausibles are established with increasing frequency in the ferment of Irish culture: here is . . . an Irish stew well seasoned with transvestism and alcoholism, not forgetting descriptions of gay sex that range from the bizarre by way of the hysterical to the transcendent."

Our Times (London)

PRAISE FOR *TURTLES ALL THE WAY DOWN*

"Mad entirely . . . dialogue to die for . . . This isn't one to read on the bus if you value your reputation for sober citizenship; on the other hand it could restore your faith in life, the universe and whatever you're having yourself."

Helen Byrne, *RTE Guide*

"Irvine Welsh should be taking lessons from Gaye Shortland. You'll laugh, you'll cry, you're unlikely to recommend it to your granny. She's not out spotting trains, she's in the driving seat, effortlessly achieving on every page a cocktail of loud music, rough sex and gritty prose that relegates Welsh and his mob to the anorak class."

Sinead Mooney, *The Examiner*

"I loved it. The true test, I suppose, is that while I was reading it at home, lots of times I actually cracked up laughing out loud on my own, so – thumbs up."

Pat O'Mahony, *The Daily Record*, RTE Radio One

POLYGAMY
A Novel

GAYE SHORTLAND

POOLBEG

Published 1998 by
Poolbeg Press Ltd
123 Baldoyle Industrial Estate
Dublin 13, Ireland

The Arts Council
An Chomhairle Ealaíon

A catalogue record for this book is available from the British Library.

ISBN 1 85371 852 1

Cover photography by Gaye Shortland
Illustrations by Sarah Farrelly
Cover design by Poolbeg Group Services Ltd
Set by Poolbeg Group Services Ltd in Goudy 11/14
Printed by The Guernsey Press Ltd,
Vale, Guernsey, Channel Islands.

A Note on the Author

Born in Cork, Ireland, Gaye Shortland has taught English literature at University College Cork, the University of Leeds, Ahmadu Bello University Nigeria and the Université de Niamey in Niger. She lived for fifteen years in Africa, spending much of that time with the nomadic Tuareg of the Sahara and eventually abandoning teaching in favour of managing a restaurant for the American Embassy in Niamey. She married a Tuareg and has three children. Now living in Cork, she is the author of two critically acclaimed novels *Mind That 'tis My Brother* and *Turtles All the Way Down*, both of which are available from Poolbeg.

To my Guiding Light
For all your courage, energy,
intelligence and generosity.

And to my cousin Nicky
Who remembered me
And paid Janis Ian's passage.

"Let's drink a toast to those who best
Survive the life they've led . . .
It's a long, long time till morning
So build your fires high.
Now I lay me down to sleep
Forever by your side."

Tea & Sympathy, Janis Ian

PART ONE

Chapter One

So here I am at last, facing a blank screen, my breath coming short. The screen is the blank surface of a pool. I am afraid of the plunge. I can't remember what's under the surface. I haven't swum in a pool or lake or the sea since I came home from Africa. I say it's the cold.

I told a friend that I have shelved my life – that it's all there stowed away in the subconscious, waiting to be dealt with sooner or later. He was in the process of moving house and he said, "Leave it there – that's what the subconscious is *for* – it's like our attic – you can keep throwing stuff up there but, Jesus, you can expect chaos if you try to bring it down again." I thought, that's marvellous – that's original thought in a world of cliché. *Don't bring the stuff down.*

But he did clear his attic. Maybe I'm moving house. *"Shall I at least set my lands in order?"*

There's the blank surface. How to take the plunge?

Maybe I could start as I did last year when I wrote a short story:

"Last night I dreamt I was putting a young girl into bed beside my husband. We were here, in Ireland, but she was African –

3

brown-skinned and slender with hair cropped close to her skull.
Though she was naked, I was unsure whether her breasts were
developed or not. But I'd been told often enough that it didn't
matter: fucking would make them grow. What hurt me was the
way she nestled close to him, her head on his shoulder, as if it
were the most natural thing in the world, and the way he folded
an arm about her in the same inevitable way . . . "

That was a powerful start. A bit mannered, granted – but
powerful.

Not true, though. I don't have any husband here and I
don't dream about Africa. That attic is firmly sealed off.

Besides, I already knew how the completed pattern
would look when that small rug was woven. I don't know
now what will emerge. But I can see the colours . . .

⚔⚔⚔⚔

I can see Khassim standing in the small bathroom of my
bungalow in Samaru, Zaria, northern Nigeria.

I had come home from the university that day and
parked under the flame-tree, eyes scanning the house for
any small signs of excitement, any clue that Rhisa was
back from Niger.

Nothing. My baby-nurse Amina, a local girl, waved a
hefty black arm at me from where she sat on the porch-rail
lazily pitching groundnuts at lizards, swinging her sturdy feet
in their white plastic sandals, my sleeping child on her back.

No Rhisa. Again, no.

Wearily I climbed the steps to the porch.

"*Sannu*, Kate!"

Amina took my books and bag from me with a little

curtsey-like bob, teeth gleaming in her very black skin, Minha stirring a little against her cotton-print back as if she sensed my presence.

Husaini was at the door, barefoot and bareheaded, blue-black hair newly plaited. "*Takafart!* Infidel woman!" he threw at me ironically by way of greeting, with his usual half-shy teasing grin. His *tagilmoust* – the eight-yard Tuareg headdress – was looped loosely around his neck. The indigo dye from it had rubbed off and showed vivid blue on his light skin, the neck of his white robe stained darker blue. For him I managed a smile of sorts but I barely greeted the inevitable bunch of night-watchmen and hangers-on sprawled about my living-room – young men who weren't Rhisa – and made for the bedroom, sick with disappointment again as I was at every sunrise, every sunset, every return home.

As I passed the little bathroom I glanced in and saw Khassim standing there, freshly washed. Afterwards, I couldn't imagine what he saw in me that day as I stood in the doorway, face flushed and sweaty from the midday sun, hair dutifully braided in the approved fashion, cotton wrapper and skimpy T-shirt of the approved Tuareg dark blue, silver earrings and dark blue beads also as required – coppery hair, blue eyes and sun-reddened skin emphatically *not* meeting aesthetic standards.

I was surprised to see him. He rarely visited – he was a married man with responsibilities, not footloose and fancy-free like Husaini and the others. Besides, though his wife was a distant relative of Husaini's, Khassim came from a different clan and spoke a different dialect.

He smiled his wide and beautiful smile, looking impishly out at me from under his lashes, hands raised to

5

shake water from his thick black curls, long muscles swelling in his bare arms. He was wearing baggy blue trousers and a white net singlet. His feet were bare. He stood there like a golden-brown gleaming satyr, grinning shyly at me, eyes full of enormous fun and mischief and awareness. I could see his nipples, erect through the network of the singlet. We stood smiling for a long moment, then I stepped into the bathroom. He moved against me without hesitation and I watched our reflection in the small bathroom mirror as he pressed his nose against mine, breathing in my breath, and his hand pushed between my legs and pinched.

How long had I known him? Six years? Why did it happen that day? How could it have happened like that? I don't know. I stepped into the bathroom, first step on a long and bitter journey.

I had just drawn back from Khassim, my blood leaping in a kind of astonished joy, when Husaini's *rat-tat* sounded against the open door behind my back. "*Shayi,*" he said, pouting his lips to indicate the little glass of tea in his hand. I took it and drank it off as he waited, the sweet golden third ritual glass. Then Amina appeared behind him, my now-awake Minha stretching her arms to me anxiously, half-twisting out of the cloth that anchored her to Amina's back. I took her in my arms, feeling the usual shock of pleasure in the moment of contact with her sweet sweaty little body.

I carried her into the bedroom and took off my bra and lay down with her. She snuggled up to me under my loose Tuareg shirt and kneaded my breast and began to suck. It was too hot. The ceiling-fan made its feeble efforts. I reached and flicked the switch on the table-fan, training the flow of air directly on us. It was near the end of the cold season, *harmattan* dust still clouding the sun occasionally in the mornings, but midday temperatures hitting the usual excruciating high. Soon we'd be heading into the hot season before the rains.

I was still trembling slightly. Husaini's smile had been as warm and carefree as ever. He couldn't have seen. The rat-tat on the door had been just a cheerful signal.

Husaini was Rhisa's first cousin and had become my right-hand man – by day. Like all migrant Tuareg from the *République du Niger* he worked as a security guard by night – in his case on a building-site. He was one of the lucky ones – many worked as night-watchmen for private families, often for a pittance. There were so many of them in Nigeria now, ever since the droughts of the seventies had wiped out their herds of camels and goats and played havoc with their centuries-old lifestyle. Migrant labour had taken the place of raiding desert caravans – now they carried ghetto-blasters home as booty, instead of slaves.

My child's father had set off north with his ghetto-blaster nearly three months before, on what was supposed to be a three-week visit home to his people in the Sahelian desert plains of Niger. I was weary with rationalising his delay: of reminding myself he was watching the phases of the moon not a day-by-day calendar like me, that he had a responsibility to his family in Niger, that his widowed elderly mother had only half a welcome in his father's family, that he was illiterate and we had different ideas of communication, that he wouldn't worry about our child knowing she was as safe with me as she could possibly be on God's earth. That he was a nomad. All of that; and underlying all of that was my fear that he simply wouldn't come back, that he'd finally married that young first cousin of his, that he'd gone to Libya to join Gaddafi's Tuareg battalion, that he'd been imprisoned, that he'd had a bout of malaria and died.

I lived day by day, making a pathetic attempt to exercise the great African virtue of patience.

I was heart-sick, day and night.

᭝᭝᭝᭝᭝

I sat in my office and watched the plump bottom in the cotton dress as the student disappeared, and wondered: is she lying, in fact? If so, such a complicated fabrication . . .

The door closed on her bright "*Sai gobe!* Until tomorrow!" and a beaming smile.

I tried to get down to work but the girl stayed vivid in my mind – the tilt of her head with its elaborate and delicate crown of little plaits, the large full breasts and jutting bottom in the short modern dress, the assurance in her emphatic voice: "So what I'm going to do to finish the essays, I will wean my baby this week so I can go and stay in the student hostel and use my friend's notes and texts. My mother will take care of the baby . . . "

All so easy for you, young mother, I thought. All so matter-of-fact. I had to go to war against your culture and mine to have my child.

All so casual. Even death.

"I have another problem," she said. "One of my essays – one of the students took it to read and I didn't get it back from him before he died – "

"Killed," I said. "Before he was killed . . . "

Was I correcting grammar or making a protest?

"Yes – before he was killed. On the Kaduna road."

I shook her out of my head and hoped to Christ no other student would pay a visit. I thought of my two-year-old in her little cotton dungarees, inside the French door that morning, pressing against the panes in an agony of protest as she watched me leave, and I wanted to get out of this dusty barren office and get home to her. To see if, by the grace of God, her father might be back from the desert.

I had to set an essay question on one of my lecture themes. I wrote: *Faulkner ignores clock time and substitutes living time. Discuss.*

⚜⚜⚜⚜⚜

I was coming out of the market in Samaru, with Husaini, when I heard it. A small crowd, the usual Hausa market mix, had gathered around the sandy area outside the shabby white building that served as courthouse. A wiry under-sized man poised on a bike, two six-foot metal rails strapped together balanced on his head. Gaudily-dressed girls casually balancing trays of peanuts and sesame cakes, gnawing at sugar-cane as they stared. An old leper clutching his begging-bowl in fingerless hands. A butcher, a goat's head bloody in his hand, a machete in the other, vultures eyeing him at a safe distance. An old woman, bright cotton headcloth drawn across her face with a gnarled hand to cover her mouth. Women, fingers pinching their lips in wonder, sleeping babies on their backs. A blind beggar-man, intent, slackly holding the stick that linked him to the small boy who led him. A wizened old man in his white embroidered robe and pillbox hat, fingering wooden prayer beads. The usual scattering of young men in their skimpy modern shirts and pants. They were all curiously silent, ears cocked like animals, eyes gazing blankly towards the building.

A woman's voice was crying from inside without let or pause, calling on God for help, over and over and over and over and over again.

"What is it, Husaini? Ask them," I said from a tight throat, in Hausa.

"*To!*" he said shortly – "OK". He twitched at the mouth-fold of his *tagilmoust*, bringing it higher over the nose, making it more formal, and went reluctantly to ask the old man with the beads.

I stood there waiting in that blinding midday, her cry biting into my brain, laying down an indelible track.

"What did he say?" Quickly, tell me.

He muttered through his veil, his clear voice muted, eyes deflected. "This is how it is. That woman, her husband took a second wife but the women refused to live together in peace so he divorced the first one. She went home to her people but she refused to give her child up. Then the husband took her before the judge and the judge said it was necessary she let the child go. But she said no one except God could separate her from her child." He looked directly at me, eyes wide in faint wonder at the woman's heroic moment.

"Yes?"

"The judge said she didn't have the truth and he told them to take the baby from her and lock her up. Because of that she's begging God to help her."

We stood for a while, then Husaini moved off and I followed him to where we had left the Land Cruiser.

We were driving along the main road when I spotted Jonathan's powder-blue Volkswagen heading in the opposite direction along the string of small stores behind the gutter and back off the road to our left. The VW stopped in front of a photo parlour. I suddenly wanted to see him rather badly, so I swung left when we reached the entrance to Harry's, the small Lebanese store, and parked there amid a swarm of dusty ragged little *almajirai* – Koranic students, who by custom begged for their food. While I made the three-dozen-times-a-day adjustment of my cotton wrapper, loosening it and tucking it in more securely at the waist, Husaini shooed the boys off, making way for my favourite beggar who came rattling up on his little wheeled go-car, cheerful and legless, propelling himself along at ground level with his stumpy hands. I gave him the usual few *kobo* and then we trudged back along the line of stores that sold Star beer, bright plastic-ware and enamel bowls. At least, I trudged. Husaini strode along, erect and graceful, with his loping swaying Tuareg gait.

The VW had disgorged a bunch of people, two of them Tuareg and likely to be members of my household. Jonathan was forever absconding with them. Yes, that looked like Ikis-Ikus in the white tunic and *tagilmoust* and the short one was Aghali, bare-headed and shaggy-haired, in his modern black trousers and orange shirt.

Jonathan had spotted us and was making hurry-up hand movements. He had left the driving-door gaping open, as he typically did. Everything with him was quick-fast – closing a car door was time-wasting.

He was very Peter O'Toole that day, light blue eyes brilliant under the brim of a straw fedora-shaped hat with a black band. "*Sannu*, Rutherford! God sent you now. Come! We will take a photo for the album!"

He spoke in an emphatic Nigerian style – he had spent all his adult life rattling around English West Africa. Ikis-Ikus's eyes were dancing through the slit in his *tagilmoust* and Aghali was grinning ear to ear. They found Europeans eccentric and hilarious and always had great fun with Jonathan.

"*Sannu*, Jonathan!" cried Husaini in the light voice that sometimes had a little husky crack in it, as if it hadn't quite broken yet despite his twenty-five-odd years. "Are you well?"

And they went through a perfect orgy of the repetitive stroking Tuareg hand-shake that usually lapsed into horse-play when Jonathan was at the receiving end. But not today. Jonathan turned to me.

"This is Musa Ibrahim," he said, waving an attractive youngish man forward. "He lectures in Art. And he is a fine sculptor." He put a hand on the guy's leather-clad shoulder and his eyes glinted at me from under the brim of his hat.

Musa shook hands and smilingly greeted me in Hausa. "*Ina gajiya?*" How's the tiredness?

"*Babu gajiya!*" I smiled back. No tiredness. Just the woman's cry still slicing through my heart.

I covertly examined this Musa Ibrahim, barely greeting the two other young Hausamen. This had to be a new love interest and I was always mad keen for Jonathan to find true love. Musa was your typical Hausa aristocrat, slim and fine-boned, with a tiny moustache mid upper-lip. Dressed very sharply in leather jacket and blue jeans, a slighter and more serious version of Eddie Murphy. Looking good, I thought, with a glance at the glint in Jonathan's eyes.

The photo parlour was the usual, with requisite bold-patterned lino, upright chairs and – an odd note – a silver wrought-iron fence by way of decoration in front of the back-drop.

"Rutherford," said Jonathan. "What's happened? You don't look well now." Using "now" as an emphatic in the Nigerian way.

"Oh, I'm OK." I'd be telling him later. We told each other everything. "Just desperate to see an Irishman – even if he is a Dublin Protestant and Trinity graduate and gay with it."

"Those are my finest attributes," cried Jonathan. "You cannot insult me! You – a stupid Corkwoman who doesn't know her arse from her elbow!"

He then got the notion of swapping headgear with Husaini. So the eight yards of Husaini's indigo-steeped *tagilmoust* were unwound and rewound on Jonathan. He had to be taught how to do it, of course, but that was sheer flirtation on his part. He'd been over this course so many times he could have done it in his sleep – and probably did: draped over the head first like the Virgin Mary, then across the mouth and nose, up and around the head as many times as it would circle, the end tucked in. The lads had a ball – they loved this stuff – and the guttural vigorous sounds of Tuareg oaths and obscenities flew throughout.

In deference to Musa Ibrahim, however, Jonathan largely kept his hands to himself.

"And much hilarity ensued," said Jonathan when the job was done, folding the cloth down from his indigo-smeared nose with a practised flick that betrayed his proficiency utterly.

The gesture was not lost on Musa. "So you want to be a Buzu, Jonathan?" he said, half-humorously, using the rather contemptuous Hausa term originally applied only to Tuareg slaves.

Jonathan laughed gaily.

My ear, however, was finely tuned to the varying degrees of anti-Buzu hostility. Stray catcalls of *"Matan Buzu!"* followed my progress everywhere: "Buzu woman" – a joke – or "Buzu's woman" – an insult. I never understood the precise implication.

To my ear, Musa's tone had been more than slightly acid.

"Not Buzu now! Tuareg! You must use their proper name," said Jonathan.

In fact, it wasn't their proper name. It was an Arab term meaning something like "forgotten of God". They called themselves Kel Tamajeq, "the people who raid", or Kel Tagilmoust, "the people of the veil".

And so we were photographed for posterity: an unrecognisable Jonathan with Musa centre-back, arms draped round each other like a bridal couple, the two Hausa lads posed on either side like book-ends, hands on hips. Me, in my willow-pattern-blue-and-white cotton *zane* and dark blue T-shirt seated on my upright chair centre-front. On my right, Husaini, like a Mafia member with plaits in Jonathan's hat. On my left, Aghali, a cut-throat Sicilian bandit with his mop of hair.

Happy Days, as they say.

Husaini skived off with Jonathan and company into Samaru village. I let him go though I badly needed his company. What I really needed, though, was a heart-to-heart with Jonathan, the regular bout of unloading that helped me make it through the days.

"There is some Buzu outside behind the house," said Amina when I got home. She gestured to the back porch.

My heart leapt. Rhisa? Amina wouldn't know him – she had come to work for me after he had left for Niger.

But it was Khassim who stood there: tentative, poised, ironic.

He was wearing his white *tagilmoust*. I went outside to greet him. A smile and we touched hands repeatedly in the traditional handshake, his middle finger hooking into my palm in traditional flirtation, his hand finally returning to his breast in that graceful gesture of salute and allegiance.

He always addressed me as *madame* with the French inflection, never using my name. He had a wonderful voice, with a lightness overlying a very male timbre. It was alive with humour but could be harsh or tumble into guttural depths when serious.

We went through the greetings in Tamajeq but then lapsed into Hausa. I generally spoke Hausa, it being something of a *lingua franca* in West Africa and light-years easier than Tamajeq. The difference between the two languages was something like the difference between Italian and Gaelic, lilting vowels versus virile consonants.

Khassim had brought the bike around to the back of the house. To hide it? My heart fluttered.

Minha was asleep on my bed, dressed only in little yellow pants, limbs limp and thrown wide in delicious relaxation. I sent Amina home.

He wasted no time. Came right against me and we kissed, nose to nose.

"I want you," he said in Tamajeq, as if Hausa were inadequate.

My cheek was against the bunch of charms in their flat leather wallets hung round his neck. I slid a hand up his right arm and felt the charms tied above the elbow. So, he had come protected and ready for battle.

We sat and then lay on the wooden-framed Fulani bed in the living-room, beneath the ceiling-fan that circled lazily and hardly stirred the thick air. I said "Wait" and went to check the bamboo window-blinds, breath coming short, and locked the doors.

I lay down with him again and embraced him, breathing him in until I was panting. What was I at? I turned my head aside and gasped in the close air. The blinds were down but anyone who came onto the porches could put an eye to the mosquito-netting and see in through the bamboo slits. We couldn't go in the bedroom, because of Minha. In any case, I didn't want to go in there. There was no way I could have sex with him. I loved Rhisa with a passionate love that had not abated an iota in five years.

Keep it light, keep it light, I thought.

I rubbed my face into the softness of his *tagilmoust*. He was wearing a mid-length tunic of the softest black cloth and I breathed deep, drawing in through the thin cotton the heady smell of oil-based perfume, tobacco, indigo dye, sweat, man.

His hand pulled at my *zane* at the waist and undid it. His fingers hesitated as they found my bikini briefs and he cursed softly. "Take it off," he whispered.

"No!" This was not going to happen, I wouldn't let it happen.

His fingers plunged further and found my crotch. "I'm begging you," he whispered in my ear.

"I can't, I can't. You know I can't." Stop. Get up. You must get up before it is too late.

His fingers probed and he kissed me.

My body sang with tension. I pulled his tunic up and ran my hands over the muscles of his back. He raised his belly and fumbled with one hand at the draw-string of his trousers. My hands slid over the soft gathered cotton and grasped at his buttocks, pulling him against me. He fumbled again and I felt him pull at the string and draw the waist wide. The weight of his warm penis fell against my naked belly.

My eyes went to the windows. "No! No!" I said in English and pushed him away with all my strength. "Stop!" I gasped my way upright and pulled my *zane* back in place. "I can't do this!" One of the blinds stirred and my heart jolted.

"OK, OK!" he whispered.

I thought, what of Khadija? His wife, my friend. What of Rhisa? But somehow I couldn't articulate those thoughts. "You'd better go. Now."

He sat up. "I'm going," he said softly. He pulled his trouser-string tight again and tied it. I could still see his erection pushing against the gathered cloth. Then he reached for me and pulled me down again and back against him. "*Shi ke nan* – that's it. I won't do anything. Let me hold you. You can't chase me like this." His voice murmured. His weight rolled back on me. My arms were full of his sweetness and hardness.

"Stop," I said. "Stop. Someone will come." My eyes flew again to the slits in the bamboo-blinds.

"I won't do anything." He sucked at my breath with his nose. His hand pulled at my *zane* and found my crotch again. I pushed against the hand, needing his fingers to go in.

He stopped and gazed at me, beads of sweat standing out on the skin of his face. "Please, madame, take the *caleçon* off," using the French word for "trunks".

"I can't."

I heard his faint sigh. I held him, our hearts hammering together. The hand left me and I felt him pulling at his clothes again.

"No, Khassim! You said you wouldn't!" I pushed at his chest but he held me tight and I couldn't move. The hand pulled at my underwear.

I thought then, it's too late. And my body went slack. A sigh shuddered up from my belly.

I felt his penis slide deeply in and then it really was too late.

I stood outside smiling at him, lightly holding on to the handlebars of his bicycle, my hands saying "Don't go."

17

Then, as I watched, the elation died from his face and he looked at me strangely. "Rhisa told me to guard you," he said, his voice deepening in his throat.

He was using the Tamajeq word *"kam"*, the feminine "you", even though he was speaking Hausa. As if my female presence were so strong he could only address it in his own language. He always did that, from that time on.

I stared at him, astonished, even in that moment feeling a painful little throb of joy in my heart that marked this reminder of Rhisa's caring.

Was this true? Would Rhisa approach Khassim, who was not a kinsman, not a clansman? Khassim, known as a man to be trusted, but still . . .

"He came to me before he left and begged me to be your guard."

Wait. Khassim was not a clansman: that meant he had no loyalty to any of Rhisa's kin. *"To be your guard."* Rhisa had asked him, not to take care of me, but to spy on my dealings with Husaini and the others.

Suddenly I felt nauseated.

Why was Khassim telling me now? It sounded like a warning but perhaps it was a confession.

I said nothing.

He rang his bicycle bell and heaved a deep sigh. A quick glance around and he kissed me.

Rhisa had asked Khassim, the only married man, the safe one. And Khassim had promised – to be my guard.

I watched him ride off and I thought, does that somehow give you the right to fuck me yourself?

Chapter Two

I didn't see him for the next three days. On the fourth day the yearning really kicked in and I was angry. I went out to saddle Chilli, the chestnut horse I had inherited from a friend who had left Nigeria. I had developed a fierce lust for tearing across the bush or losing myself in isolated places among the rocks of Kufena inselberg. To look back from afar and see ABU – Ahmadu Bello University – at a distance gave me a kind of perspective, a relief from paranoia, from the sense of threat. Around the inselberg there was a depression like a moat, as if the rock were a medieval fortification. This would be a sward of green grass once the rains came and up on the rock would be pools where one could swim at the risk of bilharzia or worse, multitudes of long-tailed monkeys watching from a safe distance. I followed the moat and circled the great rock in a silence alive with the shimmering background buzz of innumerable insects. Yet even here in this oasis of peace was the ever-present unease that comes with motherhood, the little flutter of the nerves that always must be there when you are apart from your child.

I was only ever away from her for short periods like my one-hour lectures at the university or a trip to the market.

Or a ride like this. Anywhere else and she was in her little car-seat beside me.

I should get home. I quelled the urge. Minha was safely sleeping or warmly clung to Amina's back or eating from her yellow plastic bowl at her little wooden table. Chilli had his needs, too, and I hadn't taken him out since the day Khassim had called. I rode on towards Zaria Old City beyond the inselberg.

As I rode past the gate in the mud ramparts of the city a procession was emerging. I reined in and halted to watch. A young girl passed, astride a horse decked out in full caparison right down to golden tassels on his bridle and a bright blue face-mask. My Chilli was a humble creature next to him, his rose-and-green Hausa saddle-blanket suddenly shabby. The girl was wearing a cloak so heavily embroidered with silver and gold thread it looked as though it might pull her to the ground. A huge golden tassel fell from the hood down her forehead and all but concealed her face. A rich young woman going to her marriage house. A very rich young woman. The white-turbaned man riding ahead, under ceremonial black fans and gold umbrellas could even be the Sarki, the Emir himself. They passed, surrounded by red-turbaned bodyguards and musicians in damask robes and indigo turbans flashing a metallic purple under the sun.

I wondered how many other wives would be there to welcome the *amarya*, the new wife. As the youngest, she was likely soon to be called *Mowa*, the name given a favourite wife. How many years would it take to slip down the ladder until she was *Bora*, the least favoured? I felt a now-familiar little flare of anger. It was a cruel system. And I felt they knew it: a co-wife was called a *kishiya* – a "jealous one".

I decided to go and visit Khadija. I would cut across the bush to Agric – the area where Agricultural Research was situated – and the building-site where Khassim worked.

I rode back past Kufena and cantered along farmland trails, past baobabs and palms, trusting that the beat of Chilli's hooves could be clearly heard behind the mud walls of the isolated compounds I passed. My nightmare was that a child would step out of the bushes on the trail. But even that never stopped me tearing across the landscape, guilt and joy filling my throat. Then it was open bush and rocky dried-up river-beds, with a need to move more cautiously and a real possibility of losing myself, as I knew to my cost. Today I did well, hitting the main road only half a mile or so north of the building-site.

Khadija was sitting on a mat in front of their make-shift hut – the kind of temporary shelter they felt quite at home in, being nomadic people. I looked around, hungry for a glimpse of Khassim, but he wasn't in sight. When she saw me she smiled her dazzling smile and waved a heavy golden arm. I rode up and dismounted, feeling both flamboyant and self-conscious as I always did when I arrived on Chilli, seeing it through their eyes as eccentric, unwomanly, possibly obscene – Husaini commenting laughingly on a pretty Hausa girl on a bicycle, "If she were my girl I wouldn't let her ride a bike! *Kai!* Let that saddle touch my belongings?"

Feeling a bit ridiculous because I was riding "out in the noonday sun" – *mad dogs and Englishmen*.

"Madame Katherine! You are welcome!" Khadija cried in English, pitching her voice high in a tone which was at the same time raucous and shrill. The baby, little dark Fatimatu who looked so like her father, was on her lap

21

grappling with a generous breast – Khadija, at home, always went barebreasted as was their custom. Little Yakubu, golden and curly-haired, sat against her, sheltering under the fall of her black veil, playing with the cowrie shells on the long red leather thong that bound up her braided hair. I sat down thankfully on the mat beside them. A blackened pot brimful of rice was simmering on the fire. Khadija could do all her housework from where she sat. And sit she did, in the glorious relaxed way they had, solidly on her great haunches. She was so tremendously female she made me feel lacking.

I sat there on my own skimpy buttocks, the usual great contentment welling up in me, body aching with relief and pleasure in the warmth of the afternoon sun. It was that time of day when the sun lost its savage strength and became benign, like a fearsome parent who suddenly holds out her arms and enfolds you, saying, "*See, I'm your mother – here to give you loving care – let me comfort you.*"

I watched Khadija. I wanted to be comforted like the children. I wanted to grasp her golden breasts with their dusky overlay of indigo. I wanted to lay my head on her rounded thighs and breathe in that musky mixture of indigo and sweat and oil-based perfume – Khassim's smell – the smell of the tribe.

Yakubu had been trying to poke his chubby fingers into the pockets of my jeans. I let him, knowing what he was at. Then he went right under my *takatkat* – easily done – Tuareg women's shirts were cut loose and cool, simple wide rectangles covering the arms and open down the sides.

"Yakubu! *Bastard!*" cried Khadija, pointing a supple finger vigorously at him and then prodding his head with it. "Do you want to steal Minha's milk? Minha, your woman – that you're going to marry! You have no shame!"

Yakubu pulled back and looked at his mother, eyes round in fright.

"Leave him!" I said, laughing. I ruffled his short curls – recently shaved and just growing out, a longer lock left on top. "It's nothing, Yakubu!"

Khadija's mouth twitched and she laughed and said to me in an undertone, "He's looking for his paper of meat."

"I know – and I haven't brought anything." I always brought a twist of paper with peppered meat or groundnuts for him. "Open him a tin of fish, Khadija."

"Don't worry about him! Do you know? Your friend Jonathan came over here yesterday to buy some bread! Saying that he forgot to buy bread in Samaru. And he gave Yakubu one *naira*! By God, he's a kind man!"

Probably came to lust over the labourers. Jonathan's group of bungalows was just across the main road, a few hundred yards from the site as the crow flies.

"Yes, he's kind. But open Yakubu's tin now. Here, Yakubu – give Mama the money for the fish."

"We thank you!" said Khadija and she reached for one of the cans stacked in a little pyramid on a mat by her side. Khadija had a *tebur* – a "table" – a nice little business selling cigarettes, bread, tinned milk and fish to the labourers and guards. With a mock frown, she reached out a hand demandingly to Yakubu. He put the money in her palm and then watched the opening of the can with visible excitement, starved for protein as always.

"Lie down, Katherine! Rest!" When she relaxed her voice sang along like the song of a guttural thrush, but I could always hear a little hard edge hidden deep in it somewhere.

I stretched out on my side, a narrow fringed leather pillow under my armpit, the ache of my tired muscles merging into the special pleasure of lying on the hard surface of a mat.

And I wished to Christ, as I always did, that this was it, that this was my life. The university was anathema to me. Teaching TS Eliot to chauvinistic Nigerians who really did not want us here. What a futile bloody task. This was what I wanted. All I wanted.

No – not all: I wanted to move north to Niger, into Tuareg country, on the edge of the Sahara where my heart was and where I spent every vacation, every moment I possibly could.

I watched Khadija – her flashing smile, the powerful graceful movements of her arms – breathing in her strength.

Khadija had earned her strength. She had been married off to an Ibo soldier in southern Nigeria as a young girl, sold by her uncle when she was only twelve. The devastation of the droughts had brought all sorts of greed and desperation in its train and there was a ready marriage market – the light-skinned Tuareg girls were at a premium in the south.

The enormity of it never failed to stun me afresh when I thought of it – a little girl flung out of her environment into a strange man's culture, family, bed. What seemed most terrible of all was the fact she couldn't speak the language, wouldn't ever hear Tamajeq.

She came back, of course, speaking Ibo, Hausa, some English and some Yoruba. And with well-honed southern market skills. She ran a tough little business on the building-site, salting the proceeds away in her tin trunk, with Khassim acting as her "heavy", debt-collecting on pay-day. The bra she had once worn, in her life as a smart young southern woman, now hung from one of the supports of the hut like a kind of trophy.

The Chair she sat in, like a burnished throne,
Glowed on the marble . . .

I was trying to lecture on Eliot these days. Khadija sat beside me on her straw mat, regal as Cleopatra.

Eventually she had run away, leaving three young children behind her, and had come north where the local immigrant Tuareg community had closed around her and lied for her when her husband came searching.

Then she had antagonised her kinsfolk by marrying Khassim, who belonged to a different Tuareg confederation.

I lay there, remembering. Even before their marriage she had sometimes gone to him, defying whatever Tuareg conventions still held in this foreign environment. But then she was a free woman, freed by her years of bondage and to some unspoken and undefined degree an outcast because of her southern marriage.

⚜⚜⚜

Once, three years before, we were stuck in one of those marathon queues during a petrol-shortage in Samaru, baking alive in the midday sun under the car roof during the hot season when the temperature was way over a hundred. We had been there for seven hours, since six that morning – myself and Rhisa and Husaini. *Hakuri maganin duniya* – patience is the medicine of the world.

"Look!" muttered Rhisa into his veil.

Khassim was striding along the main road heading towards Agric, Khadija a yard or two behind, billowing along in traditional black. They had probably just got off a bus from Zaria where she was staying.

"Worthless bastards!" said Husaini, in the voice with that half-broken edge to it. "Look at them."

"What's the problem?" I asked sharply. I was partially exposed to the sun where it blazed through the window and my arm was frying right through the cotton cloth I had wrapped around it to shield it. My other hand was engaged in holding my sunglasses in place – let go and they glided down to the tip of my sweating nose.

Rhisa raised a finger and, looking straight ahead, made one of his very rare critical statements: "If they were home in Niger they would be beaten." It was so out of character I was startled – he was an extremely gentle soul.

"Why?" I asked, anger stirring before I even heard the answer.

"Because they haven't married."

We hadn't married either. Where did that leave me?

"He's a useless one! He's an Ekli!" said Husaini, flicking his lower lip upwards with a forefinger in contempt.

"He isn't an Ekli!" I said, despair about my future with Rhisa welling up. "Why do you say that!" The Iklan were slaves in Tuareg society, all descendants of black Africans captured south of the Sahara, in raids on caravans crossing it or bought in the now-defunct slave-market at Agadez. "He's a free man, the same as you!"

Not even a different tribe, just a different clan, a different confederation. Khassim came from the deserts and mountains of Aïr north of the ancient town of Agadez. My brave buckos, on the other hand, were Iwellemmedan from the desert plains north of Tchin Tabaraden to the west. I was always amazed at the extent of their traditional prejudices. What price a marriage – or non-marriage – to an Infidel woman?

"All those Kel Aïr are slaves," Husaini said in his rapid throw-away fashion. "Their ancestors all had children with their slaves."

I looked at Rhisa and Husaini in the masked state of rage that had become second nature to me. Looked at Rhisa – at the long plaited hair, the Semitic features, almond eyes and golden-brown skin that brought a Minoan bull-dancer to mind. Looked at Husaini, who was like a more Caucasian version of Keanu Reeves.

The cars were moving – someone up ahead had given up and pulled out. Right, I thought, starting up the engine, I'll mint a bunch of medals for you lot, for preserving your ethnic purity so fanatically. I slammed my foot on the accelerator and put my anger into moving up the few yards – and nudged the car in front of us. Its driver was too fatigued to look around but he raised his hand feebly and, twisting it back at the wrist, gave us the customary five-finger-spread gesture of abuse – *Uwaki!* Your mother! The lads gestured vigorously in response, leaning from the Land Cruiser window – *Ubanka!* Your father! Laughing, they topped it off with camped-up *fuck-you's* in Tamajeq to the amusement of the beggar-boys standing around. My anger cooled a little. They might be fucking racists but they were my fucking racists.

Not good enough but it would have to do. I tried to think of it as an accident of history. Looking at them, I could understand it in anthropological terms. Even now, they might have stepped off Crete or Cyprus yesterday. I could understand the in-built biological urge to preserve the group intact, to survive as an entity, surrounded by Arab and black African races as they had been ever since they first set out from Libya thousands of years before.

I could understand it intellectually. But emotionally . . .

They were my friends – Rhisa was the father of my child – and it hurt.

I had known Khassim, of course, long before Khadija came up from the south to drive the Tuareg men of Zaria mad with love-sickness. I remember him by firelight, on the building-site out in the bush where he was working at the time. I used to take my Rhisa to visit him at night. I can see them even now, sitting together laughing, embracing like lovers, hanging about each other's necks, fingers entwined. I remember how I despised what seemed to me like cheap laughter, cheap affection. I watched them, eaten with jealousy. He always wore black and his hair hung then in short braids on each side of his lean beautiful vivacious face, with its high cheekbones, fine nose, and well-defined mouth. His wide and brilliant smile transformed his face, creasing it with laughter-lines. If you looked carefully you could notice a tiny white cloud on his right eye. He said that was something to do with a gun accident.

He still wore black but now his hair was cropped thick and strong and the skin on his face was coarser. Nigeria had not been kind to him – he was plagued by fevers. But he was still beautiful, the gleaming satyr I saw in my bathroom.

No wonder she had chosen him, when she could have had anyone.

She had come north and Khassim had fallen in love. I

could remember well how lovesick he was, courting her nightly. He used to come knocking at my door late at night, skiving off from his work, and I would drive him to her place in Tudun Wada, on the southern side of Zaria town. We were good friends, even then.

He must have been a marvellous lover then, I thought. Those years ago.

God, he was ardent.

And she was so handsome – straight-backed and dignified as a voluptuous princess in her tight-waisted cotton-print Hausa costume, long plaits falling from under her high turban. I remembered how he wanted her, risking his job to go to her and fend off the other courtiers who paid nightly visits to cluster around her.

⁂

Little Fatimatu was looking at me, bright black eyes snapping, small brown body naked but for leather-bound protective charms tied around neck and wrist and hips. She had been staggering around, supporting herself on her mother's thighs and the length of my body. She looked so like Khassim, had his spark of energy. Yakubu was placid and handsome, golden-brown, with petulant little lips and a head of curls, a little Greek statue, his mother's child. I wondered, not for the first time but always secretly, whether he really was Khassim's child.

"Little wretch!" Khadija swung Fatimatu onto her lap and onto the nipple. The child sucked, black eyes alertly fixed on my face, kneading her mother's other breast. Khadija looked at me ironically and said in English, "She's black like the father."

Why did you marry him then, Khadija, only to secretly disparage him?

Suddenly I wanted to ask her. My mind scrabbled around, searching for a way to ask that wouldn't be too blunt. "Khadija? Your people in Birnin Konni? At the time you married Khassim, did they agree to it?"

"*Kai!* They didn't agree! Never, never!"

"But why?"

"They said he is an Ekli! A slave! That he is black!"

"But he *isn't* an Ekli – "

"I know but they don't accept the Kel Aïr. And you know, he wasn't so black when I married him – it is his fever that made his body black."

Where's the logic there, Khadija? "So what did you say to them, at that time?"

"I said I didn't care! I wanted him! But, you know, with all this they had heard news of his greatness and in the end they kept quiet."

I had forgotten. Forgotten that Khassim was something of a star in their firmament. He had been an *elfileyga* – a bandit – in his earlier days, hiding out in the Aïr mountains, armed at a time when his people had surrendered all their weapons to the police. He had come to Nigeria, not as a migrant, but as a wanted man in his own country.

"*Kai!* I had forgotten that!" I said. There were songs about him.

"Because of that they gave him respect."

And is that why you married him, Khadija? Did his prestige as a folk hero outweigh his shortcomings in the ethnic-purity stakes?

This was my chance to ask more, to probe her defences.

Fatimatu came off the breast with an audible pop and crawled back to me. I hooked an arm about her and she pulled at my earring.

"Khadija?" I asked. "That first husband of yours – the Ibo. He had other women besides you, or is that not so?"

She pursed her lips. "He had."

"How many?"

"Two. Both of them Ibos."

"But wasn't he a Christian?"

"He was a Christian but they follow their traditions. You know, they were all pagans before. His uncle even had eight women! What do they care!"

"But didn't that worry you? Sharing him like that?"

"I was a little girl! What did I know? And afterwards I was used to it. I wouldn't agree to it now! At all! Every third night!" She sniffed her contempt, tossing back her glossy plait of hair and plunging a small stick viciously into the pot. She lifted out a few grains of rice and pressed them between thumb and forefinger, then flicked them away. "Huh! Now – that would be the day I'd pack my things!" And she took Fatimatu from me, tossing her over her head. "Hah!" she cried, pinching the child's vulva and then flicking the fingers open under her nose. "Perfume!"

I wondered afresh at the extraordinary fact that her people were monogamous. It seemed to me quite amazing and wonderful, surrounded as they were by polygamous peoples and entitled as Muslims to the prescribed four wives. Traditionally, of course, they were a matriarchal society, patriarchal Islam a shallow veneer on a culture where succession was passed through the female side and children inherited their mother's status, not their father's.

I left reluctantly soon after and arrived home to find Amina filling the teetering water-filter above her head-level with a kettle of boiling water in one hand and Minha clutched to her hip. I had told her and told her. So, at a loss as to what else to do, I snatched Minha from her and raged and ranted while, dumbfounded and cowed, she bit her hand and cowered away from me. It was bloody useless. I knew she would only register that Madame Kate was having one of those inexplicable Bature – European – fits of temper.

Husaini and Aghali came to the kitchen door, grinning, and that infuriated me in earnest so I yelled at them to go and unsaddle Chilli. I went to get a bottle of water from the fridge – all gone, of course – and heard the lads bandying that awful word *Takafart* outside. It wasn't actually an insult – just a term they had adopted from the Arabic to refer to white people – but I found it hard to stomach being called an "Infidel" on a daily basis. Fuck them and their ignorance! I took some warm water from the filter and locked myself in the bedroom with Minha. In the mirror I could see my face was flaming. I felt terrible. I had good reason to freak but yet I had shamed myself. I saw myself as the eccentric and uncouth Baturiya through their eyes. I pressed my hands against my face to blot out the image.

Minha was trying to pull down the handle to open the door. These days she was a little ball of energy – when she wasn't conked out in fathomless siestas. She was the cutest little child, small and firm, an absolute copy of her father but so fair-skinned no one realised she was African. Little as she was, she already had his slightly zany sense of fun. What she didn't have was his luxuriant blue-black hair. Khadija was always despairing about Minha's scrap of fine chestnut hair. She blamed me because I had refused to let them shave Minha's head when she was born. It wasn't too late, she kept telling me – we could start now and still have results: thick black beautiful hair. It annoyed the hell out of me, this unyielding aesthetic yardstick they were eternally wielding. Damn it, my hair was red. Just how ugly did I look to them, in fact?

I was wondering whether I should fire Amina on the spot. The next girl would be no better, though, and I was fond of Amina.

The idea of cause and effect was not popular, to say the least. What was it? Stupidity? A natural laid-back attitude? Or casual familiarity with calamity? Whatever, it was made worse by Muslim dictums about the Will of God. I was not allowed to say: if you let the child run around the open fire or open latrine she will fall in and die. That was impiety. In Kano State the previous year they had protested against wearing crash-helmets by tying them to their scooters and dragging them behind: statistics studying the relation between rampant deaths and the lack of helmets were an impiety.

Minha had picked up Husaini's *bulala* – his heavy leather whip – from the floor and was flailing at the door with it, staggering back and forth with the weight of it and falling on her bum. "*'Usaini! 'Usaini!*" she cried in her small voice and soon I heard his tentative knock.

"Leave me in peace!" I yelled.

"*Mahaukaciya* – madwoman," he said, laughter in his voice. "Open for me." He rattled the door-handle.

"For God's sake, leave me in peace!"

"God give you patience, my mother!"

Minha was standing like a little startled bird, listening to his voice outside the door.

They never would leave me in peace. I opened the door.

"*Mahaukaciya*," he said fondly and threw an arm about me. "When I go home I will tell Rhisa that you are going mad here in Nigeria."

That night I unlocked my bedroom cupboard and took out one cassette from my pathetic little bunch of tapes. I had to protect them like a miser. They wouldn't last a day if not under lock and key. This one was marked in Tuareg script – *Tifenagh* – with the symbols for "k", "ch", "n" and the dot for a final vowel: "Kacina", a northern variant of "Katsina", the town where I had made the recording two years before.

I kept the volume down and my ear to the cassette player so that the stray bodies in the living-room wouldn't hear. Even under those conditions, it was intensely exciting – the handclap and drum-rhythm moved with the barely suppressed energy of a high-stepping horse or camel held in check. I strained to follow the lead singer's narrative, all but lost in the energy of counterpointing voices. I couldn't really follow it. However, Husaini and I had translated it before and as I listened I remembered scraps: *And Khassim lifted his right foot to his left knee and resting his elbow on his thigh aimed . . . he said, "The devil take you – I am not water in a gourd for anyone to drink off . . . Let the women of my place beat drums and sing my name . . . the beautiful Muroniya will not hear that I laid down my gun . . . " With that he shot at Ekwell . . . the bullet smashed through his backbone . . .*

Great. Might as well be down home in West Cork listening to "The Crossbarry Ambush". A friend, an Englishman who fancied me, once said to me: "Why, when you come from one exotic tribe, do you want to belong to another?" I wanted to belong but their blinkered culture drove me mad. Maybe because I came from a blinkered culture myself.

And who the fuck was this Muroniya?

Some famous beauty, no doubt. Enormously fat, no doubt. No doubt Khassim used to visit her when he was on the run and no doubt between his visits she heroically refused to grant anyone else her favours. Kitty *What's-it* and Michael Collins. And no doubt if he had died in ambush she would have died of a broken heart. But he hadn't.

He was here in Nigeria and the beautiful Muroniya could go fuck.

Chapter Three

He came the following day when we were sitting on mats outside making tea in the charcoal brazier.

"Khadija's man," said the pint-sized Aghali, grinning like a leprechaun, Minha cradled between his legs. He raised his glass and saluted Khassim with it.

My heart began to hammer. I was taking some pictures and I kept at it, barely acknowledging him. Resentment against him flared up. I concentrated on my pictures. I had just got a beauty of Ikus-Ikus perched on the porch-rail holding a hand-mirror, narcissistically putting kohl around his eyes. Now I was working on one of Amina, sticking pink blossoms in the tight little arches of her hairdo, my hands trembling. The luscious delicacy of the blossoms was extraordinary against the blackness of her skin and her sturdy peasant frame.

Suddenly he was at my elbow. Startled, I looked at him and saw there was something wrong.

"Madame," he said gently. "Just now I got news of Zainabu, Sidi's woman. That she has a lack of health. She gave birth yesterday morning. Sidi refuses to take her to the hospital. They say she is calling for you."

When we reached the compound in Zaria the women were helping her outside to urinate, literally carrying her, her legs trailing on the ground. I was shocked to see her. Last time I'd seen her she had been fat. Now I could see her ribs as they hauled her. Only her breasts looked big: her milk was coming in. It hurt me to see her dressed in the grown-up Tuareg woman's garb of black *zane* and veil – my little girl of just two years ago, a skinny little ragged creature who wanted to come and live with me. I would have taken her then but that, it seemed, was not part of the plan.

I had last seen her less than a year ago as a buxom bonny young girl, fed to the required fattening-point as a bait for the moneyed Hausa *Alhajai* – rich merchants who had made the pilgrimage to Mecca and earned the honorary title. Her mother told me a certain *Alhaji* from Kano had made a good offer. I didn't tell her that the idea of bartering Zainabu out of her own culture turned my stomach.

Zainabu had been cheerful and proud, her little bright face rotund. She walked me back to the Land Cruiser and, standing there swathed in her bright Hausa cottons, had taken the heavy silver bracelet from her wrist and given it to me with the dignity and flair of a princess. She pointed inside the bracelet to where her name was written in *Tifenagh*. "Read it," she said smilingly. To please her, I sang out the sounds represented by the symbols: *"Izzeh-Enneh-Ibbe-Iwweh – Zainabou!"* And she laughed aloud and slapped hands with me.

I had looked at her that day and seen tragedy in the illusion of maturity they had created, based on white rice and sugar. Her mother would have been force-fed on the richness of camel's milk back in the desert, I thought, in the good old days before God had the notion of sending the droughts that wiped out the animals . . . *"I trust in him who has goats, has Niger, has wiped out the once numerous cattle, and left the Tuareg so destitute they began to be watchmen . . ."*

A fatted calf. For the market, if not for the kill.

I hadn't visited again. The whole business sickened me and the image of Zainabu in sexual congress with some old man or bloated businessman haunted me, disturbing me like a piece of pornography.

I kept track of the news. In the end they had not chosen a rich *Alhaji*. They had reckoned Sidi with his steady job as security guard at the tiny Zaria airport a better bet. He was a tall good-looking young man in his twenties who had a bit of schooling and spoke some French. Maybe she had wanted him. I attended the wedding but then I fell out of touch.

Remembering all this, a dull sense of outrage in my heart, I let Husaini approach the men. Khassim hadn't come with us – it was pay-day and he had to be at the building-site to collect his money – to say nothing of Khadija's debts. He would come to my house later to hear news of how we had fared.

I sat with the women. They showed me the baby, a fine little boy.

Zainabu's mother sat next to me, wizened, black veil held to her mouth, tears in her eyes as I looked at her.

"Is she bleeding a lot?" I asked.

"Very much!"

"Is she in pain?"

"Very much!"

"Why doesn't Sidi take her to the hospital?"

She lowered her head and made no answer.

Another woman leant forward and whispered, "He is afraid they will keep her."

"So? If they keep her?" I said. "As long as she gets her health?"

"They say women catch a lack of health at the hospital and die."

Infection. It happened.

"We must have patience, madame."

Fuck your patience. You'll kill her.

Husaini came back and gestured to me. I went outside with him.

"He refuses." With the usual eloquent shrug of one shoulder.

"Why?"

Husaini shrugged.

I went back to the women who stared impassively up at me.

"He refuses?" asked one.

"Yes."

They made no comment. I couldn't understand the situation. The women weren't normally so passive. Did they really fear the hospital would kill her?

"Careful!" They were bringing her back. They laid her down in her black robes, the black veil of womanhood.

Her face was pallid but she smiled at me. "Madame!" And a weak hand tried to reach for me.

"Zainabu! No strength, is there?"

"None, madame!" she whispered.

"Do you feel pain?"

39

"Very much . . . "

"Do you want to go to the hospital?"

She made a weak sound of assent in her throat.

I went out to the men and spoke with Husaini. Then I stood at his elbow as he spoke to Sidi for me, formally. "Madame says it is proper that you take Zainabu to hospital. She will take her and bring her back and pay for any medicine."

"No," Sidi replied. "We thank you, madame. It is nothing. She will get her health."

A rush of words in Tamajeq to Husaini, too rapid for me to catch.

"He says you must not worry." Husaini was expressionless.

We left soon after.

"Why won't he let her, Husaini?" I asked when we got under way.

"Useless bastard! He is afraid of spending money. You know, if she goes he must spend money on transport and medicine and food to be brought to her. All these Kel Aïr are the same." Husaini in throw-away mode as usual. He always had some peculiar slant on things.

That prejudice again. I had forgotten – this was another "mixed marriage" in their terms – Sidi from Agadez, Zainabu from Tchin Tabaraden.

I said, "My son, tell me what the song says about the young women who drink American Aid milk . . ."

He looked at me in surprise but spat his wad of tobacco out the window and started up a brisk handclap without more ado.

"No, no, you don't have to do the song for me. Just tell me what it says, in Hausa."

"*To!*" He got a kick out of our translation work and by now knew what I wanted and could deliver a text with some precision. "It says that the young women 'of America' don't drink, that there is no milk now in the bowls. Then it says that the young women stand begging, they were beautiful before but now they are all burnt with the sun and they don't put butter in their long hair . . . "

"And they only water American powdered milk and drink it . . . that's the part I remember . . . " I had lived on powdered milk myself throughout my pregnancy and the aftermath. It might even have been American aid milk. *Not for resale.*

"Hear – then it says these sisters drink misery now but only last year, when they moved camp for salt, they were like queens, and the camp was full of young men and women sinning and playing!" He finished with a flourish, eyes gleaming, as if he had some fine memories of sinning and playing himself.

Khassim was on the front porch when we turned into my house. Somehow his stance was always like a bird of prey, a state of relaxation that was poised and alert, muscles coiled for action.

"*Salamu rhaleykum!* Peace be to you!" he greeted us.

"*Aleykum essalem!* And peace to you!" answered Husaini.

"*Meniy iselen?* What's the news?" With the guttural tone in his throat that meant business.

41

I gave him only a ghost of a smile as I passed him and left Husaini to give the formal response of "*Elkher rhas!* Only peace!*" Sometimes the falsity of these conventional responses stuck in my throat.

I was sitting on my bed nursing Minha when he came and rapped on my door.

He squatted down before me with a smile and a kiss for Minha. I wore my mask of blankness while my hands sweated and my vagina contracted.

"Madame," he said. "Don't worry. Don't spoil your spirit. You know Sidi is my kinsman. I will go to him early tomorrow morning when I get off work. I'll tell him truth. If you come after with your son," meaning Husaini, "you will take her to the hospital, God willing."

A quick glance at the open doorway and he kissed me passionately nose to nose.

Husaini shook me awake next morning – he had a back-door key and let himself in every morning when he knocked off his night-job. "Hey! Hey! My mother! Khadija's man has come! He went to Zaria early this morning. He has been arguing with Sidi since. Zainabu's mother is begging you to come because Zainabu is losing consciousness." A graceful gesture of head sinking to shoulder to illustrate this. "Khadija's man says that if Sidi refuses again he will call the police."

A moment of pride, marred by "Khadija's man". Did they refer to anyone else by the name of his wife?

This time I stood outside next to the car, with no pretence of sociability. Through the open door of the mud compound I could see Khassim and the other men in the outer yard. I watched Husaini go through the formal handshakes, the sharing of tobacco, the adjustment of veils. Sidi wore no veil and his hair was cropped. He had cut off his plaits to wear the peaked airport uniform hat.

Expressionless discussion continued. The men milled about and loitered up and down.

At last Husaini came out to me.

His eyes were smiling. "He agrees."

We stood among the mass of suffering humanity in the hospital. We had taken her to Emergency but then had to go back to the nightmare reception office to get her a number and card. After forty frantic minutes and a bribe, we had a card and counted ourselves lucky. When we got back to Emergency, we were told to wait. An English friend of mine, a road accident victim, had bled to death waiting in this room. I looked at Zainabu and thought, *she's dying*. I plunged into the hospital and fearfully began to waylay doctors coming out of the wards.

I stood by the examination table.

"See that pulse in her neck. She is in heart failure. She has lost too much blood." The Indian doctor pressed hard over her stomach. "We may not be able to save her."

He glanced at me swiftly.

"Why did they not bring her sooner?"

"Her husband wouldn't agree."

They did save her and later in the week I brought her back to her home.

But by that time everything had changed for me and I was incandescent with newfound energy. The night after I had taken her to the hospital I had driven Khassim out to the university plant nursery at Bomo Lake where he moonlighted as night-watchman and spent some hours with him, in blissful solitude under the stars. I did that every night from that night on.

Chapter Four

My friend Ronald, whose wife had left me Chilli, sent me a large postcard from England. I had just written to him with my news. The postcard was marked: *Le Bain, by Léon Carré* from *Le Jardin des Caresses* 1914. It featured a cappuccino-skinned naked lady, wearing a necklace and bracelets, being assisted into a stream by a fully-dressed dark-skinned bearded man in crimson robe and pale blue turban. They are surrounded by idyllic idealised vegetation. At the lady's naked feet is a long speckled scarf undulating through the grass. It could also be a snake.

"*Dear Kate,*

Some of the details of this record are not correct eg the baobabs, the absent pubic hair etc but never mind . . ."

The plant nursery was set on the side of Bomo Lake, a magic place, a stretch of water in that dryness. The radiance of the green-blue water, liquid cool lapping against the reeds, made your skin thirst to look at it. With the sun grilling down on you, you could put your hand in it and experience the miracle of wetness. You longed to get in, to embrace it, to be absorbed by it.

Around the nursery was a ring of tall slim stately trees like Lombardy poplars which swayed and beckoned to me from a distance as I approached along the little dirt road. I never did check what kind of trees they were, precisely. I had other things on my mind. The nursery itself was a large circular sandy area partly sheltered by gigantic spreading trees and enclosed by a high fence made of straw matting. A shed with a thatched roof ran along half the length of the enclosure. Inside and outside the shed were masses of shrubs and plants either in pots or with their roots embedded in earth bound in black plastic. I never once saw any university official or student labouring among the plants, never knew when they placed them there or took them away. Rarely saw anyone there but Dauda, Khassim's co-worker, and the supervising guard – the *rangadi* – who did the rounds of various university sites on his bicycle, checking up on the watchmen. Khassim's only manual labour was to water these potted plants and the banana trees planted here and there. The rest of the time he slept, made tea, prayed, chewed tobacco, watched, and chatted with any stray comer – sword, knife and whip always at the ready. He had an emerald green uniform which he largely neglected to wear, often putting just the thick shirt over his black traditional baggy pants as a token gesture to officialdom.

At night we sometimes went inside the plant-filled shed for a little more security but usually we risked lying on a mat out under the brilliance of the stars, though that meant our clothes had to stay on. Inside or out, we were constantly in a state of alert. Not least, perhaps, was the fear that discovery could cost us both our jobs. Nevertheless, for all our fears, we could never meet day or night without somehow, whatever the odds, making love. And, however hurried or leisurely it was, it always had to be the complete act – any oral play was always quickly abandoned as we rushed towards the state of oneness. And it seemed we were protected by the magic of the place – it truly seemed like the Narnian Wood between the Worlds. My vivid blue Toyota Land Cruiser stood there day after day, stray afternoon trippers from the campus came and went occasionally from the lake, locals from nearby Bomo village passed on their way to Samaru but no one ever once walked in on us and our love-making.

Sometimes, when I arrived and walked into the wide entrance, the place seemed to glow with an almost throbbing radiance. The energy was such that even the bicycle leaning against a tree-trunk seemed animate. Breezes from the lake shuffled through the leaves and sunlight gleamed and dappled and slid over the ground. Beyond, Khassim would be sitting serene, cross-legged, in dynamic stillness.

It never occurred to me at the time – why, I do not know – but he must have placed protective charms around the place. Of course he did.

He would not have neglected to do that.

I often went there with Minha in the afternoon – officially Khassim took over from Dauda at three. Dauda was a Hausaman from Maradi, just over the border in Niger, and they had forged a good partnership. Early on, I took some photos to show Jonathan: Dauda, a long-limbed good-looking man in his thirties, in proper uniform and peaked hat; Minha in little white dungarees posing like an adult with her hand on Khassim's shoulder; Khassim making tea, pouring it in a delicate stream from one little glass to another.

We spent much of our time making and drinking *shayi* –

green tea. I never much liked the tea but I was seduced by the making of it. The ritual was lengthy and soporific. The charcoal fetched first, then lit in the circular wire brazier with the help of pieces of straw, the little red enamelled teapot of water and leaves perched atop the coals, then the wait for it to boil. Meanwhile, pieces chipped off the huge hard phallic cone of sugar in its blue sugar-paper, the lid of the pot flipped back, lumps of sugar added. The hypnotic sub-ritual of pouring from pot to glasses and glasses to pot, each glass delicately held between thumb and third finger. Finally the murky green-brown tea poured for the last time into the little glasses and handed ceremoniously to each guest. Bitter enough to curl your tongue and drill a hole in your stomach, strong enough to wake the dead, but hot and wet. More water added, boiled again, the little lid flipped back and more lumps of sugar added, the whole process run through again. And all done with the right hand only, the left hand never being used in Africa for such a purpose. The second glass and then the last: yellow-gold, sweet enough to kill. I watched Khassim go through this innumerable times, this little balletic ritual choreographed and performed with Zen concentration. I watched every day, fascinated into a sensuous hypnotic state of deep restfulness.

The act of drinking too was special: there was a standard noisy sucking up of the liquid, whether quaffed in one go, taken slowly, or passed around and shared.

Then the little teapot, with its graceful curve of spout and handle, was washed and the glasses rinsed, again with the right hand only, silver rings glinting, and with the minimum of water on a little enamel or brass tray. Khassim's teapot had been lovingly repaired by the Inaden, the special Tuareg caste of craftsmen, with decorated little ovals of brass. Then the leaves and sugar were wrapped and folded and stowed away in fringed leather pouches with exquisite care, for the next time. The tray dried with a shaking of sand and the tapping of a fingernail. The fire doused with sand.

It was a meditation, a communion, a courtesy, a welcome.

Perhaps we needed no other magic ritual but this one which paid homage to all the properties of earth, water, wind and fire and the skills of man.

I hadn't visited Jonathan for an unusually long period nor had he come to see me. He had a reason, of course. I swung by his bungalow every couple of days – on my way to or from the building-site – but, every time, there was a snazzy black car outside his door and I passed on. We saw each other as usual at the university and one day I tracked him down during lunch-time at the staff pool and we rushed through a brief progress report – brief because I couldn't bear to be out in the midday sun for too long.

It was time for a proper visit. I needed that. I parked next to the snazzy black and went to the door and knocked boldly. Through the mosquito-netting I could see he was in his bedroom. A guest who was not a guest. When Jonathan called "Enter!" and I went in, they were miraculously transported to the living-room, Cokes in hand. This time Musa Ibrahim was in full traditional Hausa splendour – embroidered pill-box hat and embroidered damask robes. But twirling his car keys on a long lean finger. He really was extremely handsome.

49

"Rutherford," said Jonathan in his dry ironic way from where he sprawled on his divan. "What are you up to now?"

What are *you* up to, I thought, but didn't say. Obviously *not* in the throes of sexual congress, at any rate, judging from the well-pressed cut of Musa.

Musa left soon after, visibly ill-at-ease, saying something about a new extension to his house and having to see the builders.

When he left Jonathan shot into the bedroom and I followed, scanning for bedrooom activity but finding nothing of note.

He pulled off his clothes, displaying the well-formed bum I was well familiar with, and pulled a little short cotton *zane* around his hips.

"An underpants might be not a bad idea, Jonathan, if you intend to sunbathe in that."

"Who's to see? Now that Musa's gone?"

"Your house-boy, for one."

"I sent him to the market. Come on now – take a *zane*, Rutherford. Look at that Bature skin. You need some sun."

"Jonathan, it's high-bloody-noon out there. I'd fry."

"No, you won't." He refused to acknowledge the difference between my pathetic Celtic skin and his tougher darker version.

Feet thrust in rubber flip-flops, sunglasses stuck atop his head and he was already in the kitchen ladling rice and stew onto two plastic plates.

I opened the mosquito screen on the back door for him. "I'm made for the mists and the bogs, Jonathan. I have to accept it."

We went out into the hideous glare where he shoved a plate and spoon in my hand and laid his nut-brown body out on a camp bed.

"You'll get cancer," I said, as I always said when he basked while I cowered. "And no matter how dark you get you'll never be a Nigerian."

"Bitch!" he said. Then, "You should get a sunhat."

"No one wears sunhats except eccentric foreigners."

He cocked an eyebrow.

"So," I said. "As I'm not an eccentric foreigner, I can't."

"So get one of those great black Tuareg veils then."

The stew was Nigerian-hot. But good. I was grateful for it. Jonathan ate much better than I did. Me and my innumerable hangers-on were, of economic necessity, on an all but meatless diet.

"Worked up an appetite, have you?" I asked, as it was time for confidences. We kept each other well informed on states of heart, mind, soul and body.

"Mmmmm."

"So? Tell me all about him."

"I told you now," using the emphatic, Nigerian-style "now".

"Tell me more. I'm not sitting stewing and frying out here for nothing."

"I'm in heaven," he said.

I grinned. "Long may it last."

"And you?" he asked.

"I'm in paradise."

"He's good at it, then?"

"It's amazing, Jonathan. This is the first man I've ever been with where I just have to lie there and wait for it and do nothing at all."

"In the much-maligned missionary position, I take it?"

I burst out laughing. "Absolutely!" He had been fascinated by my passionate defence – on feminist grounds – of the much-maligned missionary position and declared himself converted, in principle of course, after I demonstrated with diagrams. "It's the only way to go!"

"*Come*, you mean. But – the day at the pool – I thought you told me he didn't fit?"

"Oh, you know! It always seems like that at the start. Like it will never work. Like you'll never fit together."

"And Rhisa?"

"Oh God, don't bring me down. What about your Hausaman? Does he fit?"

"Like a plug in a sink – like the neck on a bottle of Star beer – like mortar and pestle – "

"OK, OK, enough lyricism already – Jesus! Ummmm – I take it you're the mortar and he's the pestle?"

He grimaced. "Yes. The usual problem. As long as I'm at the receiving end he doesn't have to think he's queer." There was a whiteness and tension around his mouth for a moment.

Oh-ho. Snake in the grass, problems in paradise. "Hope I didn't interrupt things earlier?"

"Oh, no. He really had to go see the builders about this extension. His two young nephews have been living with him – his sister's children – to be educated or whatever. The rich uncle syndrome. Space is a problem. He always has to come here as it is."

Oh, dear. Was space the only problem? I doubted it.

"Hey!" said Jonathan, looking brighter. Mischievous, even. "He says their hair has gone red since they've been with him! His nephews. He was joking about putting boot-polish on it!"

I hesitated. "You know . . . I think that's protein deficiency."

He looked astounded. "How do you know that?"

"I read it somewhere. Are their stomachs distended?"

"I don't know."

"I'm a bit vague now, but I definitely remember that about the hair colour. He's probably not feeding them properly. Probably just giving them the bit of rice or guinea corn. Saving on food expenses. Trust a bachelor! Tell him he must give them meat!"

Jonathan looked comical, at the thought of the thoroughly-modern-Musa making this kind of mistake. "Jesus, how am I going to tell him that?"

"You're asking me?" I said, ruefully, thinking of the dusty gold-brown colour of Yakubu's curls which Khadija seemed to be blind to, for all her fretting about Minha's hair.

When I arrived at the plant nursery Khassim was preparing to do *salla*, the prayers of *la'asar*, the period before sunset. I sat and watched intently but discreetly as, squatting, he went through the graceful mime: the washing of the hands up to the wrist three times, then the mouth and nose and face, then up to the elbows three times, over the head, then feet to the ankle. But never with water, always with imaginary sand, bringing his desert heritage down here with him. Not for him the blue plastic kettles pious Hausamen carried around with them for the purpose.

He rose to his feet and stood erect, relaxed, like a swimmer preparing for an Olympic high dive. The murmur of the prayers came across the clearing to me as he went through the exercise, the kneeling, the bending, the touching of the forehead to the ground, the final relaxed moments where he sat back in kneeling position, legs to one side, in meditation.

I thought of Husaini's teasing efforts to get me to say the *Shahadah* – the declaration of faith. "Say it now! *La ilaha illal-Lah Muhammad-ur-Rasulullah* . . . say it!" *There is no god but God and Muhammed is his messenger.* If I recited it once I would be officially converted so I stubbornly refused as a matter of principle. Damned if I would. They could take me as an infidel or not at all.

To be honest, though, it never seemed to matter much to them. The Tuareg were notoriously lax Muslims.

Khassim finished his prayers and smiled across the clearing at me. We sat for a while and smiled ironic smiles at each other.

Today I had set myself a little task. I was still fretting about his lawless past and I needed to ask him about it. There were so many things I needed to ask him but never did. When we talked, it was about dreams. I told him about my longing to live in Niger in the desert and my passionate envy of expatriates who did live there, like the American missionaries and Peace Corps. I told him that if it were possible to find work teaching English in Agadez I would be gone tomorrow. His dream was simply to live the life his people had lived for thousands of years, free, self-sufficient, accountable to no one. In his dream-image he was working at the well with his sons and his brothers and Iklan in a sweat of excitement and effort, drawing water for a countless herd of beautiful white camels – or sitting at night before his tent under the stars with a woman who was the envy of the whole world. In my dream, of course, I was the woman though I knew I didn't qualify. For one thing, I wasn't fat enough.

So our dreams dovetailed but neither of us, for our different reasons, could go to live in Agadez. He was wanted and I was unqualified.

These were the things we talked about, besides everyday gossip, never anything more disturbing. I never could bear to shatter the tranquil surface of the pool in our Wood between the Worlds. There were other worlds beneath that surface, many of them menacing.

That day, however, I steeled myself and asked him some questions as the sun set. So I asked and heard about the hiding of swords and guns in the desert rocks, heard about the life of an outlaw – not the heroic version but the true version – from the man who had suffered it, not the poets who wrote the songs.

I made myself listen when it was my practice to close my ears, resenting as I did their blinkered clinging to the age-old depredations which would finish them off in the modern world. When the French had tried to educate them they hid their sons in the desert and sent the sons of their slaves to school. Now they had only the slimmest of representation in a government and military dominated by Hausa and Zarma-Songhai. They were helpless, already heavily dependent on western Aid and hounded by five different governments, their nomadic kingdom straddling as it did the modern sates of Algeria, Mali, Burkina Faso, Niger, Libya. And these outlaw antics could only make the situation worse.

"But how is it you did not feel the fear of death?" I asked. "Or did that not worry you?"

"You know," he hesitated and looked at me, his face red with the light of the setting sun. He continued almost in a whisper, as if he were imparting a great secret to me or a shameful one. "I was a fighter when I was young. Look!" He raised a hand, splaying it for me to see it in the red light. "When I get angry I lose myself. I see a red colour like this all around me, like a mist. Everything is red. Like

55

your face is now." He stretched a hand as if to touch my face and then gestured vaguely at the rose-tinted landscape around. "I remember nothing when the mist clears but while it is there I fight like a devil."

See red. *He sees red.*

Time and again it happened. The sensual roots of our emotions and language exposed to me.

He took out his *taba* – his tobacco – tied in its dusty little rag and opened it up. I waited and watched while he went though the balancing of the leaves on the lower lip, the initial chewing, the addition and grinding of the tiny piece of potash between his teeth, the spitting of the juice and eventual poising of the wad on the lower lip.

"Is it true," I asked, "that until now you are wanted by the government in Niger?"

"They are looking for me," he said abruptly.

"But what was the reason you fled from Aïr in the end? Did it become too difficult to stay?"

He spat a stream of juice and worried the wad of tobacco between his lips. Then he looked at me. "I got into a fight with a chief's son – from one of the neighbouring drum-groups. I won." There was a kind of fear and wonder on his face. "My sword went away with his hand. That sword there." He pointed with his lips to where his sword leant against a tree. His grandfather's sword. "His right hand." He clasped his wrist to show me, reliving the moment. "I had to leave then and I cannot return. If his father and brothers do not kill me, they will call the police to do it."

"So that is why you never go back?"

"I have not seen my family for ten years – except when they come here. My mother died and I couldn't go back. Only a thousand kilometres – two days is enough – and I could not go. Patience is everything." He smiled at me. "I will stay here until Nigeria kills me. Or until the Kel Tamajeq take up their swords again."

"That won't happen, Khassim."

"It will happen. Without a doubt."

***

It was one o'clock in the morning and NEPA, the Nigerian Electricity Board, was up to its usual tricks. No light. No water, either. No bath – the bath was full of stored water as usual.

I had just come back from Khassim's plant nursery and I had a nine o'clock lecture. Unprepared as yet.

On top of that, the diarrhoea that was a way of life for all of us had suddenly struck. Life was at its Nigerian best. A touch of malaria, now, would be the icing on the cake. And I had forgotten to buy mosquito coils. I sat on the bed where I could swat the mosquitos away from Minha. The screens on the doors and windows didn't really keep them out unless you were super-vigilant but I hadn't used a mosquito net on the bed since I was a greenhorn.

Hunched there on the side of the bed, sweating in the close fan-less heat, mosquitos buzzing unimpeded around my ankles, I squinted at my TS Eliot by candlelight.

The Waste Land. Sahara. "Sahara" meant "waste-land".

Phlebas the Phoenician, a fortnight dead,

Forgot the cry of gulls, and the deep sea swell

And the profit and loss.

Christ, they've never seen the deep sea swell . . . or a gull.

But how strange. My Touaregs' alphabet was derived from the ancient Phoenician alphabet. They must have seen the deep sea swell long centuries ago.

I wrote: *Explain Phoenician. Check they know what a fortnight is.*

Profit and loss, OK.

O O O O that Shakespeherian Rag –
It's so elegant
So intelligent . . .

I scribbled on my A4 pad: *line 128 – note that Shakespeherian is not a misspelling – can anyone tell me the correct spelling? Can anyone tell me what a rag is? Not the common meaning – something to do with the rhythm. Syncopated – i.e. transference of accent to normally unaccentuated beat. Jazz.*

Check they know meaning of elegant.

Christ. Those six lines should take up the hour.

I sat upon the shore
Fishing, with the arid plain behind me
Shall I at least set my lands in order?
London Bridge is falling down falling down falling down
Poi s'ascose nel foco che gli affina
Quando fiam uti chelidon – O swallow swallow
Le Prince d'Aquitaine à la tour abolie
These fragments I have shored against my ruins
Why then Ile fit you. Hieronymo's mad againe.

Jesus Christ.

I wrote: *Does anyone know what a nursery rhyme is?*

I could hear it: "*Mrs Rutherford? Why must we learn about British culture?*

I wrote: *The Waste Land makes a statement about the decadence and disintegration of European civilisation . . .*

I thought, can't go wrong with that . . .

My eyes were closing. Minha's sweet little body beckoned.

I blew out the candle and lay beside her. The mosquitos got to work.

Chapter Five

Khadija was having her hair plaited. She lay at ease on her side like a seal basking at the zoo, leather pillow under her armpit, head propped on a hand. Dark-blue glass bracelets glowed on her wrists. Raechita, an older Tuareg woman with a well-lined face, was smearing blue hair-gel on her palms and rubbing it into the loosened hair. Raechita was wife of Abdulaye, one of Khassim's co-workers on the building-site. She lived across the main road where her husband had somehow acquired one of the "stewards' quarters" – servants' quarters – that belonged to Jonathan's group of bungalows. She had approached us that day, brazier in hand to beg charcoal, her long black *zane* trailing in the dust, and Khadija had press-ganged her into plaiting her hair.

"*To*, Raechita, listen," said Khadija. "God brought you. Now-now we were talking about marriage – Kate was asking me about marriages where there are two women. Tell her your *histoire* about your stay in Agadez with the Arab."

"*To!*" Raechita took one side of Khadija's hair and twisted it up into a knot out of the way. "Hear." She spat a stream of tobacco and poised the little wad on her lower lip. She began to work on the other side of the hair with a decorated blunt-edged instrument like a knife, dividing it into strands. "I was married when I was a small girl. My father married me to a friend of his, an Arab in the town of Agadez. He was a big trader. My mother had died, so after the marriage, instead of keeping me at home until I grew up, my father sent me to stay with the Arab's family when I was still a small girl. Hear! I was so young that when I first had a period I didn't know what it was. It was he who told me and showed me everything – how to fold a cloth for the blood, how to put it on." She stuck the hair-knife into a lock of Khadija's hair and with eloquent hand gestures showed us how he had shown her. "I had gone in the night to urinate and when I saw the blood I started to cry."

In the night?

I sat, heart racing, afraid to ask.

Afraid to ask.

I had gone in the night to urinate . . . and he showed me . . . what did she mean? Surely she hadn't actually been sleeping with him before she began to menstruate?

Nothing in her face, no guilt, no anger. No shame.

"After that I became pregnant three times," fingers raised for emphasis, knife held against her palm with her thumb, "but I miscarried every time and his mother began to talk to him against me saying that he should divorce me, that I couldn't give him children." She went back to her work on the hair. "But he wanted me and didn't listen to her. Then she began to force him to take a second wife. So I went to him and said: 'To. Take a second wife if you want to. But that day I will pack my things and go. I will not agree to stay like that.' And then, by the will of God, I became pregnant again and I gave birth to my daughter Fatoni who is now in Agades. Praise be to God! But because of his mother my husband took a second wife. He didn't tell me until he brought her home. And that day I packed my things and I went to him and said: 'To. It is enough for me. Let us part in peace.' And I left."

So many years after and the pain still clear on her face.

She had stayed in Agadez, not returned to the desert, so she was not parted from her daughter until hard times had driven one of her sons, by a later marriage, south to Nigeria.

"Until now," she said, spitting out more juice, "Fatoni's father takes care of me. I made two more marriages and even after my third husband died Fatoni's father didn't leave me hungry. I am only in Nigeria because I followed my son here." She had divided the hair in a complicated pattern, giving Khadija certain tresses to hold. She suddenly looked piercingly at me. "Madame, don't you ever try to enter a marriage with two women." She grasped the knife fiercely in her fist and gave it a little emphatic shake. "You hold to your habits. Your habits and ours are the same. So the time when you marry you will feel the sweetness of your husband, you alone!"

And there it was again – "*when you marry*" – my five-year-old relationship with Rhisa always ignored.

Later, hair freshly gleaming in a complex weave of little tresses, Khadija got busy and swept the dirt area around the hut, bending from the waist as they all did and working the handleless broom which was basically a bundle of twigs. I watched her, my brain ticking over compulsively as ever, filing, categorising, weighing up differences, assessing comparative worth, storing information, collecting facts to report to Jonathan, fascinated, wearing myself out in my efforts to understand. In this instance, I was wondering why no one in this part of the world had ever experienced the *eureka* moment that had resulted in the broom-handle in Europe: the notion that it would be a bloody good idea to attach a stick to the broom and save the strain on the back. Women's backs, slaves' backs – was that why nobody cared? Of course, the end-product was stiff spines in Europe and supple spines in Africa but it still bothered me that the moment of illumination had never dawned. Surely wood wasn't in *that* short supply with the rain-forests to the south. Wouldn't wooden spoons be a damn sight more efficient and comfortable than plunging the hand into the communal stew-pot? Of course, I reminded myself, the Tuareg did have wooden spoons. And ne'er a need to sweep the sands of the desert.

I lost focus on my meanderings as Khassim and Elhassan, a first cousin of his who had just come from Agadez on a visit, arrived back from the market.

Khassim had bought a gift for Yakubu, a pair of long cotton trousers with a draw-string at the waist, but when he tried to put it on the child he found that it wouldn't come up over his distended little stomach. He stroked Yakubu's belly with his fingers, laughing ruefully.

Christ. They saw it as healthy fat.

I kept bringing tins of powdered milk but it was no good. Khadija would drink it off herself in an attempt to add to her girth or sell it to the labourers or give it to passing guests and hangers-on. The little tins of evaporated milk and fish were always there for her *tebur*. Never for Yakubu. She sold them and added penny to penny in her big tin trunk.

There had been a major disaster a year before when a young guest, a kinsman of Khassim's, had prised open the box, swept all her savings away and fled – to Libya or

Lagos, no one knew where. The story was that Khassim himself was paying her back the money, since it was his kinsman who had stolen it. It figured.

Rhisa and the others thought it all pretence and seethed with resentment. If they ever asked Khassim for a loan he said he owed Khadija such and such and had no money. If Khassim needed a tin of fish or condensed milk he paid her right before all their cynical eyes.

I wondered. I thought she was tough enough to make him pay in earnest.

And she had lived in a trading environment which none of them understood – her southern Ibo women would be powerful market women.

I knew for a fact Khadija never bought anything for the family, like food or medicine or clothing. That was Khassim's responsibility. And so she salted away her money with her beloved little son's distended stomach before her eyes.

On the other hand, Rhisa and company could be right. They were so *married*, that pair – they had all sorts of systems going. I was intrigued to hear Husaini assert once, to my astonishment, that Khassim and Khadija weren't truly married – that he had never paid the bride-price. That Khadija had used her own money to pay the bride-price to her kinsmen, pretending it was Khassim's. Trust Husaini to come up with that. Possibly he was more observant than anyone else – in any case, all his pronouncements were made with a cheerful naivety that robbed them of any vindictiveness.

Khassim sat down beside me. I forgot about brooms and spoons – and wheels for that matter – about protein deficiency and money habits and power-struggles and watched his face as he played with his little daughter. She was so painfully like him. She stood, tiny legs straddling his knee, little arms planted on his thigh bearing her weight, head back, sparkling black eyes focused on his face. A beautiful, fit little infant like all the ones still on the breast. It was after they were weaned that things went wrong. Khassim laughed deep in his throat and there was some quality of embarrassment to his laughter which I couldn't interpret. Could it somehow be because of me? Had I let the veil drop for a moment and had he seen my envy glaring out at him?

Some expletives from Khadija drew his gaze. "She's angry now," he said mischievously, ironic. "She's working. Always when she's working she's angry."

And there was such a depth of affection and familiarity in his gaze and in his words it made me quail. A squawk from Khadija and a thud. She had tripped on her trailing black *zane* and fallen on her hands and knees. Khassim chuckled and Elhassan called out some teasing comment I didn't catch. They slapped hands, laughing.

Khadija laughed with them and, throwing the broom aside, came and sat with us, her great bosom heaving. I thought it ridiculous that the little bit of exertion should reduce her to this gasping state. She'd have a heart-attack eventually at this rate. My anger against the fattening process went so deep I felt vindictive about that. Serve her right. And him. And all of them. Insisting a woman should carry all that weight. Like camels storing fat against drought and famine.

"*Ekli*, are you mocking me?" she asked Khassim, breathless, smiling.

"Never! *Teklit*, we are giving you respect for all the

work you have done," said Khassim fondly, responding with the pet-name they used between them – *Ekli*, *Teklit*, slave, slavewoman – and cutting me to the heart.

She was late with the food and I was glad. A few other men arrived, greeted us and sat.

"*Teklit*, the day is passing," said Khassim without any particular inflection. "I must go back to the market around two. To collect a loan."

A reprimand! I was pathetically pleased.

"The rice is nearly cooked," she said blandly in a fashion that made it sound like an observation of her own rather than a response to his statement.

Shortly after, we ate. The men, five around the bowl. Khadija and I with the women's bowl to ourselves. Rice cooked in red palm-oil, tomato, onion, stock-cubes and a few pieces of meat here and there for the lucky ones.

Khadija's sweeping blitz had certainly thrown her off course. The rice was mouth-burningly hot. She had put too much ground chilli-pepper in. I felt as if it were taking the skin off my mouth.

The spoon went round the men's bowl. After a couple of rounds Khassim cleared his throat. "*Teklit*," he said mildly, "the pepper is much!" Another reprimand on behalf of his guests.

I gloated secretly.

"There's pepper!" was her response. An acknowledgement rejecting all guilt and blame.

I ate, pleased she had blundered with the pepper but eaten with despair. It was like that between them, formality masking an intimacy that belied his feelings for me.

I went straight from there to Jonathan, needing comfort, but found him sitting with his two hands in the icebox of the fridge.

"What the hell are you doing?" I asked laughingly. But then I saw his eyes were red-rimmed. "Are you OK? What's happened to your hands?"

"I'm OK," he grinned ruefully. "One of my time-saving plans that went wrong. I was cutting up a huge pile of chilli-peppers thinking to make a massive amount of meat stew to freeze and store. I burnt the hands off myself. It's been a couple of hours – they're OK now. I keep coming back and sticking them in here. It's working. Jesus, the pain at the start. I couldn't believe it." He shuddered.

"Well, believe this! I came here to tell you a pepper story! I've just nearly got my mouth burned off – Khadija overdid the pepper in the rice." And I told him the little story.

I expected him to listen with his usual eagerness, filing it busily in "the computer" with that far-seeing look of intelligence in his eyes, the whirr of the brain ticking over almost audible. But he bit his lips and looked even more white-faced.

I thought he was just distracted by the pain.

Finally, he shook his head. "Those Tuareg women. They're unbelievable. Imagine a Hausa woman speaking to her husband like that."

"It's killing me," I said. "How *married* those two are. What a *couple* they are."

Jonathan gave a wry grin. "You say it's killing you but, actually, the truth is you'd kill for a story. It hurts you but, you're so fascinated by it, you're smiling as you tell me. And not just because Khadija fucked up and disgraced him with her hot pepper." He shook his head again. "You know what you are? You're a writer in your soul. If you don't have drama you go out and create it. You're not living a life. You're writing a story."

I shook my head impatiently. Everyone was forever urging me to write about the Buzus. It irritated me. I didn't see why I had to justify my relationship with them.

"Musa was here," said Jonathan.

"Oh?" There was something more than his hands burning him up.

"Came just after this happened. I was in such pain I was crying. Crying, imagine! I said to him, 'If this is what you do to the little girls who fool around, it's a wonder they ever have sex in their lives again!' Because he told me they rub pepper into their genitals. The pain must be horrendous."

And I was dying inside all over again.

"And what did he say?"

"He just shrugged his shoulders. And said he would never do such a thing himself. But I told him to get out. I was furious. He went."

"He'll be back."

"I know." He took his hands out and sat with them hanging between his knees. They looked pretty raw.

"How are things with him? Otherwise?" I asked tentatively.

He was silent for such a long time, staring at his hands, that I thought he hadn't heard me.

But some instinct made me wait.

"He's getting married," he said.

Elhassan, the guest from Agadez, was curled up on the mat fellating the child. Yakubu giggled and drew his legs up, his little penis erect as his uncle repeatedly took it in his mouth.

I couldn't bear it, fascinated.

I said nothing.

"This is the good thing about a male baby," he said laughing at my stare. "You can't do this play with a girl."

Yakubu pulled his uncle's head down by the hair. Elhassan began to suck again. Yakubu laughed hysterically, threshing with his legs.

I sat in a sweat, my skin prickling. Angry, genitals pulsing.

"*Bastard!*" Khadija's plastic sandal slammed across the hut. Something scuttled through the straw matting. "Bastard of a mouse! Until I kill him! Bastard! Robber!" She retrieved the sandal and came back smiling quizzically at my expression of astonishment. "Did you see him? Doesn't he have the heart? To come here in the sun looking for my guinea corn?"

Khadija as warrior. I felt diminished by her prowess. I was terrified of mice.

Khadija leant from the hips over the pot, lifting the blackened lid, scooping a grain of rice out with a piece of straw. She pressed the rice between thumb and finger and pursed her lips. "Yet!" She joined me on the mat, plumping down heavily.

I heard the bicycle before she did. Khassim. Yakubu heard it too and was distracted from Elhassan's play for a moment – then he gasped in surprise as his uncle's mouth came down again.

Khassim took a brown-paper parcel from the carrier of the bike and approached with his long-limbed stride, pushing the veil down from his smiling mouth with a long finger. "Madame!" And the formal handshake with the secret little bite of a fingernail into the palm of my hand.

He grinned at Yakubu's giggles. "OK, Yakubu? What's this laughter?"

He handed the parcel to Khadija and a huge piece of steak all but spilled out. "It's for you two. I must go straight to work. Eat it *all*!" A big circular movement of a long forefinger. He was off to do his moonlighting.

Elhassan sat up and adjusted his *tagilmoust* while Khadija exclaimed shrilly over the meat, questioning Khassim about it. He answered her as he fumbled in his pocket and took out the knotted handkerchief that held his tobacco. I watched him as he stood there with his characteristic graceful tension, going through the little tobacco ritual, all the while his quizzical gaze fixed on me.

He looked as though he were trying to communicate something. Then Elhassan slipped his feet in his sandals and got to his feet and I realised what it was. Elhassan was accompanying him to work.

My whole fragile world swayed and crashed. I could have burst into tears. They walked to where the bicycle was leaning against the fence behind the hut and, with much laughter, began to discuss whether they could both manage to get up on it. I was devastated. Did I matter so little to him? How could he so cheerfully go off with Elhassan? A night without him would kill me. Without the daily pledge of sex between us everything would be thrown into terrifying doubt.

"Well, we thank you for the meat!" Khadija cried after him as they at last wobbled off, Khassim awkwardly bedecked with cheap Chinese flashlight, knife and traditional sword, Elhassan precariously perched on the carrier.

"*Kai!* We have luck!" she said, indicating the meat.

I stared at her, feeling the intimacy and affection between us. My secret was a kind of power I had over her assurance.

What would she say if I told her? What if she could accept it? What if it could always be like this? If I were part of the family? If Khassim married me? Would it really be such a blow to her pride? They were Muslims after all. And she had been in a polygamous marriage before. In any case, wouldn't her shrewd business sense win her round, if nothing else did? What price a rich Infidel co-wife who could set her up in a proper business? I had no money – but she didn't know that. She probably had more stashed away in her tin trunk than I had in the bank.

I couldn't continue like this. This hole-and-corner stuff was slow torture.

I would tell her. I must. I'd beg her to let him marry me.

"How will we cook it?" she was saying. "The fire is cold. On the stove?" And she cooked it by throwing it on the large circular enamelled top of the primus stove. I had never seen that done before.

I remember eating that meat very well. It was surprisingly good – quite tender. My heart was racing. I knew that as soon as we had eaten the last bite I would say, "Khadija, I want to marry your husband."

My fingers trembled. I thought she must surely notice. Khadija, save us all. Say you'll accept me.

She made sure the last piece of the meat went to me.

I ate it and said nothing.

Chapter Six

When the knock came to the French window he sprang to his feet and practically cowered, in the time-honoured stance of the man caught with his pants down, one hand holding his trousers up. Frightened as I was, I still registered that he looked utterly craven and stupid standing there like that.

NEPA was on the blink again and shadows from our candle danced on the wall. I hesitated – then blew the candle out. We stayed still, quaking, and whoever it was went round the back. More knocking.

They would wake Minha.

Voices. Christ. They might settle down on the back porch.

Eventually there was silence. I went and peered out through the bamboos.

No one.

I went back. "They're gone."

"I thank God."

I lit the candle again. He was still standing there, holding his pants.

I hardly dared to say it. I knew I was teetering on a precipice. "How is it you are afraid like that? How is it you feel shame like that?"

71

He stared. "Khadija would go mad!" he said.

Why, I thought, why? Why would she go mad? And why did it matter if she did? Every negative feeling came crashing into my heart. All my hopes. The hopes so secret I'd been hiding them from myself. My hopes that he might choose me above her. My hopes that maybe he was strong enough not to care if people knew he was screwing the Baturiya. The hope that he loved me. The hope he might tell her. The hope we had a future.

I despised him.

"And what about Rhisa?" he asked. "Contempt for me is what he would feel if he knew."

Contempt for *you*. Oh, your good name is the only important issue in question here.

"And you?" he asked with slight aggression. "Don't you care? You are cheating him and you don't feel any shame?"

I was floundering. Was that all we were supposed to feel, then? Shame?

"I don't feel shame," I said, my voice trembling. "My wanting you is too much."

His chest was heaving a little. "In truth, with me too, it is so."

I thought, say it now, the moment is passing. "Khassim?"

"What?"

"What if you marry me? Would Khadija not agree?"

"To divorce?"

"No – I mean . . . if you were to marry me without divorcing her . . . "

"Two wives!" He was startled. "She would never agree."

I was silent.

He didn't really want me, I thought.

We did make love. I could never say no to that. But I was shaken.

I had been fooling myself.

So this was the deal again. Furtive passion in the dark. Another man who would not have the courage to say, yes, I was his woman.

Jonathan's electricity generator was whumping away in his garage when I arrived. He scuttled out, opened the door and scuttled back into his bedroom without a word. I carried Minha in and deposited her on his living-room divan.

When I went in he was stretched on his bed, in khaki shorts, pale and sweating from an attack of diarrhoea. "I have the runs," was his feeble greeting, a commonplace one in Nigeria.

I stood in the middle of the floor in my black Buzu robes and told my story like a one-woman Greek chorus.

"God bless the man," said Jonathan in rueful wonder. "He's monogamous."

And I was perversely proud that he was. In a secret corner of my soul there was a gloating thought: *light-years ahead of your Hausa polygamist, Jonathan.* "But I'm scared. I just want to pull out. The signs are bad, bad, Jonathan." And suddenly I started to cry with the despair of it.

"I know, love. I know." He sighed. "You want him. And you want him to yourself. The party's over."

"Oh, God. I've been here before," I sobbed. "It's terrifying to feel the pain starting in. Why does the joy go so soon and the bloody hunger come on?"

"I guess we're made like that."

"I want to pull out *now*. I know what's down the road,

73

the rest of the story. But . . . maybe it's not really that I want him to myself . . . it's more like wanting to belong to him than wanting to possess him."

"What are you saying? That you want to share him?" said Jonathan sharply.

"Yes, I'm saying that, I could agree to that."

"God, maybe you should try it now," he said, intrigued. "Surely he'd agree? For all you say, *nobody* is monogamous here. How can he be?"

"I told you. It's to do with the status of their women."

"There's a fine irony." He shook his head and went "tsk-tsk" in wonder. "He wouldn't have the capacity to be so intense about you but for that."

It was true. But there had to be a way around this. "Honest to God, when I sit in the evening with Khadija and the children, I really believe it could work."

"Mmmmm," he considered it gravely, doubtfully, gnawing at his thumb, and shook his head.

"*You're* doing it," I said.

"I'm trying – and not in the Nigerian sense of succeeding. But . . . Kate . . . look . . . hang in there if you can . . . sometimes it is true half a loaf can be better than no bread. If you can fix up any system where you can have each other – with a bit more security – "

"I know. It's the old story. If I only had a bit of emotional control . . . "

"Look – there could be a marvellous piece of living ahead. And no need for hunger pains. But talking of control . . . " He plunged for the bathroom, grimacing.

I sat and waited.

He came back white-faced.

"You OK?" I asked.

"Yeah."

"Are you taking something for that?"

"I'm trying starvation."

He lay back gingerly.

We listened to the whine of the generator.

"God, I know what I wish," I said suddenly.

"What?"

"I wish this thing with Khassim would grow with such force that it will make its own way and take over and be part of my life forever."

"Then thank God for that, girl! And do the right things."

"Like what?" I asked.

He smiled weakly. "Be patient."

I smiled back. "Be cheerful."

We smiled at each other, grinning at the challenge. "Be calm."

"Be a comfort."

"Be sexy," he said.

"Be fun."

"Be *available*," he said.

"Be docile."

"Be helpful."

"Emmmmm . . . be a good listener."

"Be a good *cook*!" he said.

"Feed him red meat," I laughed. "And fresh milk from the farm!"

His stomach visibly heaved and he clutched at it.

"Sorry," I said.

"Emmmmm . . . be closer to Khadija . . . " he said, cocking a shrewd eye.

"Are you accusing me of manipulation?" I said. "Let's

see . . . OK . . . help write his lectures for him when he takes days off for dirty weekends at Kainji Dam Hotel?"

"Bitch! How do you know I did that?"

"A lucky guess," I grinned. I had seen the notes.

"Help him build an extension to his house for his new wife?" he said, wincing at either his stomach or the memory. The extension had been for Djibrilla, the *amarya*, of course.

"More gifts for the kids . . . ?"

"Guilty again . . . but who told you?"

"Saw the Michael Jackson T-shirts."

"OK . . . right . . . let's see . . . give him ready and lavish loans promptly on request?"

I stared at him and suddenly took a downward plunge from our little high into depression. "How much have you given him?"

His mouth twisted. "Not prepared to say. Not chicken-feed."

"Yes," I said. "More . . . money."

"*Always* more money," with a heart-felt sigh. "Much more money."

We brooded for another while and then, with great difficulty, I told him the fellation story. For once, I got no sympathy. As I might have expected.

He said, "It sounds like a wonderful custom to me."

I didn't have the energy just then to launch into our usual exploratory debate so I sidestepped the subject and fished the few photos I had taken of Khassim and Dauda at the plant nursery out of my bag.

"God," said Jonathan, staring a black-and-white one I had taken of Khassim in profile. "He's fantastic. This one's got it all – the humour, the looks, the energy, the intelligence. And I can tell he's a rogue! Oh, what a man! I could sink my hands into those curls right now. Rutherford, you've got to have a child with this one."

Diarrhoea and all, poor Jonathan was generous as ever with his energy and enthusiasm.

Musa had married. The wedding had actually been ready to roll by the time he told Jonathan the well-churned typical story: his family had arranged the marriage, she was his cousin, he didn't want her, there was no way he could go against his father, it wouldn't make any difference.

We and every other unattached Bature we knew had heard it all before.

Jonathan was heart-broken but was soldiering on. He was very much in love. This was as good as he could ever expect in Nigeria, he said, and perhaps it might work?

There was something else I had to tell him, something I'd been shying away from since I arrived. I got to my feet again.

"Rutherford, sit down now! You're making me nervous."

I had a habit of staying on my feet when we had our discussions, walking up and down as I talked, like I used to do with my mother in her kitchen long years ago. "I'm OK. I prefer to stand."

"Sit! Have you never noticed? I never stand when I can sit and I never sit when I can lie down. Conserve your energy and counteract the effects of gravity! Particularly vital for me at the present moment."

It was true. He spent as much time as he could afford stretched out on that bed, recuperating from the customary whirlwind pace of his active life. That was Jonathan. No half measures.

"Oh, you don't see all the sitting and lying down I do daily on Tuareg mats," I said.

"I've heard about it," rolling the eyes. "And I envy you." He stared at me soberly. "You know – it got to me the other day when you described how you and Khassim went through all that farcical stuff that afternoon – you know, at the nursery, when Dauda hung around and Minha wouldn't sleep? And you wanted to screw?"

I nodded with a grin.

"And you actually went into the shed and did it anyway when Dauda took her down to the water for a minute? You were seeing Khassim that evening in any case! I couldn't get over the fact you couldn't be together at all without having to screw. I thought, Christ, why am I putting up with this sparse attention from Musa? And his bloody marriage."

"Khassim has a bloody marriage, too."

"Doesn't seem to stop *him*. I think Musa must be terrified he won't get it up for Djibrilla if he spends his seed on me or something. He's pathetic at the moment."

My heart selfishly sang. I ravenously gobbled up anything, *anything*, that insisted Khassim loved me.

"You know, Rutherford – your Khassim is living proof that sex happens exclusively in the brain – there ain't no way he could be doing what he's doing on simple testosterone."

"Do you really think so?"

"And there ain't no way he could be screwing the wife, too. Which amazes me because they always *are*, you know."

"Are what?

"Are shagging the wife."

"Always?"

"*Always.*"

"Why always?" I didn't care for this bit.

"Oh, it's a way of keeping her suspicions at bay. Give her a quick fuck once in a blue moon, keep her quiet."

"Well, he says he isn't."

"Do you believe him?"

"I don't know. I think I do. Like you said, I don't see how he could be doing us both." But he could – a quick fuck once in a blue moon – of course he could.

"Well, at least I don't have to wonder. My guy's breaking his gut trying to prove his manhood on his bloody Djibrilla."

She'd be pregnant soon, I thought, looking at the bitter twist to Jonathan's mouth which had nothing to do with the cramps in his stomach. How does he bear it? I'd go mad. He was bound to crack eventually. "Play it cool if you possibly can, Jonathan. And watch your step a bit . . . Musa is part of the Hausa establishment. That means there could be repercussions if you . . . offend him."

"Oh, hell, so what? You and your paranoia! Me and my shadow have run the gauntlet of Immigration before. I've been abused and reviled good-oh but they haven't got rid of me yet. That Immigration bastard is the spawn of Satan, granted, but what he's after is just a little *dashi* to grease his palm. I've told you before – if they throw me out of this university, I'll go to Kano. If they throw me out of there, I'll go to Sokoto. If they throw me out of there, I'll go to some god-forsaken secondary school!"

"What if they throw us out of the country altogether?"

"On what grounds?" he asked.

"Well . . . in my case, they're scared of Gaddafi and his luring the Tuareg into his special battalions . . . you know

I've been accused before of spying for Libya. And of smuggling people without ID across the border."

"Which you do."

"No big deal. Just dropping them off at one side and picking them up on the other. But they can make that hang me any time they want. Not literally, I hope."

"Nonsense!" he said. "I can see you here forty years from now with a full household. Masses of children. Goats. Chickens. Flora and fauna. A stable of stallions – both human and animal."

"Forty years from now I won't be up to it."

"You? You will be."

I wouldn't be here, up to it or not. The Nigerians periodically deported all their Nigeriens, heaving them all back across the border into Niger. They had done the same in the south a few years before, shoving a great multitude of non-nationals over the border into Benin, regardless of the fact most of them were from Ghana, not Benin. I had good reason for my paranoia. The Tuareg would not be allowed to stay indefinitely.

"So you were impressed by our planting?" I asked. Jonathan had come to visit a few days before and had seen how we were enlarging our garden area, planting a line of trees around the back. Basically, I was working on privacy. More paranoia. "You shouldn't be. My Buzus are driving me nuts. They think I'm mad. They hate work of any nature. Nothing is worth any effort – life is about lounging about on mats, being waited on. They're so damn superior."

"Kate. They ruled the Sahara for thousands of years. Of course they feel superior."

I was silent.

"Any news of Rhisa?" he asked after a moment.

It was hard to say it. "I've been meaning to tell you." It stuck in my throat. "A couple of guys came down from Tchin Tabaraden a few days ago. There are rumours he's got married." I didn't look at Jonathan.

"That cousin of his?" came his voice quietly. "The one in that photo you took when you were up there?"

I nodded. "So, you see, we're in precisely the same boat."

"Do you believe the gossip?"

"I've no idea," I said with great weariness. "You know how it is . . . versions of versions . . . gossip is their life's blood . . . everyone swearing blind on his version . . . third-hand reports masquerading as the horse's mouth. Short of getting in the Land Cruiser and going up there, there's no bloody way of knowing. Correction: getting in the Land Cruiser and going up there wouldn't make the slightest difference. I know it of old – I'd get up there only to be met with a wall of lies and subterfuges as shifting as the bloody sands they pitch their tents on. Jonathan, 'twould drive you fucking mad. You end up wondering if your head is on backwards. Truth is a concept they have no particular interest in."

"But you *do* think he's married?"

"Probably."

"Oh, poor Kate . . . "

Poor Jonathan.

I brooded as I drove home.

No, I wouldn't be staying much longer in Nigeria. Much as I longed to put down roots, I knew I too was on shifting sand like the Tuareg tents. That bastard of an

Immigration officer would never let me and my Buzus in peace.

Jonathan was all right, probably. If they didn't get him on the gay thing. He was embracing the modern Nigeria and modern Nigerians. He had television, for God's sake. He was boosting their self-image. I was flirting with a race they hated in a covert way, a bunch of people who had taken them as slaves for centuries and were now delivered into their hands as destitute underdogs. And I had been blatantly harking back to the past ever since I came to Nigeria, had gone to live in villages, worn traditional costume, digging and delving for all the reasons we should go back not onward.

Jonathan was staying. I didn't trust that I could.

In any case, I wanted to be in Niger. As my Tuaregs did. They weren't really lazy and I knew it. They were migrants. Their hearts were in the desert and nothing outside had any reality. How wrong they were. What they perceived as a passing disaster – the droughts and their after-effects – was probably the beginning of the end. A culture extinguished.

Rhisa in his simplicity had never seen the reality. Had never understood what I was trying to do for him and his family. That I was offering not just love but a kind of salvation. That the best part of his game was to stick with me.

And meanwhile the Sahara was marching on.

Chapter Seven

The first rains came, brief and sparse, but immediately a flush of green ran across the landscape and a ravishing freshness filled the air.

We were driving past the building-site early one morning, on the way to the cattle-farm at Shika to buy the fresh milk my desert dwellers craved, when we heard a high-pitched hail from far across the grass over near Jonathan's house.

"It's Khadija," said Husaini, his voice dripping with disgust. "She cries like a police car."

And again I wondered at the depth of the hostility. I spotted her over by the bungalows moving along in a fashion that seemed to tip her forward on her great weight, a heavy arm lifted as she hullooed. She hooted again, a long-practiced long-distance hail designed to carry across empty desert. I took the next right turn and circled back.

In a moment she was panting at the window of the car, "It's Khassim! He is very sick! His fever has come back! I was looking for your friend Jonathan to take him to the hospital but he isn't there!"

Heart in pain and in triumph again in an instant. Serve her right. Why did she act as if he were her responsibility when she had to turn to me?

She climbed in and we drove to their hut.

He was indeed very ill, burning with fever, barely acknowledging me, eyes glazed.

And the usual dilemma: whether to give him Nivaquine? Whether to take him to the hospital for a shot which would blast the malaria out of him together with whatever bit of acquired immunity he might have? Better leave him to battle it out. Or die? I had nearly died myself from malaria some years before.

I never knew what to do. I had seen some of the Tuareg refuse treatment, veering to what seemed like the point of death, but rising victorious on the third day. What was the use giving him quinine when he wouldn't continue taking it? I could feed him tablets day by day – but what would happen then when I wasn't there to do that?

In the end, as always, his degree of temperature frightened me. I lost my nerve and we ended up at the hospital where we gave up in despair and exhaustion after a wait of four hours in the usual horrendous queue. The bout of fever had passed by that time in the usual deceptive manner of malaria. We went to one of the local drugstores and bought a course of treatment there instead.

A thought struck me. "Khadija? Have Yakubu and Fatimatu had their needles?" I meant their infant inoculations.

"No. I'm afraid of needles. You know, there was one baby in Tudun Wada who became a cripple after one."

"But, Khadija, all the babies in Nigeria have them – you know that!"

"Fear is what I feel. When I heard about that baby." She pursed her lips doubtfully. "You know, those needles sometimes are dirty."

"We'll take them to the university clinic. The needles will be clean there. We must. You know how many children die of measles in Niger! And meningitis." I was on dangerous ground and I knew it, talking of death and her children in the same breath as if I were trying to put the evil eye on them.

"*To*," she said shortly and I knew there would be opposition to any efforts I would make in that direction.

On the way home Khadija asked to pass by Zainabu's place. I glanced at Khassim and he made a weak little gesture of assent, dry-lipped.

The women were singing to a brisk hand-clap when we arrived, voices rising over the compound wall. I knew the song.

"*I want Sharaibu . . . My heart is breaking but I must have patience . . . I want Sharaibu . . . For years I've wanted him . . . And until the world is destroyed I'll want him . . . My heart is shredded . . . My heart is like a tarred road with cars going over it . . .*"

"Madame!" Zainabu came bursting out of the compound to meet me.

She embraced me warmly and drew me inside by the hands. Caressing me, thanking me. Her face was rounding again. She looked startlingly different, in coloured *zane* and a white lace traditional blouse, her head wrapped in a Hausa coloured headcloth.

The other women rose to greet me, her mother among them with the baby in her arms.

Zainabu took the baby. "Look at your son!" she said to me.

I could hardly bear to look. I could hardly bear to see the great breasts burgeoning on her slight frame. It was grotesque, obscene, the child enormous against her small stature.

I smiled and concealed my anger and disturbance. But the anger was like a dull fire in me. I couldn't see the child as other than a parasite, sucking the life from her.

They wanted us to stay to eat or at least take tea but we pleaded Khassim's illness and they waved us off, glowing with warmth. They were happy. They were not a failure after all. I had saved them. Sidi wouldn't be divorcing her.

As we drove back to Samaru Khadija pulled at my *takatkat* and pointed out a little white house all on its own on a rise far back from the road. She said, "I don't know why – maybe because I was born in the desert – every time I see that little house I want it. There, away from everyone."

I was surprised and touched and thought that this little dream of hers showed how truly she loved Khassim. Her and him. Isolated.

And jealousy stirred.

We have the same dream, I thought, remembering Bessie Head's *Maru*, and how her strange aristocratic hero achieves his dream: the outcast woman he loves and a little house with a water-tank fixed to the side. Bessie's people listened to their gods. As soon as the rains began Maru would plant rows of flowers on either side of the path leading to the door – sunflowers, was it? Or was it daisies? Just as he had seen them in his dream, *"so simply and precisely did he translate his dreams into reality"*. I was fascinated by that phrase ever since I had first read it, as if it held a profound truth just beyond my grasp. Some saving miracle.

I was hooked on simplicity, haunted also by the image

of her heroine settling into Maru's village as a teacher, in a little house, with its bit of polished lino on the floor and its simple bed and table and chair, from where she could watch the smoke from the evening cooking-fires rise into the sky.

I asked myself: why is *my* simple dream so daring that the world has to go into convulsions rather than let me have it?

I glanced at Khadija. Why shouldn't we share such a dream together?

I went the following week to collect Khadija and take her and the children to the clinic for the infant vaccinations.

She told me she had diarrhoea.

The following day I went again.

She couldn't leave the building-site because Khassim was gone to Tudun Wada and there was no one she could trust to guard their belongings.

I realised it wasn't going to happen unless I pushed harder. But I didn't want to push. I didn't want to take sole responsibility. I was afraid of infant vaccinations myself and I knew it was quite true that children were sometimes crippled. A clumsy or ignorant nurse, a stab of a needle too close to the spine – it happened.

Khadija was pounding grain with vigour, standing over the wooden mortar, the pestle as tall as herself.

"He has gone to Tudun Wada – to visit that bastard girl! I know what they are doing!"

"What girl?" I asked, heart suddenly in mouth.

She tossed the end of her black veil, weighted at the corner by the "household" keys, more firmly over her shoulder exposing her bare breasts. "That ugly girl! Thin like a stick!"

My heart skipped a beat. "*What* are they doing?"

"He is *eating* her!" she cried, the heavy pestle coming down with a slam, and her breasts bounced.

Eating. The great Hausa all-round, all-purpose word. She meant fucking.

I was filled with alarm and took care not to react. And I was astonished that she should say this to me. A wife saying this about her husband in so casual a fashion? Her vigour was coming more from the effort of pounding than any emotional disturbance. It didn't fit. I couldn't fit it in with anything I knew.

"Doesn't that worry you?" I asked.

"Let him!"

Let him?

"I have my own money. If he continues I will pack and get the bus to Birnin Konni — you know my people are in the bush there! I don't care!"

She started to work up a rhythm with the pestle and her breasts bounced as the hollow thud rang out pleasantly.

It had been at the back of my head all along, tempering whatever guilt I felt about Khassim. Even without me, how long would they last anyway? I could give him up and then she'd divorce him in no time on suspicion of what he was doing with some girl or other — or they would quarrel about money. I steeled myself to ask. "But why do you think that? That he's eating her? What makes you think that?"

"Because he is *not* eating *me*!"

Joy to the World.

"He keeps saying he's sick or tired. Not too tired or sick to go to Tudun Wada, though. Leave him! He'll see! He'll drink trouble yet!" She sniffed and tossed her plaits. "Come!" She dropped the pestle and beckoned me inside the low-roofed hut. Then, "Wait," she said emphatically and, squatting, took the key tied to the corner of her veil and opened the padlock of her tin trunk and threw back the lid. I was unable to squat comfortably like her so I settled on the bed as she rummaged and drew out something firmly wrapped in a headscarf. She opened the knot with her teeth and unfolded first cloth, then paper. It was a framed photograph. She handed it to me. It was her but almost unrecognisable. A large black-and-white photo. Thick long black hair loose to the waist, trousers and a white sleeveless tunic-type shirt to her hips, high-heeled sandals and a white plastic handbag with a short handle. The bra underneath, no doubt.

"I give it to you!" A sweeping emphatic gesture of a palm towards me. "But don't let Khassim see it."

I looked at her inquiringly.

She pursed her lips satirically, a gleam in her eye. "Before, he wanted to smash it and tear it up. He doesn't want the other men to see it."

"Why?" Stupid question and I knew it.

"Because of the trousers!" Her voice swelled with the humour of it. "He thinks they will say I was a prostitute! You keep it! I give it to you!"

"*Kai*, Khadija, you keep it! You should keep it!"

"Take it! He will burn it some day. Better you have it."

"Well, then, I'll keep it for you."

"But don't show it to the others!"

"I won't."

"Let me tell you. I had photos of my children too – the children I had with the Ibo – but he tore them up."

A dull ache started up in my heart. "Truly?"

"He is jealous!" she cried laughingly in English. "You know men!"

I wondered how she felt about her Ibo children. Were they somehow less her children than Yakubu and Fatimatu? How did she leave them? How could she laugh? "Khadija . . . don't you feel the lack of the children you left behind?"

"Very much! But I must be patient. I will see them again." She had just lifted a dark blue velvety dress from the trunk.

"Will you go south to see them? You can't."

She swivelled around, still squatting, and faced me, her face close to mine, the dress over her arm. "Even if I do not go, they themselves will come looking for me. Let me tell you! It is always like that. They always look for the parent who is gone. I heard that in Agadez many French soldiers married our women and had children with them. Some of them took those children with them when they left. But those children, when they grew up, all came back to look for their mothers in Agadez. It is like that. Whichever parent they are with, they always go back to the other one. There was one girl – she stayed in France for twenty years and then one day she returned and came to her mother's door in the town of Agadez and said 'Come and embrace me! I'm your daughter!'"

So this was how they comforted themselves. The faith they lived by.

"Look at me!" Khadija said and she held out an arm. "My skin has risen! When I think of them finding their mothers."

Sure enough, her skin was covered in goosepimples. I marvelled.

This was it. *The Tempest. The Winter's Tale.* The lost and the found. The daughter returned. Wholeness restored. I suddenly knew that Shakespeare's audiences must have been just like Khadija. Must have reacted like her, not with their minds or their critical faculties but with their bodies in the blood. We had lost it. We could no longer experience that shock of wonder.

She shuddered. "Patience, Katherine. Patience is the medicine of the world. I will see my children again." Her glance fell on the dress over her arm. "I forgot! Look!" She lifted the dress up. It was midnight blue with masses of gold and silver embroidery running down the front. "I wore this when I was a girl but now it is small for me." It was straight and slim. "I want to sell it. It would be exact for you!"

It was made of some sort of synthetic material with a velvet-like surface. And it was cut very tight. I would sweat like a horse in it. I would have no use for it.

"Do you want it? I could get thirty *naira* but I will let it to you for only fifteen."

"OK. It's good. I agree."

"I thank you!" She folded the dress and handed it over without more ado. "Listen," she said in English. "I will tell you a secret. If that bastard continues, I will use this money to take the bus to Birnin Konni – to my brother's place across the border. I will take it on the road outside. I will be gone before he knows."

I found Jonathan savaging a mango.

"Chop some mango now," he said.

I shook my head. "Hope you've washed that."

He waved a sticky hand.

I told him the latest on Khadija. "She says she will take off for Sokoto."

He shook his head. "No, she won't. They never do. It's an extraordianry thing but they cling like limpets when the man is having an affair. Even when they don't know. They seem to sense it and there's no getting rid of them. If she does go, she'll be back like a yo-yo. Mark my words."

He was devouring the mango avidly but as if I had caught him in a guilty private act, pulling it into a starburst of strands with his teeth as he sucked off the flesh.

Why did it make him feel naughty? Did it remind him of some erotic act?

"I honestly feel she's ready to go. I feel a bit guilty," I said.

He wiped some juice off his chin. "Surprise, surprise."

"No! Not very guilty!" I said with some heat. "Jonathan, they may be monogamous but the turnover is terrific! I could make a massive sacrifice and give him up – and as sure as God made gooseberries she'd walk out on him next month or next year!"

"I thought only the men could say 'I divorce you'?"

"The women walk out . . . I've heard them . . . you know, two weeks into a marriage and they're back home . . . 'I couldn't stay with that kind of thing,' they say."

I was wishing I had my camera to capture him and his mango, now reduced to the stone with its starburst strands. Then he dropped it into the plastic dish and looked at me more guiltily than ever.

"I once had a go at your Husaini, you know," he said.

"You did *not*!"

"I did actually. About a year ago. He came here to greet me so I thought there might be something doing."

"*And?*"

"Oh, he turned me down but very nicely. Humorously. Nice guy, your Husaini."

"Nice guy? I'm surrounded by dark horses."

He was licking his fingers.

"Why did you think of that just now?" I asked.

"I remember I was eating mangos the day he came."

Oh, I bet you made a performance of that!

"I wondered," said Jonathan. "Did he never make any advances to you?"

"Oh, a few tentative things in the early days. A little flirtation. But he's Rhisa's cousin, you know, so he can't anymore – since Minha's birth I'm his sister or mother or something. He even calls me mother sometimes."

"Nothing like incest to add a bit of spice . . . "

"Oh, I quite fancy Husaini . . . but in a mild and comfortable way. I do feel very maternal towards him, I suppose . . . well, I don't know . . . we're . . . pals."

There was a pause where Jonathan opened his mouth to say something and changed his mind. I looked at him sharply.

He mouthed again and then said it. "You know – eh, your Rhisa once made an advance to me . . . "

Jesus.

"Never told you. But I think it might help if you know now."

The shock was immense.

"Oh, it was very mild – " He waved a hand vaguely.

"What? *What* exactly did he do?"

"Oh, it was just a touch-up . . . "

"*What* did he do?"

"Oh – well, he just put his hand on my butt and

93

squeezed it – in the kitchen. I just looked disapproving and that was that. I did it for you, Rutherford."

I would never know. There was no way of knowing. Normally so clear-sighted, when it came to my Tuaregs Jonathan could sometimes go way off the mark.

This was *his* fact, his truth.

I would have to deposit it in that area of my brain where I placed facts that were fiction and fictions that were facts.

"They have such fantastic buttocks, those Tuareg – but I'm despairing of ever getting my hands on them," said Jonathan with a sigh. "Have a mango. Chop."

Khassim and I lay together on a mat in the plant nursery in clear white moonlight. He was suffering from another one of his fierce bouts of fever. They were becoming more frequent as the rains came on and mosquitos flourished. His fever puzzled me. I had treated him for malaria but yet it returned. He complained of pain on the left side and I figured his spleen was swollen. I had heard this could happen from repeated attacks of untreated malaria. I began to think there was some irreparable damage.

We had made love as always, nevertheless.

He had turned me over on my stomach, as he sometimes liked to do, and my heart had sunk into a little trough of disappointment but I let him go ahead. It would make it easier for him and he was ill. He knew I wasn't keen so he whispered in my ear how much pleasure it gave him – the weight of our bodies on his penis as he pushed in, the curve of my buttocks against his belly – he hardened even more as he whispered and he took me swiftly with strong efficient strokes. I loved to feel that tremendous vigour but I never invited him to do it this way. I was greedy, every orgasm with him too precious to lose, pinned down on my stomach like a turtle on its back. I needed to wrap my legs around him, get the stimulus of his groin on my clitoris, come with him.

Rhisa had once told me laughingly that sweethearts faced each other for sex or sexual play but that married couples did it from the rear – spoon-position. I was secretly aghast. I supposed the reason was that married couples have surreptitious intercourse surrounded by their children and other sleepers in a tent, while courting couples are off in the sand-dunes. Though Rhisa made the rear-entry option sound like the more exciting one. Well, watching camels all their lives . . .

"God, you're a wonder," Khassim breathed as he withdrew. "God, the man who got you when you were a girl drank sweetness. I have never felt sweetness like that in this world."

Oh Jesus, I thought guiltily, is it the diaphragm he's feeling? I used it as little as possible, taking huge risks and never taking it out to add more spermicidal jelly in his presence, no matter how many times he came. I could buy the pill over the counter in Samaru but was afraid to use it while I was still breast-feeding Minha a little. This time I had inserted the diaphragm on the way, stopping in the dark on the road to do so, not for contraceptive purposes but because I was afraid I was starting a period and didn't want him to know. He never commented on the diaphragm. It seemed to me he simply didn't notice it and this had led to several detailed discussions with Jonathan about what a man was likely to feel or not to feel, with a negative verdict on the penis as an intelligent or sensitive instrument.

I was afraid to tell Khassim I was using it for fear of some sort of Muslim objections.

Menstruation was the bane of my life. A hint of a period and sex was forbidden in Islamic morality – maybe he wouldn't have cared about that but he did believe that contact with menstrual blood would leak the power from the charms he wore. I had at times managed to fool him right through, if we only met at the nursery in the dark and the period was light, and I always cheated on the first and last days. Anything to avoid five days' abstinence which was a nightmare. I felt a kind of guilt about my periods, as if I were failing him when I bled.

Later he lay with his head in my lap and electrified me by articulating plans to divorce Khadija. "I'll take her home to her people soon," he whispered. "Then after I can send her a message saying I'm divorcing her. That is the best way to do it."

The night lit up with his words.

He turned and lay on his back, head still on my lap. An arm went back and around my hips and he murmured from dry lips in Tamajeq, "No buttocks."

I froze in shame, my face flaming in the dark.

In an attempt to rush past this embarrassment I blurted, "Khassim? You know I am using medicine to prevent a stomach?" A pregnancy, I meant.

"Yes."

"Do you want me to continue using it?"

To my horror there was a prolonged silence. He made no answer but abruptly rose and, fumbling for his tobacco, slowly left the nursery.

He was angry with me, surely. I had never felt his anger before.

My world threatening to fall around me, I adjusted my *zane* and followed him outside.

I found him squatting by the lakeside, chewing his tobacco.

"Why did you leave me?" My voice was shrill.

"It's nothing."

"Nothing? I asked you a question just now. Give me an answer."

He was silent for what seemed like a long time.

"You know," he said slowly, at last. "I haven't divorced Khadija yet and we haven't married yet and you are talking about children."

I was speechless and furious. And I quaked as I tried to interpret what he was saying. Never mind his words – what was he saying, really? What? He could only have children with Khadija and I was to be denied? He was satisfied with this furtive love and had no intention of giving me more?

All the alarm bells were ringing.

"You must have patience," he said. "Patience will fix everything."

Patience. *Hakuri. Tazaydart.* The great African virtue.

He had no intention of divorcing Khadija. It was all pretence with him. He is terrified of the idea of me being pregnant, I thought. Terrified with the shame of having a child with an Infidel. I knew how Rhisa struggled with those feelings.

Go. Go now. This is the end.

"I'm going," I said and strode away. He didn't come after me.

Go. Go. It's the right thing to go.

I got in the car and was well down the dirt road when I

97

started to cry. I pulled up and let myself cry, great gulping sobs of pain.

What was I doing? I couldn't go away like this. What else was there for me if I turned away from him? So what if we never got further than this? I wasn't capable of leaving him.

After some time, I turned the car and began to drive back, cold and numb now.

And then I saw the bicycle light wending its way along the road, winking out of sight at times.

I halted as we drew level.

"Madame!" His hand grasped mine where I clutched the window frame and his touch was heaven returned to my battered soul. "Go back to the nursery!"

I drove on and he turned the bike and followed.

I cried again helplessly as I felt the steel strength of his arms around me and the heat of his body against me. Too hot. The skin of his face was clammy after his exertions.

"You're sick!" I sobbed. "I forgot."

"Don't worry, don't worry! I am never sick when I am with you."

He pushed me down on the mat and we made love again desperately and I reached out for my pleasure as if it were to be a pact with God and when it came it came keenly as though my belly were a papaya split open between the hands and I swore I would never leave this man in this life.

He shivered after and lay back with a groan, his tunic soaked with sweat.

I was insane to have put him to such strain.

"Khassim! It would be best if I took you home." I was desperate to back-track now. "The fever – "

"It's nothing, it's nothing . . . "

"No – can you leave? Can you tell them you got sick? I can't leave you out here."

"They won't know. The *rangadi* has been here earlier. He won't be back. We can go."

"Can you leave the bike here?"

"I can lock it, yes."

"Give me the key."

I rolled the bike into the shed as he slowly began to gather up his few things. I came back for the mats and the brazier and when I came out he was still feebly tying his *shahi* things together.

"Come here!" came his voice weakly across the moonlit space.

I went.

"Madame, listen to me. I have been thinking about what we had better do."

"Never mind now – let's carry you home!"

"Wait a little! The plan that I have made is this: you must get work in Niamey. At the university. We will leave Zaria altogether. Because of Rhisa. Because of Khadija. And their people. If we go there together, his people will leave us in peace. I will take Khadija to her people in the bush at Birnin Konni and then afterwards divorce her when she is safely settled there." His chest was heaving and the voice was weak. "Do you agree?"

"Yes!"

"There is something else," he said.

"Yes?"

"You know, I don't have a *carte d'identité* from Niger and I can't travel without one. What I will do, I will go soon and steal across the border at Zinder. I know a soldier there

– a Tamajeq – he is a relative – and if I can give him the money to bribe some officials he can get me a card. His name is Issa. A *capitaine*."

Go. Soon. Steal. Border. Soldier. Bribe. All those were words I had learnt to dread.

"But you are wanted in Niger!"

"There will be no problem as long as I don't go to Agadez."

I dropped him at some distance from his place. He would send for me in the morning if he had not recovered, to try to get hospital treatment once more.

Niamey! In Niamey, the capital, I could get work.

I had been in Niamey before. What I remembered most was the extreme conglomeration of ethnic groups there. The city was on the river Niger where it made a short run through the country between Mali and Nigeria. I remembered the Pont Kennedy with camels and women dressed in more garish colours than I was used to in Nigeria, an astonishing mixture of ethnic groups: Arabs, Fulani, Tuareg, Kanuri, Hausa, Zarma, French, Americans, groups I did not recognise. I had thought at the time that surely this was a place where myself and my entourage could blend into the mix and be secure. It seemed so cosmopolitan and the French had stores where you could buy cheese and wine and paté and chocolate – amazing to a resident of Zaria, Nigeria, where tinned hummus imported by the Lebanese was the height of luxury. The bread in the street stalls was French baguettes instead of the horrific sweet inedible gummy stuff the British had left in Nigeria as their legacy. Niamey had first-class hotels where you could drink cocktails and, despite the extreme poverty of the country as a whole, the French, running the place on uranium revenue from the mines at Arlit, had made sure that there were no electricity cuts or water cuts.

But it was in the extreme west, far from the northern deserts I craved, in a kind of knob like a horse's cropped tail protruding from the body of the country – or, in fact, exactly like a fish's tail, the rest of the country a fish reaching its gasping head deep into the Sahara as far as Libya to the north-east.

My heart lifted. A new life. Hope, after all.

Chapter Eight

When I got home the day Khassim was leaving for Zinder, my house was full of people and gear. Two other men were travelling with him.

"My God," muttered Husaini as he met me at the door. "You'd think it was a fucking pilgrimage." He said this in Tamajeq as if only his own language could give vent to his resentment.

I laughed. "Where's Khassim?"

"There in the washroom with Khadija," he answered. "Maybe she didn't have a wash for ten years . . . " His voice was heavy with irony.

My heart beat faster. I walked through the living-room, saluting the men who were there. As I passed the bathroom door little Yakubu ran past me and opened it. Did I stop? Did I stand and look in? Or did I just glance as I passed by? Khadija was squatting in the bath, water gushing over her from the spout of the water-heater. Her arms were crossed over her heavy breasts. Her body was golden and opulent. Khassim stood beside the bath, wearing his robes and *tagilmoust*, scrubbing her back.

"Shut the door!" she shrieked, raising her eyes without lifting her head. "Shut the door, Yakubu, for God's sake!"

I went on to the bedroom and sat down at my writing-table. I bit my knuckles until they showed angry marks. The fucking bastard! How could he do that? In my house? In my bathroom! In the bathroom where I had fallen in love with him.

"*Sannu*, madame!"

He stood there, hand outstretched. I barely touched his hand and gave a cold hello. He felt the coldness. But did he understand? Probably not.

Khassim left for Zinder and I began to count days. A day to get up there, a day to find this *capitaine*, a day to do business, a day to get back, a day to spare . . . five days . . . call it a week. I'd be lucky. In Africa things always took at least twice as long as you expected . . . twice? Three or four times as long. Or longer.

Traumatised as I was by Rhisa's long absence, I found the waiting extremely painful.

On the eleventh day little Yakubu developed a fever. I treated him for malaria but his temperature climbed and climbed. Khadija was calm, as always. We waited until the following day but he was worse. She seemed reluctant to take him to the hospital and I didn't want to take all the responsibility, but I thought of Khassim and was afraid not to. We took him to the hospital. I recognised the doctor who treated him, a very young American. He said it was most likely meningitis. They took some of the spinal fluid to test it and gave him some injections. In his right thigh.

I left Khadija with him at the hospital and drove home wondering how many more painful days must pass before Khassim returned. I had given him as much money as I could. It still mightn't be enough to cover the gifts and bribery that would be necessary to get the card. And what if he got another violent outburst of malaria? My heart ached. I was hungry for him. I felt as though my soul had gone to Zinder with him.

In the afternoon I took Husaini and went back to the hospital.

The young doctor took me aside. "Well, it isn't meningitis. The test was negative. It looks like polio . . . but surely he's been inoculated?"

"No – he hasn't." There you go now, Khadija, I thought, in despair and anger. You and your dirty needles.

"But surely he's been through the usual infant programme? I thought all the women go to the clinics now . . . " His eyes were fixed doctor-fashion on my face.

Where the fuck do you think you are, I thought, Boston? "No – no. These are bush people – migrant workers. They're very suspicious of hospitals and medicine." And you should fucking know that, berk.

His eyes shifted. I didn't understand his hesitation. His shifting glance.

He brought his eyes back again. He was trying. He was young. "It never occurred to me that he mightn't be inoculated against polio." A pause. "You know that we can only hope for the best? That there isn't any treatment?"

"Yes, I know."

I left Husaini at the hospital to buy some food for Khadija and keep her company for a while and drove home to relieve Amina of Minha. As I passed the Albarka cinema in Tudun Wada, with its massively elaborate wall-decorations of traditional motifs in yellow and dark blue, I pulled in. I needed a drink. Among the clutter of hawkers and beggars who immediately surrounded the car there was a little girl with something covered with a piece of wet sacking on the tray on her head. "*Baturiya! Baturiya! Coca?*" pulling back the sacking to reveal a cluster of Coke bottles. The drink was tepid and fizzy. But wet. Someone was trying to sell me a decorated calabash, "Cheap-cheap!" A bunch of dusty decrepit little *almajirai* clanked their enamel begging-bowls against the window-frame of the car. I scrabbled for my sunglasses, needing a mask. Just then, a group of black-robed Tuareg women approached, catching my attention automatically. Didn't know them. Maybe from Mali. One of the women pulled her veil back and showed me an emaciated baby at her breast. I was horrified, striken to the heart. What was it? Dehydration? Malaria? Was the mother so malnourished she couldn't feed it? "*Yunwa!*" she said – the Hausa word for hunger and her hand went up eloquently to her mouth and then swept into a begging gesture towards me. Despairing, I gave the few *kobo*. I could have done more. I could have taken them home. What was the use? Short of adopting that child and every child, they would continue to die needlessly.

I set off for home. The thought surfaced on the high wide bypass from Tudun Wada to Samaru, rising to the surface like a fish lunging for food. My hands were suddenly slippery with sweat on the wheel. I pulled over to the sandy verge and sat with the engine running, grabbing at the medical dictionary I had taken with me from home, propping it against the steering wheel, hands shaking as I turned the pages. My sunglasses slid down my sweaty nose and fell off into my lap.

Polio. There it was. Yes, there it was. *Injecting any muscle which is incubating the polio virus can result in paralysis of that muscle . . .*

105

Jesus. What was the incubation period? He'd been through that, surely, when he'd been injected? Surely he had. He was already sick. Surely incubation was before the symptoms came on?

A bicycle was approaching.

I reread the dictionary. It wasn't clear.

The bike drew closer. A clean, well-dressed, white-haired young man whose skin was all in patches of black, of red, of yellow. A piebald man. He passed, staring back at me with tiny eyes behind white lashes. I thought of him strapped to his mother's back as a baby. Their courage was stupendous. Though if he was a first child she had an excuse to shun him, refuse to feed him, leave him on the rubbish-dump to be rescued by her co-wives, Hausa-fashion.

I watched the bicycle grow smaller in the rear mirror, the man's white robe billowing.

I put my head down on the wheel, my head full of the buzzing silence around me and wept quietly for a while.

That night I woke to hear a rapping on the glass of the French window in my bedroom. Heart knocking, I peered through the glass. A white-robed figure stood outside. It moved closer and Khassim's dark eyes peered back at me over his white *tagilmoust*. I fumbled at the key and pulled the door open. He stepped in, stood his sword in the corner by the door and then stood poised for a moment – always wary, always the wild animal strange to interiors. I went into his arms, into the joy of soft fine cloth over the hardness of his body, the musky smell.

He pulled the *tagilmoust* down and rubbed his face hungrily against mine.

"Wait," he said and pulled the heavy outer robe off over his head.

"Did you go home?"

"Yes. I heard the news of Yakubu." He breathed in my breath, nose to nose.

"And the papers? The card?"

"I got them."

We fell back onto the bed and my hands fought to get to his skin under his tunic.

"God," he half-sobbed. "I was so tired. Coming here, I thought I wouldn't be able to do anything with you. But I can't see you without wanting you." He pulled his tunic up and loosened the string of his trousers. I opened my *zane* and felt the heavy beautiful weight of his penis against me. He pushed into me and I wrapped my legs around him and waited, as I always did, for the plunge into the glittering void.

When we walked into the hospital ward a few hours later, at first light, Khadija pulled her veil up over her mouth and her eyes filled with tears – the first I had seen. She didn't otherwise acknowledge his presence. He stood staring at Yakubu and then laid a hand on the child's curly head. Then he made a sign to her to follow him. I watched them avidly through the window as they stood outside on the concrete walkway talking, their stance somehow antagonistic, a good yard's distance between them. Was that just propriety? He took his new ID card out and showed it to her, explaining, excusing his absence. She kept her head up proudly. I sensed a whiff of accusation and blame between them. Or was it just pity for each other? Was it his pain she couldn't bear? Was it love?

They had such dignity. They were well matched. I hated her.

We took Yakubu to the doctor's house some weeks later. He had recovered well from the fever but there was no movement in that right hip and leg. The house was a shady bungalow, with verandahs front and back crammed with plants and massive old red-brown pots and dark wood artifacts from the pagan south. We stayed on the verandah. Khadija sat on a Fulani bed, Fatimatu on her back, while I stayed standing with Khassim. The doctor's young wife offered us lemonade which we refused. She gave some to Yakubu, who was in Khassim's arms, and he started to drink thirstily but then winced in surpise at the cold – he had never had a drink with ice cubes before. Khassim sat Yakubu next to Khadija and she put an arm about him, supporting him. I remember the colours and pattern of the blanket on the bed quite clearly. It was one of the beautiful creamy-white blankets we called "camel blankets" woven of rough hair and decorated in bands of rusty red-brown and dramatic black.

The doctor knelt and tested Yakubu's knees for reflexes with a little rubber mallet. There was no response in his right knee. Khadija remained completely impassive throughout. I didn't look at Khassim.

The doctor lowered his head. "I'm sorry. I'm sorry. There's no response."

"Does that mean there *will* be no response?"

"It does mean that, yes."

"No hope?"

"None. Of course, a course in physiotherapy will improve his condition to some degree."

Khassim was watching my face. He abruptly got up and walked into the garden and around the side of the house. I followed him. He was standing there fumbling with his tobacco. He looked at me, a kind of serene pain in his eyes. I told him, full of pity and pain for him, full of the self-importance of being a private tragic chorus, full of greed to claim his attention in this intimate way, full of the lust of demonstrating to the spectators that I had a share in this family. Glad of anything that destabilised their dependence on each other. Full of guilt. He gazed and said nothing and then went on with his tobacco ritual.

It didn't occur to me that I was breaking the taboo: predicting the future.

Chapter Nine

I arrived at the building site to find everything changed. All the Buzus on their feet, milling about. With a shock I saw Khadija seated on her trunk, possessions piled around her, everything trussed and strapped. She greeted me with the usual woman-to-woman irony. "We're moving!"

"Why?"

"Khassim had a fight with the foreman. He told me to pack so here I am."

"He's lost his job?"

"He left it," she said gaily.

Christ. I was furious with him. And her. Just like that? Pack: and she packed. I couldn't begin to understand her response. But she would laugh anyway, whatever she felt. She would always put an unperturbed face on things. She was an aristocrat. Head on hand now, she smiled at me.

"What did they fight about?" I asked.

"There were some bricks stolen from the far side at Abdulaye's working-place. The foreman fired him, saying that he had taken *dashi* to let some thieves in. Khassim entered into an argument with the foreman and said that if Abdulaye was fired he also was leaving."

Fuck you, Khadija, fuck you and him and the strength

of your partnership. What's this? Wifely duty? Pack and she packs.

"What about your *tebur*?"

She shrugged, sitting there looking highly amused.

Always no criticism.

Never any criticism.

"Why don't you talk to him!"

"*Kai!* The men, this is how they are!"

"But where will you *go*?"

"Maybe Niger," she said in English.

Christ. "All of you?"

"No, no. He still has his work at Bomo."

She was leaving. This was what I'd been praying for. I'd have him to myself!

I should offer to take them to stay with me. My pulse quickened. Maybe that was the way forward. I didn't feel it at the time but that moment was a kind of crossroads for me. If I had made the other choice perhaps everything would have gone differently. If I had committed myself to Khadija. If I had made the choice that would bond us. But I hadn't the courage. Or the generosity. I wanted my privacy, the small degree of it I had left. I wanted my individual soul, my house, my child, her husband to myself.

"You can't go, Khadija. What about Yakubu's medicine? You know the doctor said he must start going to the hospital every day!"

"I know but . . . "

"Look," I said. "Stay here until I come back. My friend Jonathan over there has a steward's quarters he's not using. I'm going to ask him if you can stay there."

"We thank you!" she called shrilly as I left.

111

I watched Yakubu drag himself around the dirt yard of the quarters. No power in the whole right leg and hip. I was taking Khadija and the children to the hospital daily. They strapped him to boards and taught her to do things with poultices and bandages. She did it conscientiously but not with much faith.

I had little faith myself. It was all so pathetic and pained my heart.

We had just returned exhausted and parched from a visit there. She pulled off the tight pink T-shirt she had worn with a huge sigh of relief and threw her black veil over her head. "God, but our things have sweetness!"

"Truly!"

She passed me the enamel bowl of water and I drank deeply.

She then drank herself. "Yakubu says it was the doctor's needles that spoiled his leg!" she cried gaily.

Khassim had said the same to me in his own style. Quietly, non-committally, with just a faint hint of reproach.

The thought was there. If I hadn't taken Yakubu to the hospital he wouldn't have been crippled. But to really reprove me would have been an impiety: they knew that God, not I, had decided the fate of their son.

I knew it was my fault. I had let it happen.

Also, I knew that on some hidden secret level I was glad about it because I was glad about anything that disrupted the smugness of their happiness together.

The clouds were bundling black over the house and, expecting rain, we were all crowded inside, sprawled out on the floor messily making tea, charcoal brazier poised on a rusty powdered milk-tin lid, small milk-tins full of sand serving as tobacco spitoons, cassette player beating out the vigorous almost frantic rhythm of a Tuareg song, the place alive with the smells of damp bodies and the puddle Minha had just created near the front door. Husaini had an arm thrown around me, his turbaned head pressed against my cheek, teasing me about my Tamajeq, trying to get me to repeat the more guttural sounds. Into this appalling moment, of a hundred possible appalling moments, stepped the Immigration Officer.

The hot-eyed, xenophobic chauvinist we all feared. The man who threatened to deport an American friend of mine who had come to Nigeria accompanied by her two teenage sons. She had no right to have these sons living with her – where was their father? The man who had threatened to deport an English couple who were not legally married. She was a whore and he was a pimp. The man who had threatened to deport an Irish friend of mine if she did not, that very day, return to the Nigerian husband who had beaten her black and blue and kept her locked up for days.

None of those people were, in fact, deported. My friend returned to her husband, the couple got a Nigerian marriage certificate, the American mother ate humble pie and got a letter of permission from her ex-husband to have her sons live with her. And, no doubt, they all paid *dashi* – or *goro* as it was still called since the good old days when gifts and bribes were in the form of kola-nuts.

As the big muscular policeman and his younger side-kick were ushered in the door by a wild-haired Aghali, the wind suddenly whipped up outside, sending dust and leaves and pieces of paper spiralling, slamming the doors of the garage to and fro, making Chilli whinny. Making our visitant seem like the devil himself on a medieval stage.

I rose and stepped forward to meet him, knowing that my face was smeared blue from contact with Husaini's *tagilmoust*, conscious of my dirty bare feet and the fact I was naked under the Tuareg shirt with its open sides.

Husaini and the others rose with their customary courtesy to go through the greetings with the policeman but then, while I prayed they might go discreetly into the kitchen, they went back to where they were lying on the floor. Count yourself lucky, I thought. They were just as likely to troop into the bedroom and climb *en masse* on my bed.

The Immigration Officer opened his mouth and spoke but just then the thunder cracked. A bolt of lightning flashed across the sky and suddenly the rain came down, pelting in an insistent torrent on the roof, running in vigorous rivulets along the porch, lashing through the mosquito screens. I couldn't hear what he said.

With a sense of nightmare, I gestured towards an armchair and the policeman sat down, stiffly, his peaked hat on his knee, his car keys jangling silently against the backdrop of noise. The younger one stood at attention behind him. They stared at the dishevelled bunch of people who shared my life. Aghali shoved an armchair under the sidekick's rear, practically toppling him into it. Then, to my intense embarrassment, he went and lay down on his side behind Husaini with his left arm flung across his hip, close as lovers.

I sat on the chair opposite the policeman and held a hand to my face in a pathetic attempt to cover the blue smears that I knew must be there. I tried to keep eye contact with him, aware that it was considered rude to do so, but willing him not to drop his gaze to the tangle of bodies on the floor between us. I didn't at first see the letter he was holding out to me.

I took it and opened it with trembling hands.

It was a summons to come to the Immigration office that day.

"What is the problem?" I asked.

"Come to my office in Zaria in the afternoon," he said.

"But what is the problem?"

"I cannot say."

Ikis-Ikus smilingly handed him a glass of *shayi*.

He thanked him – "*Na gode*" – drank it off and handed the glass back.

"Is there a problem with my visa? With my work?"

"If you come I will explain the problem."

"So there is a problem?"

"We will discuss in the afternoon."

Abruptly he rose.

A chorus of farewells rose from the floor.

"*Sai an jima*," he said to me. Until we meet.

He was sitting behind his desk reading a document when I entered, his ill-will smouldering on his face like a visible vapour.

He ignored me for what must have been a full minute.

When he looked up I handed him the summons with a tight little smile, and sat down tentatively, my sweating and trembling hands clutching my passport in my lap.

I was wearing my most typically Hausa costume, a cotton *zane* and tight-waisted matching top with a pelmet-type flounce around the hips and elbows, in a light maternal blue cotton with white embroidery around the scoop neck and white piping around the edges. With a matching turban. Very proper, very modest, very feminine, very un-Tuareg. I had tucked the plaits that made me look more like a Tuareg woman out of sight.

He was reading the summons as if he had never seen it before.

He looked at me.

"Where is your passport?"

I handed it over deftly, with assumed meekness, and he brooded over it at length while I cringed inwardly, knowing he was counting the many entry visas for Niger.

I thought of Minha ouside in the Land Cruiser with Jonathan and Husaini. I had brought her in case I was to be abruptly whisked off to Kano Airport without returning home to collect her. I had brought Jonathan for support and to make business arrangements if that happened. I had brought Husaini because I always brought Husaini. My bag at my feet was full of official documents, photographic negatives and my other most precious possessions. And all the money I could muster.

I had not managed to find Khassim to tell him what was happening.

I would have preferred to cling on to Minha but if I had brought her inside there would be questions about her father, her nationality, her religion and mine, my marital status, God knows what.

No doubt there would be, anyway.

"Where is your visa for Libya?"

So it was that. A mixed tide of relief and apprehension swept over me. This was serious but the Libyan spy thing was the one accusation that had no foundation whatsoever. I could defend myself from this one.

"I have never been to Libya." A nerve in my face suddenly started to jump, twitching my upper lip.

"But you speak Arabic."

"I speak Hausa." Smile, I told myself, smile. "I don't speak any Arabic."

"What do you do in Niger?"

"I go there as a tourist." I smiled, the nerve in my lip still jumping.

"So many times?"

"I think it is very interesting." Smile, now – a European just-into-a-little-junketing smile.

"Why do you have all those dirty Buzus in your house?"

The crudeness of the question shocked me.

"One of them works for me. The others are his friends." I smiled: I am just an insignificant woman not likely to cause any trouble and terribly pleased to spend my time appreciating African men.

"But why do you allow them in your house? They are worthless people."

"I am trying to learn their language." I am a harmless woman and I am fascinated by Africans. I despise European men. You are my idea of a really exciting male. "I am interested in languages."

"*To, ji . . . don tuwon gobe a ke wanke tukunya.*"

I stared.

"What did I say to you?"

"You said: it is for tomorrow's food that the pot is washed."

"Do you understand what it means?"

Was he threatening me?

"I understand," I said uncertainly. Was it a threat?

He tapped on the desk with my passport. "Those Buzus are spies. For Libya."

"The ones I know have never been to Libya. They are

117

just young men – they don't have enough money to go to Libya. They are just simple people from the desert. They haven't even been to school." I laughed my amusement and contempt for these ignorant creatures from the bush.

"Do you know a Buzu man called Elbeka?"

"No." Great puzzlement. "Elbeka?" I knew him. He had been arrested the previous year for smuggling Buzus into Libya through Chad.

"He is in prison. He was a Libyan spy. He was living here in Tudun Wada before."

"I don't know him, no. Maybe I've met him but the name means nothing to me."

There was a protracted silence.

He hadn't asked me about Minha. He *must* ask me. I had planned to tell him her father was studying in America, that we would marry when he came back. That he might believe. I thanked God that my child was so fair-skinned – I thanked God for the chestnut hair – a story like that could pass. A sudden panic took me: what if he asked for her father's address?

"You can go," he said.

I stood by the Land Cruiser, shaking in reaction, ready to throw up at my own hypocrisy and betrayal. My betrayal of my friends, my child, her father. My betrayal of myself. "I'm out of here, Jonathan," I said. "I've got to get out of this country."

Everything was telling me to leave. Only some days after the episode with Immigration, I went with Husaini to see an Englishman who had said he was interested in buying Chilli.

I had gone with some of the other staff to one of the bars in Samaru one afternoon and had met the guy there. He taught geography. He had bought me one of the great green bottles of Star beer and as the sun set we had danced to simmering southern high-life music in the yard. I had liked him quite a bit.

I pulled up in front of his bungalow and we knocked and waited. I saw him crossing the living-room barefoot, wearing safari shorts and blue tie-dye T-shirt. "Hello, Brian!" I called cheerily and he opened the door with a smile and a hearty greeting in his Birmingham accent. I stepped into the cool interior with relief and Husaini stepped forward behind me, a smile on his face, hand out-stretched for the customary greeting. But in that moment, while Husaini was still on the threshold, Brian took a single stride towards him which brought him so close they were actually touching, Husaini's courteous right hand pushed right against his breast, the smile dying on his face. The Englishman said nothing at all but held his ground, staring Husaini in the eye until he backed off and, pulling the *tagilmoust* up over his exposed face, turned and made his way back to the car.

I was hideously embarrassed and could feel my face flame, but such was my long drilling in Zarian social niceties, other than that I did not react at all. My years of constant effort never to impose my indiscretions on the establishment flooded me with a kind of guilt. I had blundered. I had made a fool of myself. I had stepped over the mark and brought my dirty sweaty uneducated Buzu who spat tobacco and squatted to pee and had lice and wore no underwear into the house of a civilised man.

I should have known better. I did know better. I'd had long training with Rhisa. Usually I had the sense to leave the man who had fathered my child and who slept in my bed nightly outside the door like a dog, in his place, as was proper.

I took care not to embarrass my host further and sat and

119

accepted a Coke and ice and talked about Chilli and offered the latest funny stories about the hopelessness and ineptitude of Nigerians, about corruption and lies and NEPA.

Then I left, waving a cheery hand, making promises about Chilli. OK! *Ta-ra! Bye-bye! Cheerio!*

I couldn't look at Husaini. I couldn't bear to think of that moment when the smile died on his face, his graceful bewildered hand pushed against his chest. What made it worse was the fact that he had left himself open to insult in good faith, in trust. His face had been uncovered. He had been smiling. His body-movements were liquid and free. He would never have greeted another Tuareg like that, with his veil down to his chin, with unrestrained body-movements, with a smile. He had trusted his dignity to that ignorant uncouth bastard and had it slammed in his face.

And I had left him down shamefully. I was so conditioned to live this half-life, doing my thing for all to see but never imposing it on others, that I had not recognised the Englishman's action for what it was: a grievous insult to Husaini and by extension to myself.

The house was quiet for once when we got home. No one in evidence, not even Amina. I pulled up and took the key from the ignition and turned to look at the silent but apparently relaxed Husaini. *He* didn't move to get out, just sat there looking at me with the faintest trace of a smile on his face, a faint question in the eyes. I reached out and put my hand over his. Hypocrite, I thought. He turned his hand over and laced his fingers through mine. He didn't need comfort. But nothing I could do would ever be adequate to make up to myself for what I had done. Or failed to do. I leaned over and kissed him on the mouth. He made a little startled sound and smiled bashfully like a kid and looked half-serious and closed his lips and laughed at me with his eyes. When he just barely started to smile I kissed him again. His mouth was dry and warm like a child's.

Jesus, enough of that.

I pulled back and we both laughed aloud. He still held my hand. I treasured the moment. It wouldn't be happening again.

And I wouldn't be selling my Chilli to that dork in safari shorts.

I couldn't bear the hypocrisies of my life any longer. I had to find integrity.

In an enormous stroke of luck, the head of the English Department of the University of Niamey came as external examiner to Zaria. I asked him bluntly for a job for the coming year and he said yes, warning me that I would be taking quite a drop in salary. I couldn't have cared less about salaries and when the contract arrived from Niger a month later I signed with great joy and trepidation and awaited confirmation.

When it came I resigned from ABU with a light heart, and secretly began to pack up my life in Zaria.

I said nothing to Husaini and the others.

I took Khassim with me to the big market at Sabongari. I couldn't take anyone else because they would wonder at what I was buying. The huge market women, most of them southerners, called *"Baturiya! Baturiya!"* and smiled big-lipped brilliant smiles. And as always, stray calls of "Buzu woman!" followed me everywhere. We bought fine cloth for Khadija and Yakubu and found a Buzu tailor who would make the embroidered clothes they would wear and carry as gifts when they left for Niger. We bought the tobacco and tea and sugar and batteries she would carry. For me, we bought a large tin trunk with a sprayed-on design of elephants. An ugly, strange, noisy thing with treacherously sharp corners and edges. I imagined the spray was probably something lethal. But the trunk would serve its purpose. Khassim carried it on his head back to the car, but holding it in place with his hands, a big grin on his face. That was strange to see. In a world full of people miraculously proficient in carrying things on their heads I had never seen a Tuareg man do it.

I arranged with Jonathan that he should be my executor, so to speak, when I went on to a better world. I would have to leave most of my things behind, especially as I had decided to sell my beloved Land Cruiser. The whole business of customs and export and import tax was too intricate, too unreliable. I could imagine losing the right to enter Niger at the border itself on some pretext to do with the car and having to pay some massive bribe. Or it being confiscated in Niger. Besides, I needed the money to make the move. I could replace the car afterwards.

And so I cheerfully made my first colossal mistake. Well, perhaps not my first.

I don't remember that it hurt to let the car go but it must have.

I sold it to a young bearded English guy, remembering my amazement and joy the day I had bought it, the incredibly powerful feeling of being in charge of this great machine. He agreed that I should hang on to it until I actually left for Niger.

Jonathan would hold a "garage" sale – without the garage – to get rid of the stuff I left behind and would store my books and calabashes and ceremonial masks and wooden carvings. My Tuareg stuff would go with me, of course.

Chapter Ten

The rainy season was drawing to a close. It was almost time to go.

We were publicly cheerful and secretly elated.

We were sitting in the shade of the huge central tree in the nursery one afternoon when Dauda arrived. I turned my head and watched him enter on his bicycle, not knowing that my life was turning with the whirr of his wheels.

He had been away for a week on a trip home to Maradi in Niger.

Khassim rose to greet him, smiling broadly, and they went through innumerable handshakes. But then he came and sat with unusual solemnity. More greetings were exchanged with the usual surface ease and, on Khassim's part, more than the usual enthusiasm. Asking Dauda about his day, his health, his work, his house, his wife, his children, his news, his trip.

Dauda answered. Fine, fine, every last thing was fine.

Khassim went to get the tea things and started into the ritual.

They chatted about Maradi and Niger but I could see that Khassim was becoming increasingly aware of Dauda's restraint and a certain tension set in.

Then as he mixed the sugar in for the second glass Khassim asked again, "So how's the news?"

"I have news."

"*To.*"

Dauda dropped his gaze. A hesitation, an intake of breath. "Friend, *Capitaine* Issa has been arrested."

Khassim was raising the little glass by its rim. He handed it to Dauda with a steady hand.

"And they are looking for you."

My heart dropped like a stone.

"To." He handed the second glass to me.

There was a long silence, Dauda's eyes fixed questioningly on Khassim's face.

"What happened, friend?" asked Khassim, hands still moving through his little tasks.

"There was a plot for a *coup d'etat* and Issa was in it. With other officers from Zinder. From Maradi and Agadez also. Most of them Hausa but with a few Tuareg. But there was a spy among them. Friend, they are looking for everyone Issa helped to get an ID card. I've seen your name on a list at the police station in Maradi."

Khassim's hands were very still on the kettle and teapot.

"They will be watching at all the border-posts, without a doubt," said Dauda. "You must not go to Niger for any reason."

After Dauda left Khassim lay back on the mat, stiffly, like an old man. He stared silently at my face as I sat and wept.

At last he spoke. "When Yakubu is finished going to

the hospital I'll send Khadija home to her uncle at Birnin Konni with a message to come to meet me in Sokoto. He will help me steal my way across the border at Konni."

Not if you're dumping her on him, he won't, I thought.

He looked at me as if he read my thought.

"I won't divorce her yet."

But I knew this talk of Konni was just to comfort me. "But even if you steal across the border you must pass police checks at every town between Konni and Niamey."

He was silent for a long while.

My mind scampered here and there wildly, scrabbling along that border looking for a point of entry.

"What of Gaya? Could you cross there?" It was a border-post to the extreme west on the banks of the Niger.

"I don't know. Maybe," he answered quietly. He fell silent.

Gaya . . . surely their security wasn't that tight?

After a while his voice came slowly again, as from a distance. "What I will do . . . I will steal across in the place where the border comes closest to Niamey . . . at Kantchari in Burkina Faso . . . over there in the west."

"But you must go through Benin to get to Burkina Faso! That's – wait – that's six border-posts you must pass!"

Six border-posts, all hazardous, all capable of refusing entry or exit on a whim. All potentially requiring hefty *dashi*.

"And maybe until you go south as far as Jebba to cross the river and after that north again – that's – I don't know – it is more than a thousand kilometres or what exceeds that!"

He stared as if he had not heard me.

"And there still will be police-checks inside Niger – " I said.

He interrupted me. "If I reach Niger I can buy a camel. I will ride through the bush until I reach Niamey. If I don't get a camel I will go by foot until I reach where you are in Niamey."

"How many miles – kilometres – is it from the border to Niamey?"

"Maybe about one hundred."

I took what looked like the ruins of my life and went and wept with fresh despair, standing before Jonathan in his bedroom.

"Valium time," he said, like any Dallas housewife. But I was afraid of that and refused. Then, while we argued pros and cons Musa Ibrahim arrived and, though Jonathan protested, I beat a retreat.

He followed me out to the car. "Jesus, Rutherford, why don't you just call it off? Can't you just stay? Christ, Kate, aren't you doing OK here? At least you're together – "

I got in and slammed the door with a sob. "I can't, Jonathan. I cannot bear any more of this hole-and-corner stuff. I want to be with him – openly – without this tension – "

He leant on the window. "Then, girl, take the situation and subtract your first thought from it! Get him to tell Khadija and take you as second wife, for chrissake! And stay!"

"He won't do that. He's afraid, he's ashamed – he's bloody *monogamous*!"

"Then *you* tell her. Really, Kate, it's gone too far! You must."

"I would – honest to God, I would – " I broke off and

stared at my tear-streaked face in the side-mirror. No you wouldn't, I suddenly thought.

"What?"

"God . . . maybe I wouldn't." I looked at him. "I'm afraid of her too . . ."

"But you've often said you feel she might go for it – "

"I want him to do it. I wouldn't have the guts."

"You *would* have the guts! You have guts and to spare!"

"It's no use, Jonathan. I *can't* do it anyway without his permission. I can't. Don't you see? If I take his – his – power – his dignity from him – "

"I know, I know. But, Kate, think seriously." He pressed at his temples with his fingers and fell silent.

"*He* can't continue either, Jonathan. I think the tension is killing him. He keeps getting sick and it frightens me."

Jonathan closed his eyes and massaged his temples. "I just don't get it. How can there be such a difference? How can Musa waltz a wife in on top of me and expect me to grin and bear it and presumably waltz another in on Djibrilla any time he fancies – when Khassim – oh, for God's sake, Kate, you have to give it a go!"

"So you think polygamy works, do you?" knowing the answer. "A little self-control, a rational approach, is all it needs . . . you find sharing him with her – "

He raised his head. "*I* find it *fucking* degrading! *I* find it feels like I'm a disposable receptacle for his *cock*!"

Musa was peering out from the living-room window.

"Well, sweetheart, you won't be sharing him very long if you don't get in there," I said. "He's getting impatient."

Jonathan glanced back at the house, then turned back to me. "Oh, Jesus," he said, his face twisting as if he were going to cry, "go for it, Rutherford. It's worth every drop of blood. Even if you do have to be the little-fucking-mermaid!" He gave me a little rub between the shoulder-blades and went slowly into the house.

The little-fucking-mermaid? What was it? Something about knives driving up through her feet at every step after she assumed human form . . .

I felt much better but when I got home, Husaini, who had a fever and had got someone to stand in for him at work, looked at my face and immediately asked, "What has happened?"

I shook my head and said "Nothing, nothing".

But he held me by the wrist and kept saying "What is it, Kate?" And I started to cry all over again and couldn't stop. He didn't ask any further, just held me in his arms and rocked me, as we sat together on the Fulani bed. As he rocked me and stroked me he stared off as if into the distance and muttered in Tamajeq to himself. Then at one point he burst out in Hausa with "Worthless bastard! To do this to you! What does he care!" and my heart gave a jolt that silenced my tears abruptly, thinking of course he meant Khassim. But he meant, I then realised, his beloved kinsman Rhisa.

The following day I arrived at the plant nursery mid-afternoon with Minha to find it deserted.

I waited for a long time in the silence while Minha scampered around. We went out to the lake and back but he didn't come.

I checked inside the shed and saw that his tea things were there, rolled up in his mats. So he had been there earlier and wherever he was now he intended to return soon.

What kind of emergency could have drawn him away?

I waited; but now I felt the rise of a hot tide of hurt and pain. If there had been a real emergency at home he would have taken his tea things. This was just some jaunt, one of those silly demands his people made on him or some whim of his own. Something, in any case, he had put before seeing me.

Or, somehow, because of my over-emotional state, he was avoiding me.

I called Minha, my fragile world splintering around me again, and left.

I dropped her home with Aghali and on some pretext left again, worried and fearful, and drove back, stopping at the entrance to Agric. I could go to Jonathan and beg a beer but then I'd have to go to Khassim later with beer on my breath. I was desperate to call to the quarters but my courage failed me. It would kill me to walk in there with this uncertainty as to what was going on. What if Khadija had found out? I drove on to the nursery.

The sun was making its abrupt dive into night when I arrived. I walked into the circle of trees and called into silence.

No one.

I went again to check his things in the shed and they were there, unmoved.

I stood in the dim silence. Suddenly his dumb possessions – the mats, the spare shirt hanging from a nail, the blue-and-white streaked plastic kettle – frightened me. They were like things one would inherit on a death. Their silence spoke of the terrible unspeakable absence of the human creature who used them and filled them. I stood and stared until I shook with tears.

It was well and truly dark when I heard the bicycle bell.

He came tearing into the compound and dropping the bike strode towards me. "Madame!" he called breathlessly and held me fiercely.

I asked no questions – just to bury my face in the white softness of his *tagilmoust* and feel his human warmth and the heart thudding in his chest was enough.

"Wait – wait," he said, voice deep in his throat, but I clung to him while he dragged the mats out of the shed.

We lay and embraced. "I felt fear that you would be gone," he said. "But I have brought something for you – something sweet." And he smiled his beautiful smile. "No, not that!" And his voice was guttural again as I loosened the string of his trousers and grasped his penis.

He sat up but I didn't let go and held his penis in both hands as he fumbled in the leather wallet around his neck and took out two pieces of paper.

"What are they?" I asked, indicating the paper with my lips like any Tuareg, while I held him. "Show me."

He opened both papers. One was typewritten and had an official stamp. The other was hand-written in Arabic. "The small one is a *malam's* paper. Don't touch it until you wash your hands or you will lessen its power!" And he leaned forward and kissed me, and his penis pushed more firmly into my hands. "I will read it for you – no – you read the other – their talk is the same."

The typed one was an affidavit from the court in Zaria. "*I, Khassim ag Amodi of Samaru, Zaria, make oath and say as follows . . .*"

He had sworn that he was husband of Katherine Rutherford of Amadu Bello University, Zaria and the father of Minha . . . It was stamped *Chief Magistrate Court Zaria* and signed by the Commissioner for Oaths.

One *naira* paid.

The British had indeed left a wondrous heritage behind.

"You must take these to Niamey and show them to whoever asks where your man is. Even Rhisa himself, you can show him. And tell them your husband is coming."

And I bent and took his penis in my mouth while he put the documents safely away and took his *tagilmoust* off and put it aside.

And then I kissed him and took him into me and closed about him and grasped him and the stars glittered and blurred like diamonds through my tears and I prayed to God to give me just this one thing in life, this man, and I cried "Give me! Give me! Give me!" in a jumbled Hausa-English as I began to come, calling on God and Khassim as one and the stars rushed towards me.

⁂

Face alight with excitement, laden with plunder from the markets of Nigeria and whatever spoils he could coax out of me, Husaini left for a visit home to Tchin Tabaraden. I let him go with a warm embrace, a sizeable gift of money to buy sacks of millet in Tchin Tabaraden to carry out to the family encampment, photos of Minha, beads and a roll of soft black cloth for Rhisa's mother, a few kilos of tobacco for the men of the family, a supply of emergency malaria treatment – and no word that he wouldn't find me when he came back.

He embraced me in his warm, shy way and I felt a

nervous tremor running through his body. Then he looked in my face and asked intently, "What will I tell Rhisa?"

I shook my head and let him go.

Afterwards I wondered. He had asked as if there was something I could say that would make a difference. How could there be? It had been Rhisa's choice to stay away. But, in any case, my mouth was sealed. I could say nothing that would tempt him to come back to Zaria now.

A week later, I drew up alongside the quarters and parked the Land Cruiser. Khadija was standing in front of her door and, seeing Minha, came running heavily to meet her. She fell to her knees and scooped Minha up in her arms and I was astonished to see her face was wet with tears.

When I asked her why, she laughed ruefully and wiped her face with her hand like a child. "I don't know," she said. "You know, you haven't brought Minha here since two weeks. I was sleeping yesterday and I dreamt that she was lost. When I saw her now I felt something in my heart." And she pressed a hand to her breast.

A week later we left Nigeria, without saying goodbye.

PART TWO

Chapter Eleven

And so I was reduced to nothing. House gone, job gone, family gone. Car sold, horse sold, friends and books abandoned in another country. All those years reduced to this – me and Minha in a small flat.

Me and Minha and Khassim's affidavits. I looked at the precious pieces of paper. The English one read: " . . . *that at the time of her birth, her name was registered in her mother's maiden name. That I now make this statutory oath so that her name can be known and called Minha Khassim . . .* " The typist had written "modern name" instead of "maiden name". Someone had substituted "maiden" in biro and initialled it.

Numb with grief and fear, I had left Khassim in Zaria with the money to cover his trip and all its hazards – the transport, the camel, the bribes. And a lump sum he would give to Khadija when he sent her to Birnin Konni, to tide her and the children over until – until when?

I was sick with fear when I thought of him attempting the trip, leaving Zaria secretly and travelling alone. The reality was that my whole world could fall down a well somewhere in West Africa and I would never know. As a pathetic bulwark against that nightmare I had given him a few envelopes addressed to me at the university in Niamey, conscious meanwhile that envelopes bearing a foreign name could help to hang him if he were arrested. And could get me deported. Of course, it never occurred to me to give him a telephone number. I simply didn't realise there would be a functioning telephone service in Niamey.

With my dream almost in my hand, the dream of possessing him merging with my dream of living in Niger, I blindly pressed on. The impetus carried us both on – when, as Jonathan had said, we could simply have stayed where we were, in our oasis in Zaria.

And pressing on seemed the only way to be rid of Khadija.

It was all surreal. Here I was, in a bright foreign watershed in my life. The rigours of Nigeria now seemed like familiar comforts.

Here, instead of our bungalow under the flame-trees we had a bright simple little flat on the first floor, a small bedroom with brass bed and air-conditioner, a tiny little room off it with a cot, a shower adjoining a little French-style kitchen with a big stone sink, a small square balcony with a view of the Niger. French baguette and brie on the table. Real coffee, chocolate – wine had I not been half a Muslim. The living-room window was just over the entrance to our block and overlooked a little communal garden. There were only three low blocks in all, sprawled along the road, and our flat was on the gable end of the last block. Definitely not high-rise land.

It was ideal, really. For me and Minha. But a million miles away from Bessie Head's little house with the sunflowers. When Khassim came we would find a local house and compound. Yet, this was university housing at a nominal rent and we needed the money. I fretted over this dilemma.

Across the street was the Hotel Terminus with first-class food, a swimming-pool and *telephones*, for God's sake. The French had planned a railroad running all the way from Dakar on the Atlantic coast to Niamey and this hotel was built as its terminus. The railroad had never been built.

I had laughed when Denis, a Frenchman who lectured in English and was married to a Tuareg woman, told me about this terminus without a starting-point, a terminus to nothing.

"I hope that's not an omen," I said wryly.

He was too polite to comment but I almost heard the mental click as he registered and analysed my comment. I had spun yarns about the reasons why Minha's nomadic father was delayed in Nigeria but I knew my state of tension must have been palpable.

We were driving in his Peugeot truck, looking for a playschool for Minha. Now, with no extended family to take care of her, I needed to hire a baby-nurse immediately or send her to school.

Denis and I were two of a kind. He invariably dressed in a suit of blue cotton – baggy trousers and mid-length tunic in the humblest local style. I took it to be a kind of personal uniform. It was, more precisely, monastic garb. He had originally come to Africa as a Catholic missionary brother. Now he considered himself a Muslim of sorts, had a Tuareg wife and troop of children and applied his sense of dedication in other directions.

I liked him enormously but the thought of his marriage filled me with envy. It was that easy for a man. Choose a girl. Negotiate with the family. Pay the bride-price. *Fini*.

Why was that denied me? Why was I not allowed to make that simple choice? Why should the world consider him socially responsible but dismiss me as immoral at best, a lunatic at worst?

We met with difficulties in finding a playschool. We found a French one but they rapidly pointed out we weren't French, as if this deficiency hadn't occurred to me. The Americans would take us quite cheerfully if we paid an exorbitant sum for the privilege. Then we found an ideal school run by Nigerien women, only to be told they didn't take *les blancs* – the whites. I tried to protest that Minha was not, in fact, a "white" but Denis hushed me up and we left with elaborately courteous farewells.

"What was that about?" I exploded, back in the truck.

"It is state-subsidised – they can only take Nigeriens."

"But Minha is Nigerien!"

"Legally?" he asked politely.

"No." Then I thought of Khassim's affidavit. "Oh, yes, in fact. I have a legal declaration of parentage."

We were negotiating a roundabout in the bizarre French way where it's *priorité* to all and sundry and everyone just crowds on. *Fraternité Travail Progrès*, I read, on a large sign in the centre.

"It might be better for Minha to find another school," said Denis. "I noticed there were no mulatto children there."

Mulatto! I was aghast. I knew the word wasn't necessarily pejorative but there was no word in northern Nigeria for children of mixed parentage – apart from the casual "mixed" or "half-and-half". I thought of the staff school in ABU where the kids scattering into the yard looked like a spilled box of Smarties. Christ, this really was a different country. I was baffled. As far as I knew, the French had always been into miscegenation in an enthusiastic way. Unlike the Brits.

We eventually found an overcrowded zoo-like school, where Zarma teachers strained every nerve to keep huge herds of kids inside large rooms. It filled me with alarm but it was cheap and within walking-distance of Terminus, so that was that – *shi ke nan*.

Denis was cautious, to say the least, in his dealings with the establishment. The day of my arrival he had taken me directly to Immigration where a glowering officer had promptly threatened to deport me for entering without a work visa. I had protested and was about to touch the departing officer on the arm in appeal when Denis grasped my elbow in alarm and muttered, "*Don't touch him*". We did get the visa but Denis's reactions made this world seem a more threatening one than Nigeria had ever been.

So much for my idea of a brave new world.

Some days later in the late afternoon I forced myself to venture out of the flat with Minha, but almost quailed and retreated before we got half-way down the street. My feeling of isolation was becoming neurotic. I was full of fear that someone would address me in Zarma or French. This was utterly irrational: I hadn't used my French in years but Hausa was widely spoken.

This area – the tail of the fish in my image of Niger – belonged to the Zarma-Songhai who dominated a country extending diagonally in a huge waterless block some 2000 kilometres into the Sahara. The Hausa, in fact, made up over half the total population – over twice the number of Zarma. But the capital was the Zarma stronghold and I . . .

well, what was I? A Hausa speaker, a pseudo-Tuareg, a pseudo-European by this time. My Tuareg made up only eight per cent of the population, and their centre Agadez was a thousand kilometres north-east. I felt threatened.

I forced myself on down the street, Minha trotting cheerfully in front of me in a little lilac cotton dress. Her hair was just long enough to be tied in skimpy little bunches on top of her head. The hair that they saw as a blemish. Maybe Khadija was right – maybe I should have let her shave it. I thought with a pang of Yakubu, pulling himself manfully over the ground with his useless right leg and hip, a little top-notch of hair on his shaven head.

We reached the end of the street and turned into the grounds of the lavish Grand Hotel, scuttling into the lobby past a platoon of traders hawking their wares outside the main door. Out on the terrace a mixture of Nigeriens and expatriates were lounging about, viewing the river, drinking beer and eating little peppered kebabs.

If I had been Khadija herself in her black robes I couldn't have felt more out of place. I was the tramp trying to crash a state banquet, with my dusty feet and cotton *zane*. I ordered a beer and a Coke from a hovering waiter in red cummerbund and sat there, pretending by virtue of my skin-colour that I belonged, that this was my scene. I imagined sitting on the mat outside Khadija's hut and wanted to weep for the ease and comfort I had felt then.

What in Jesus' name was I doing here? *Oh, whither hast thou led me, Egypt,* indeed.

Minha was OK. She trotted about, charming people, leaning on their knees, grinning up at them. A bunch of Nigerien men gave her pieces of meat and she chewed away, dribbling. They laughed and gave her groundnuts. I should watch her – she could choke on either the meat or the groundnuts.

I stared at the broad river, with the stage-set interest of the narrow Pont Kennedy sprawling out over it. Across on the far side was a broad splash of greenery in the midst of which I could see the mud walls of the university.

A constant stream of camels and vendors passed over the bridge and the river below was alive at the edges with flat-bottomed wooden boats. I thought again of my image of Niger as a landlocked fish and suddenly longed for Ireland. I saw it, full of savage melancholy and lilting life out there on the grey seas. I'd die here for homesickness if Khassim didn't come soon, without Husaini and the others to laugh it all away.

I went back "home", heart-sick. I had given up my family, all that laughter. I put their photo on the wall: Rhisa, Husaini, Ikis-Ikus, Aghali. The eyes laughed out at me. That was acceptance. That was love.

Among my photos I came across the terrible terrible one that Husaini had once commented so eloquently on – of Minha and me in Madrid. It showed us crossing a little wooden bridge in Madrid zoo against a background of weeping willow branches. I had Minha, a wee scrap of a creature in a wee scrap of a cotton dress, balanced on one hip and a large bag over the other shoulder. I was dressed in a bright swirling skirt and a black Tuareg takatkat. So far, looking good. But the expression on my face was agonised. I could still feel the pain of the weight of that bag. In the bag was my camera and zoom lens, my films, my photos, my precious Tuareg jewellery, my Tuareg knive, fossils from the Sahara, books, stuff I had written, writing

materials, a few books, my passport and all my official
documents, baby equipment, some underwear, money in
four currencies – God knows what else. It was a stopover
on the way home to Ireland and I was carrying in my
hand-luggage all the belongings I hadn't trusted to
Nigerian Airways.

Husaini had looked at the photo and said, "Truly Kate
and Minha were lost there."

And I had never heard so elegant a statement.

I suddenly saw, through his eyes, how bizarre it was:
battling out there on my own with no loved ones,
obsessively determined to visit the bloody zoo for no good
reason and against all odds. And against the sheer physical
agony of carrying that weight of belongings.

"Truly Kate and Minha were lost there."

We were lost now. I had ejected Husaini from my life as
if he were a bad tooth to be drawn. I needed him.

The Madrid photo seemed an emblem of my life. An
emblem of my present situation, out on a limb once more –
moving further out, my child on my hip, to the extreme
swaying tip of the branch: *"Look at me!"*

The morning I last left Ireland, my mother in a rare
moment had put her arms around me and said, "You're my
baby! Cry – cry – why don't you just cry. Ah, why must you
always do it to yourself?"

And I did cry but dumbly because of the hidden dark
things inside me that always made me go out there and be
alone.

Looking at that shameful photo, that day in Niamey, I
thought my grim agonised face as I plodded through the
zoo said everything about my will and obsessiveness.

It would have served me well if I had stuck that photo

up beside the one of Rhisa and Husaini. But it hurt and shamed me and I stuck it back in the bundle out of sight.

Every day at the university I stood on the first-floor balcony with the mud crenellations and stared northwards where the sand shimmered in the heat until my eyes swam, willing him to step out of the landscape through the palms, longing desperately for that moment. My fear that he would come to grief somewhere on the long hazardous road was so great that I blotted it out, giving imaginative form only to the moment of his arrival.

Every evening I lay comatose with Minha on the little metal bed on the balcony, surrounded by spiralling smoke from mosquito coils, and watched the moon waxing and then waning. Knowing he was watching, too, wherever he might be.

But he didn't come.

October passed. Then first quarter again. November. A new month for him, blatantly painted in the sky.

Why no letters? If he were in difficulties somewhere *en route*, would he not have sent a letter? My lurking fear was that he had been arrested and they had refused to let him write.

The moon rounding to a full. How could it not draw him now, if he were well and free to come? The days became a torture. I mulled over the calendar obsessively, always checking the phases of the moon.

I lay on the balcony in the evening with the calendar in my hand. It was a Nigerian one, with pictures from some arts and culture festival. *One fine day you'll notice* – I'd been through it all before with Rhisa. I imagined how ridiculous it would be if Madame Butterfly sang that same wonderful piece repeatedly throughout the opera and for several different men? All with the same exquisite passion?

And yet, ironically, only *now* did I understand what the opera reached out to express: the fierce reality of biological passion. What a fool I had been to deny it, while I pussyfooted with intellect and religion, pondering over the relative values of *agape* and *caritas*, piously denigrating their questionable relation *eros*.

No one had told me.

The Catholic church had been careful not to tell me, snipping away slyly under our skirts, doing a neat job of psychological excision. So neat you could hardly see the scars when the light was poor.

One night Minha woke up crying "I want Baba". She meant Khassim. She had seen him making tea. She had been back to the Wood between the Worlds.

I wanted to believe it was an omen. That he was on his way.

Desperate for even a partial release of my anxiety, when Denis came by to take me to work, I spoke to him about not hearing from Khassim. I didn't dare to go into the political stuff, which would implicate him.

He shrugged expressively. "In Africa, people do not expect a letter. They just wait for the person to come."

I knew. *Hakuri*. Patience. I must have patience.

And I thought: if he does not come I will make a very sad old woman.

At the university a little package awaited me. I recognised the writing, almost identical to my mother's. My cousin, Nicky. The Irish stamp, a convoluted little mythical animal. It was a cassette he had taped for me, a selection of Janis Ian

songs. God bless him. I was in such tenuous contact with my
own culture I knew nothing about Janis Ian, had no idea she
had become a household name with "At Seventeen" – oddly
enough the only song I disliked in the selection. I listened to
the songs that day and thought, how curiously apposite: this
husky-voiced lady from my distant world with her anguish,
her yearning, her loneliness, the delicacy and precision of her
expressions of sexual love – all that and more riding those
vigorous rhythms and soaring above it all into hope and gold.

Before the dawn and the light, here comes the night . . .

Every day I joined one of the many taxis that shuttled
dernier fleuve across the Pont Kennedy to the university.

Before my first lecture I had felt – I always did first term –
as if I were about to board a space shuttle to the moon run by
Nigerian Airways. I couldn't seriously be expected to do this.
But lectures turned out to be less stressful than in Nigeria.
Classes were smaller – no more formal lectures to students
crowded in on each other's laps. And the standard of English
was lower here than in Nigeria, English being the second
rather than the first European language acquired – they all
spoke three or four African languages as a matter of course.

*"How many times do I have to tell you to squeeze the
toothpaste up from the end?"*

The text was illustrated with a cartoon of a woman
ranting and crazed and a bewildered defensive man.

"What kind of characterisation is this?" I asked. I
wanted them to say it was comic or caricature.

A hand raised. Gambo.

"Yes, Gambo?"

"That is bad characterisation, Mrs Rutherford."

"Why, Gambo? You understand it's exaggerated for effect?"

"It is bad because no woman would speak to her husband like that."

Jesus. My last state was worse than my first.

I had to get out of teaching.

Dreams. So much and so many, my whole life streaming through my brain.

I dreamt of the West African coast and staying in a hotel. I wanted to swim, telling myself that Lawrence of Arabia had made it to West Africa and swum there, giving himself to the powerful waves with their mighty undertow. But I met with all the West African difficulties. The hotel door didn't lock so I couldn't leave my belongings unprotected. I had no swimsuit – the man who hired them out was not "on seat". I took a bus, got out at the wrong place, had passed the hotel, had left an important bag behind with my passport in it. I asked directions of some giggling young people who made me angry with their stupidity. I did get to the water finally, wearing men's underpants and a short bathrobe. Jonathan was there, eating Danish pastries and drinking Guinness and begging me to go and persuade a taxi to "traverse" the beach. "The roads north are just like this," I said. "The tires are the problem."

I wrote the dream down when I woke in case any of it might be important but saw it was not.

But the thought of Lawrence had touched a nerve. I thought, "Where has it all gone?" How did I become reduced to all this grief? Was there no way of beating a little more romance out of life? None lurking on in some hidden corner? I had shared a country of the spirit with Lawrence once upon a time, before Africa took me and caught me in the trap of my femaleness. But wasn't that my victory? That maturity? Wasn't that precisely where he had failed? He had never negotiated his sexuality and had finally grown to recognise that. Tried to negotiate it in darkest Dorset with a birch-wielding young Scotsman.

Lo, with a little rod I did but touch the honey of romance
And must I lose a soul's inheritance?

Like Oscar's, Lawrence's story had run out of romance. Had ended in disgust, guilt, seclusion, perversion. "Home".

I slept again and woke with my heart thudding.

What if he did not come?

Jesus, would the man not come and save me? He was to make sense of it all.

But something had woken me.

There was a letter lying inside the front door, a thin blue envelope. Denis sometimes brought me mail from the university. The envelope with my handwriting and a Nigerian stamp. Showing Cattle-Fulani. A *Nigerian* stamp. He was still in Nigeria. I read the post-mark: *Zaria*. I couldn't read the date.

I stared at it numbly while the thin paper of the envelope grew sodden in my sweating hands.

He hadn't moved. All my moon-gazing was delusion. All my dreams about the hazards of West Africa were delusion. He had never moved. Khassim was still in Zaria. Sitting in Zaria. Nor loving me enough. Unable to move.

Shaking with nerves, I opened it. Tifenagh script. The message was in *Tifenagh*.

I steadied myself. *Don't panic. You can read it.*

The standard opening symbols were familiar and clear to me. I read: "*Wa nakk Khassim . . .* " It is I, Khassim . . .

I stood where I was, there behind the door, and struggled to string the symbols together. My Tamajeq

147

wasn't up to it. He should have used the script to write in Hausa – but that would never have occurred to him – I should have thought of telling him. But I had imagined him using a Hausa letter-writer.

I mouthed the sounds, singing them out in the required fashion, listening for the sense. Minha came trotting from the bedroom in her little underpants and stood, her head dropped way back as she stared up at me open-mouthed.

Bits and scraps became intelligible: *I want you. Khadija. Birnin Konni.* The root consonants for "to go". But what was the tense? Gone? Is going? Khadija was going – going – gone – to Birnin Konni.

I sang it out, stringing the sounds together and Minha began to laugh in little bouts of chuckling that shook her whole body, thinking this was a game or nursery rhyme.

The root-consonants for *iran* – to be ill. But I didn't understand the tense or the person. He had been ill? He was ill? She was ill? Something about going back to work. "Come" repeated three times in combination with a word that baffled me: six symbols spelling out k-r-s-m-t-y. I sang it out: *Ikeh-ireh-iseh-imeh-iteh-ee*. I had never heard the word. Then, in a flash I had it: *Kirsimati*. The Hausa word for Christmas.

In sudden joy I spread my arms wide and pressed my body hard against the coolness of the wall by the door. Out of the corner of my eye I saw Minha grinning up at me roguishly. She gave a little indrawn chuckle like a cluck. I laughed aloud and grabbed her up and hugged her fiercely.

He was coming at Christmas.

I swung my bag over my shoulder, grabbed Minha's sandals, hustled out of the flat, locked the door and rushed down the stairs with Minha on my hip. She clung to me, bewildered now at my breathless haste.

I had to find someone, anyone, who could read Tifenagh. And there was Denis's truck parked down the road just beyond the Terminus entrance. He must be visiting in one of the other blocks of flats. I reached the truck and waited there in an agony of joy and impatience. There was a load of mangos in the open back. I touched the rosy skin of one. It was glowing with heat. I wanted to eat one. I put Minha into the back of the truck, belatedly testing the metal with my palm to see if it were hot enough to burn her feet. It was fairly hot. I put her sandals on. The soles of her feet were rosy like the mangos. I hoped they weren't scorched. She grabbed a mango in each hand and bit one. The juice ran down her chin. I should have washed the mango. Still clutching the mangos, she ran up and down, liking the ringing sound her plastic sandals made on the metal floor. I stood there, wild with joy, while she ran and ran.

"*Berish*! Certainly!" cried Maryam, Denis's wife, when I asked her to read my letter. She was a thin dark woman from Agadez, very pretty, not too young, wearing the white Agadez *takatkat* with its bars of red embroidery in a noughts-and-crosses pattern. She had been about to tie a blue-bead necklace around Minha's neck. Now her teenage daughter took over the bead-tying, and Maryam sat up cross-legged and straight-backed on the mat, the better to concentrate.

She read it with confidence, breaking off a few times to exchange rapid-fire comments with her daughter. When she did, in my impatience I urged her on. They thought this funny and countered it with laughing cries of "*Tazaydart*! Patience!"

In a mixture of Tamajeq and Hausa they conveyed

Khassim's letter in detail. Khadija had gone. He had travelled to Benin. He had been ill.

He had gone back to Zaria. He had got his job back.

But it was I who was to come at Christmas.

"Are you sure?" I asked, sick with dismay. "It was he who was to come here!"

"No, no." She shook a long finger emphatically. "Three times he is begging: '*Come to Zaria at Christmas*.' He says come at Christmas, at the time of the holidays, and you will travel back together to Niamey."

The closing expressions of love and desire caused much hilarity and mutual slapping of hands, "By God, the man has loneliness for you!"

I laughed with them and indeed their words were a small salve to my wounds.

Eventually they asked me, "How did that person learn Tifenagh?"

I was startled. "He is a Tamajeq," I said.

"*Kale, kale!* Never! Never!"

I was made uneasy by their astonishment. Was Maryam not married to an "Infidel" herself?

We women ate together – Denis eating by himself, incongruously seated at his rough-hewn wooden writing-table. We drank tea and unease and dismay began to lift. I went home with a calm heart, a singing heart, my mind clear again, the sadness I had feared would always be with me evaporated.

I will go, I thought.

I'll go for the screw, I thought, already lapsing into Jonathan-mode. And to pick up my books from Jonathan.

Chapter Twelve

We raced through the darkness along the *route nationale*, the narrow tarred road that led due east along the southern border of Niger over one thousand four hundred kilometres as far as Lake Chad. It cut through the narrow belt of barely arable land that was an extension of the Hausaland of northern Nigeria. The colonial powers had ruled a straight line as far as the lake, cutting Hausaland in two, so that at Birnin Konni I would cross a border where on one side the Hausa inhabitants spoke French and on the other side English. *Birni* – it meant a walled town. No doubt it had some kind of glorious or bloody past. Now, it was a scrap of a border town.

The little barren villages by the roadside were no more than homesteads, their giant round mud grain-containers with domed thatched lids looming like space stations on a fictional lunar landscape as we passed.

The bus – a type of mini-bus with extra seats crammed in – swayed with its weight of passengers and the mountain of baggage tied under tarpaulin to the roof. I slept fitfully, clutching Minha on my lap, bruising my bones against the ledge of the window to the left, the head of the man on my right lolling in his sleep on my shoulder. I didn't mind his lolling – in fact, I felt privileged. He was one of the very

151

exotic bush Fulani – or Wodaabe as they called themselves here in Niger. He was wearing a leather loincloth under his striped loose-weave sideless tunic. His large conical straw hat, decorated with bits of copper and brass and soft black birds' feathers, was stowed between his long sinewy thighs. Beside him was his wife, looking like a London punk in bright white plastic shoes with mock lace-ups, bouffant rolls of hair and dozens of huge brass and tin earrings inserted around the whole circumference of her ears. Their faces were decorated with delicate little tattoos. They sat like exotic birds on swaying branches among the humble Hausa farming folk.

We had been travelling seemingly endless hours already, covering the four-hundred-kilometre stretch to Birnin Konni and at this stage every minute was agony. At Dogondoutchi, named for the high rocks around the town, I bought stuff from the windows of the bus – tepid bottles of Coke, groundnuts and stiff sheets of peppered dried meat so thin that the light of the kerosene lamps on the trays of the vendors shone through. I wasn't hungry but needed anything to relieve the monotony and ward off the torture of fitful sleep. Hours before, at Dosso, Minha had gulped tepid Cokes down so avidly the nappy she was wearing for the journey became sodden and had long since leaked into my lap. There was another in my bag but I hadn't the energy to make the effort to get at it, wedged as I was between the window and my unconscious neighbour. Somewhere east of Dogondoutchi I dragged the nappy off her and threw it out the window into the sand beside the road, a gift for some passing goat. I bunched a *zane* under her and prayed.

At a certain early point in the journey you learned to

hang on desperately, drink when you could and pray for a slow puncture so the driver would call a halt and you could empty your bursting bladder. A fast puncture or a blow-out and you died. What made it all endurable was the humorous spirit of *cameraderie* that burst into instant life between the passengers. We were brothers-in-arms, chain-ganged convicts slammed into physical intimacy, enduring each other's sweat and smells, sharing out our water and food, our emotions washing through us as if we were one organism – energy, excitement, fear of the police, despair at delay, hunger for the eventual relief of pain. And above all, patience.

"*Hakuri maganin duniya* – patience is the medicine of the world," the old man behind me repeated like an aspiration and with increasing frequency. "*Sai hakuri!* Only patience!"

If the bus tossed itself off the road we would all die together. No one survived these crashes. We would bleed to death patiently at the side of the road, moaning "*Sai hakuri!*" to each other. I wondered what the Wodaabe word for "patience" was.

I was as happy as I had ever been. I was on my way to Khassim and this was as near as I had ever been, or ever would be, to being an African. In that bus no one could deny our common and equal humanity. I was a woman, a mother first, a Baturiya after.

At Birnin Konni we would cross the border and get a Nigerian bus, equally crowded without a doubt in the world, to get us to Sokoto. Then, with luck, we would squeeze into a green-and-yellow taxi in good condition to sweep down the four hundred kilometres to Zaria. We had set out from "home" at six o'clock on Friday evening – the

153

very knife-edge start of the Christmas vacation – but it had taken our bus two hours to gather enough passengers and strap on the luggage. I expected an equal delay at Sokoto in the morning and dreaded what might happen before that, at Birnin Konni, arriving as we would in the early hours – *in sha Allahu* – God willing.

I thought it might take some eighteen hours continuous travel to cover the thousand-odd kilometres to Zaria. If we hadn't to queue for petrol in Sokoto. Corruption was such that supplies like petrol and gas were bartered off illegally well before they hit Sokoto in the far north. And of course there were the many casualties on the marathon journey north from Lagos – I had seen them – tankers on their massive backs having driven off the roads.

⚜⚜⚜⚜

We made it in twenty tough hours.

I was sick with excitement as familiar sights spun into my vision when we at last neared Zaria and could hardly breathe as we sped in the road past Shika village where I had once lived in a mud hut. At two o'clock the taxi dropped us and our bags on the road only a hundred yards from Jonathan's bungalow. Heart beating in my throat, I trudged to the house, eyes all the while nervously fixed on the row of "quarters" behind it. But wild horses wouldn't have drawn me over there. I was so terrified of what I might find. I might find Khadija.

At four Jonathan drove me, exhausted and quaking, to Khassim's plant nursery. I didn't even know if he would be there.

Jonathan stayed by the car, down the dirt road a little

distance from the circle of trees. He told me much later – in a later life – how it stuck in his mind: that picture of me walking down the dirt road to my fate, in my wine-red *zane* and Buzu pigtails – my bottom bouncing, as he said. So vivid was his description, I now see myself through his eyes, from the back. But I see myself look back – I definitely did turn and look back at him poised in the door of his powder-blue VW, elbow resting on its roof, dark glasses fixed on me.

I walked into the circle of trees.

Khassim was alone, cross-legged on his mat, bareheaded, in his black tunic.

He sat still where he was, staring as if I were an apparition, until I was standing before him. Then he clutched me about the legs and pressed his head against my thighs. His body began to shake convulsively but I didn't realise he was crying until I felt the wetness of his tears through the thin cotton.

I buried my fingers in his hair and felt the slender skull beneath, the reality of him.

He pulled me down to face him. I knelt back on my heels. His face was lined and thinner, the skin coarser, his hair dull. Like a pet who has been neglected in the kennels while the owners are on holiday.

He's sick, I thought, with fear.

"What happened with you?" I asked gently. "Why didn't you come to Niamey?"

"I tried, by God! But fever overcame me there in Benin and my money was stolen . . . " He fell silent, staring at me in wonder.

"What is it?"

"When I saw you now," he whispered, "I thought you

155

were a spirit. Because yesterday I had a dream. I was sleeping here by day and I dreamt you came to me here like this and I reached out my hand to hold you. And you handed me a sugarcane. I was taking it from your hand when you turned away and were gone. I was left here holding the stick of sugarcane."

I was the self in that dream, the light ironic ghost – *and she laid her hand on me and this she did say: 'It will not be long, love, till our wedding-day'* – I was the painfully beating heart hidden beneath smiles and light touches. How can you be so whole, Khassim, in your responses? I was both actor and spectator and my performance was perfectly tuned. Teasing. Playful. Proud. Don't let him see the pain you've been through and don't trust this.

"Come," he said, drawing me by the wrist. "Come." The familiar thickness in his throat.

"I can't. I can't. Jonathan is waiting for me there on the road."

"For God's sake, madame, for God's sake! Five minutes. Five minutes is enough."

"I can't. I am coming later. I'll come back at six." But in my head I was already lying under him – I wanted him badly and Jonathan would wait, no problem. "I can't now." Punish him. Make him wait. What was the matter with me? What was it? It was anger. It was hurt. Under the smiles. Cutting through the desire. Make him wait.

"Madame – two months! I *cannot* wait."

"No, I must go." I pulled back firmly. The very first time I had said no to him.

His eyes gave in, filling with uncertainty. "I'll walk with you to greet Jonathan."

"Thank God I came," I said as we drove off. I thought, the man loves me. I suppose I didn't doubt that.

Jonathan's face was alight. He had really feared for me. "I see it all now," he said. Strangely, this was the first time he had seen Khassim and me together. "It's lovely – your relationship. The lovely, easy, ironic thing . . . "

I was so grateful and astonished that tears pricked my eyes. "Easy?" I sniffled. "Hell, if you thought *that* was easy and ironic!"

"I could see it," he said, with a little nod towards me. "I know he's very ill but I could see how it was. And what a majestic man he is!"

"Oh, God, Jonathan, he's so sick!"

"But glad to see you . . . "

"Yes . . . "

"How glad?" giggled Jonathan, silly with relief for me.

"Oh, you were waiting now, so I don't know! We didn't do anything," I said, pretending annoyance. But I was glad, glad, so glad – so glad to be back in the security of this joking relationship, the only relationship that reinforced the link between Khassim and me.

Poor Jonathan, always so generous, always strong enough to give support whatever. There was a very big "whatever" in this case: Musa's wife, Djibrilla, was pregnant.

"You *didn't*! Why didn't you?" he wanted to know.

I started to go over the details and he shook his head and bit his lip and got that far-seeing gaze in his eyes.

"What?" I asked.

"Him and his sugarcane." He laughed softly. "He's incredible."

He was.

157

"So did he never leave Zaria at all?" asked Jonathan.

A shadow over the flash of sunlight.

"He did. He says he did." What if he hadn't?

"Has Khadija gone?"

"Yes." The great proof of his good faith.

Jonathan pulled up in front of his house and jerked the keys out of the ignition. He looked at me, gnawing at a knuckle. "So what now?"

⚜⚜⚜

"I went," said Khassim in a murmur, eyes closed, as he lay on his back in the nursery, forearm thrown across his forehead, right arm holding me close to him. "I sent Khadija to Niger with the children. My work I gave to Dauda's brother – I was lucky I did it like that, because he gave my job back to me without dispute when I returned." Our old old position, laced together on his mat, his blanket over us against the December chill, the bright full moon above us. "I reached Jebba where there is a long bridge and we crossed the river there where it is very wide. But after that the fever caught me and with difficulty I reached Ilorin, a big town. But I went ahead and entered another transport, a big lorry, then and there, and passed the border into Benin." He drew my head closer to his chest and leaned over me to spit some tobacco. And close as we already were, the tender pressure of his hand on the back of my head thrilled me. He lay back. "After that, madame, the fever overcame my strength. I lay for two weeks in a town called Parakou and while I was in the fever my money was stolen – though it was here, in my *porte-monnaie*, against my chest. I returned to Zaria like an *almajiri*, begging money from station to station."

Jesus. That must have killed him. My nightmares hadn't been so far from the truth, after all.

He looked down at me from under his forearm, tobacco on his lower lip, face was full of pain. "Madame, it is enough for me. I have made a plan. I will go to Maradi. There is another *capitaine* I know there – another Tamajeq – Sideka ag Mowka – he is from Timia in Aïr. He will help me."

"But you can't cross the border," I murmured against his breast. "They will want to see your card."

"Listen. I already have arranged to buy a company ID card from an Agadez person on the building-site – I will use that if I must and say my *carte d'identité* is lost. But I will not cross the border where the soldiers are – I will make my way through the bush and beg God that I do not meet with the horse patrol."

It was crazy, I knew it was crazy, this going back to put his head in the lion's mouth. But all these dangers seemed dreamlike while I could hear the steady beat of his heart under my cheek. I stayed silent. Anything, anything, I thought, anything as long as I don't have to do violence to my soul and part from him again.

"What do you say?" he asked abruptly.

"I will go with you. I will not leave you again."

I would stay right here in Zaria if necessary. But, I thought then, how could I? Without my job, my lifeline?

And I wanted to go on, not back.

He thought for a long while, his lips twisting on his wad of tobacco.

Finally he released me gently and sat up, crossing his

legs. He spoke, voice deepening with the seriousness of what he had to say. "Listen, madame, we will go together to Maradi. But then you must leave me and go back to Niamey until I come. They will be suspicious if they see me together with a Baturiya – it will bring danger for you and for me and for Sideka."

No, I thought, no. I must stay with you. But when he spoke with that authority that I was afraid to argue with him. "OK," I mumbled.

"*To*, if that it how it is we will spend only a few days here. I feel fear that Sideka will leave Maradi. I heard some rumours that he will be transferred to Zinder. But he is in Maradi now, without a doubt. I must go soon."

My heart was heavy in my chest again. A few days? All that pain again and so soon? I couldn't, couldn't leave him. It could not be expected of me.

Then he came to his knees and straddled my body smiling, letting his trousers fall down over the swell of his hips and his heavy erection, and I forgot the agony of parting, seeing his eyes and teeth glint in his dark face and his hair wild in silhouette above me against the bright full moon, the stars a gleaming crown about his head.

Chapter Thirteen

Four days later we left. Jonathan was driving us to the carpark. It was nine o'clock. Khassim had gone to Samaru and he wasn't back.

He had slept with me in Jonathan's spare bedroom but his fever had returned, mounting towards midnight but waning towards dawn. Two days before, I had taken him to the hospital and they had treated him for malaria once again but it hadn't helped. I was now as sure as I could be with my amateur medical knowledge that he had a damaged spleen.

I had held him, held him, every waking moment aware of the infinite preciousness of him . . .

Day by day until we've satisfied
The longest night, side by side . . .
Love won't be denied . . .

I woke to feel his penis erect against my buttocks. It was the first time I had slept a night long with him and woken to the morning with him. A sweet joy Khadija knew every day of her life.

But she was gone, I had won in the end.

He made no attempt to wake me but entered me from behind and I wanted to weep with joy at the sweet familiarity of the trespass. As we lay there, sweetly joined, it seemed we could never be parted in this life.

At six he had stumbled off to wind up his affairs and there was a small death in that parting. He had already sold his bicycle and given back his uniform but he had to collect the sword he had given to a kinsman in Samaru for safe-keeping after Khadija left.

"Where is he?" asked Jonathan, leaning on the roof of his car, door open, ready to leap in and go. "You'd need to be off. This fucking sword! Why does he want to try to carry a sword through the border in these circumstances?"

"It means a lot to him. He won't leave it. It was his grandfather's sword."

"Fuck his grandfather. Are you going to ruin your life now for a sword?"

I contemplated that for a while. "Well, at least I won't be ruining my life for a camera. Remember how I used to have to hide my camera in tins of powdered milk when I was doing my desert trips?"

"Don't you have your camera with you? I thought you had."

"I have but now that I'm a *bona fide Université de Niamey* employee and heading for the capital, not the bush, it's not a problem."

Jonathan shook his head and gnawed a knuckle. "What the fuck are they doing to those Tuareg that they're so uptight about anyone taking a few photographs!"

"What indeed."

"What have you got yourself into, Rutherford?" Jonathan sighed. "And where is this man now? At this rate you could have grabbed a few more hours' sleep – you look wrecked – you shouldn't travel today – it's too much. You'll kill yourself – and him."

"He says he must go. He's nervous this Sideka might be transferred. We can't miss our chance, love."

"Kate . . . ?" His tone had changed.

"What?"

He was gazing at me, leaning on the roof of the car, his head propped against a hand. "You know . . . you're going to make it. I've seen so many people fall by the wayside. Give up too soon when the thing was just within reach. It's extraordinary how that always happens. But you – *you're* going to make it."

"You really think that, Jonathan?"

"Yes, I do. But don't let him die. Just don't let him die. If he dies you've lost. Keep him alive and you're still winning. You *will* win eventually."

I looked at him with love and gratitude. "You're giving up on Musa, aren't you?"

He grimaced. "Can't stay in there. Letting him save his strength for Djibrilla until she gets pregnant next time round and he can let off some of his steam in my direction again. Too much for my . . . self-respect."

I threw an arm around his shoulders and hugged him, wordlessly.

"No more mileage for me," he said. "But you – don't you give up, girl. What you have is too real, too good. It's got to work. Hang on in there – "

"*Baba zuwa!* – Baba coming!" Minha was pointing, eyes wide.

Khassim was coming, with a slightly jerky high-stepping gait that alarmed me. The walk of a very sick man.

"Let's get going," I said, my heart quailing. "Don't forget to remind me to pick up a box of Kleenex on the way."

Funny. For me, a box of Kleenex. For him, a sword. In

163

the midst of our crisis, we were enmeshed in detail. A box of Kleenex on a par with his life. The way of the world. Lives and strength frittered on useless detail. I suddenly felt that if I could only slice through the frippery I could arrive at essential joy.

By the time we reached Katsina, five hours later, he was desperately ill again. We changed taxis, by a God-granted stroke of luck finding one that was leaving immediately to pick up some big-shot *Alhaji* in Maradi and bring him back to Nigeria. I couldn't imagine what that was about – big-shot *Alhajis* all owned fleets of flashy cars. Some cloak-and-dagger customs scam, no doubt. The driver was only too keen to take us – he didn't have time to tout for passengers. I paid through the nose, of course. And was afterwards grateful.

Khassim laid his head on my shoulder and I treasured him all the way to the border, while his fever surged and glazed his eyes. The taxi-driver, whose name was David, all but drove me insane with his concern. He was a Christian from the Jos plateau to the south-east, a stocky man with heavy lips and a sloping forehead. He was also a man of frightening energy. Despite his deadline for the *Alhaji*, he stopped three times – once to get water for Khassim, again to buy aspirin, again to buy sugarcane for Minha. He wanted to drive us back to the hospital in Katsina, take us to find some bush medicine, find us a "rest-house". I kept smiling until my face ached. No, we needed to get to Maradi. Khassim had a brother in Maradi. He would be fine when we got to Maradi. His brother was travelling to Mali tomorrow and he owed him too much money – we had to get to Maradi.

In between times David yapped on incessantly about his *Alhaji* client – his prowess in the marital field and the extra-marital, his prodigious drinking, his vast number of cars, houses and girlfriends, his trips to Mecca on pilgrimage, his gargantuan appetite and equally gargantuan corruption.

"If he has so many cars, why are you picking him up in a taxi?" I asked cautiously.

"Ah, dis man be too too clever! He make like he be a small somebody! For de police now!" And he smiled a huge and blissful grin, basking in the reflected glory of the *Alhaji*'s wiles.

"But don't the police know him? They must if he passes here all the time!"

"Aaah, but de man be too too clever . . . "

Khassim was stirring painfully. I knew there was no way he could walk across the border as he had planned. We would have to risk going through. When we stopped in the border-village of Jibiya to change our money in the market stalls I asked him, whispering, whether he wanted to stop and go back. He mouthed in Tamajeq "*Endawit!* – Let's go!" and made a feeble forward motion with his hand.

We slid cautiously up to the border post. This was always a moment of great tension. It was never one hundred per cent sure that you would get through. It needed papers perfectly in order, car in perfect shape, no illegal items, plus a bribe of a suitable size in the palm of your hand or stuck between the pages of a passport. And there was the perennial problem of currency: it was next to impossible to get traveller's cheques so everyone carried illegally-changed currency. Obliged to declare your money on the customs form, you were therefore obliged to lie every time. That was fine – no problem – if they didn't then search you.

"Buzu," said David. "Rest! Stay." He and I got out.

But an ebony-skinned soldier in khaki gestured silently to Khassim to get out, too. Khassim painfully climbed out and staggered against the car.

David immediately began to protest loudly in English: "De man be sick now! Too, too sick! De brother he dey stay in Maradi. Let de man sit down here!"

A single gesture from a muscular arm silenced him and directed us up the path to the customs building.

We stood inside, in front of the main desk, waiting, Khassim swaying against me, Minha on my hip.

The Chief Customs Officer was a yellow-skinned, rather plump man, dressed in an impeccable knife-edge light-khaki uniform. He was writing and ignored our presence. When he eventually looked up he gazed at us blankly.

David burst into speech, in Hausa. "Greetings, Captain. For God, hear me. I brought this Buzu from Sokoto but he has no health. He has a fever. Look, with difficulty is he standing!"

The official stared at Khassim, expressionless. Then he said, in English, "Take that diguise off!"

I hid my shock and muttered to Khassim, "He said you should take off your *tagilmoust*."

Khassim hesitated for a long moment, then complied slowly, eyes cast down.

"Why do you come here in disguise?" asked the officer contemptuously, again in English.

Hot anger surged in me at the insult. I worked on not reacting.

166

"God give you patience, master," cried David in Hausa. "It is not a disguise! It is his traditional costume from his village!" Then he leant forward conspiratorially and added in English, *sotto voce*: "You know de man be bushman now!"

The officer laughed and I thanked God. He turned his attention on me, still grinning, lounging back in his chair. "Baturiya, is this Buzu your husband?" he asked.

"*Yes*," I said. Christ. Wrong answer. He had been just teasing me.

The officer grinned even more broadly. I couldn't tell whether he believed me or just thought it was a good joke. "Hassan! Sule! Come and hear," he called and two younger men entered. "Hear this Baturiya! She says this Buzu is her husband!"

They looked at me, round-eyed. They looked at Khassim and laughed.

Khassim was too sick to follow what was being said, though normally he would have understood such simple English with the key words "Baturiya", "Buzu" and "husband". He stood dry-lipped and yellow-faced and smiled with the effort of a sick man when they laughed, not understanding why. And I saw him as diminished by it. Standing foolish before them, stripped of his dignity as he was stripped of his *tagilmoust* – strange how such a relatively harmless act could be such a violation.

"Where is your marriage certificate?" the officer asked me, leaning forward, with mock officiousness.

"I don't have one. We had a Muslim wedding – in the bush."

He sat back again, greatly diverted. "You are a Muslim?"
"Yes."

One of the other policemen asked, grinning, "Is this his child?"

"Yes," I said vehemently.

David the taxi-man bounced into the exchange again. "He is sick! His brother is in Maradi. Look at him! He needs a doctor!"

"Your passport," the officer said to me, serious again.

I rooted in my bag, one-handed and awkward, unable to find the passport until the taxi-man grabbed Minha from me.

I handed the passport over and the officer scanned it.

"Where is your ID?" He snapped his fingers at Khassim.

"It is lost," answered Khassim in Hausa, dry-lipped, swaying on his feet. "Here is my ID from work." And he handed over the company card.

The officer scanned it briefly and handed it back. Suddenly he laughed again, good-humoredly. He waved a hand. "*To*, taxi-man! Pass! You and your Buzu! Take him to the hospital in Maradi." He held out a paper to me. "*Matan Buzu*, you will fill up this form."

Matan Buzu. Buzu woman. The sweetest words I ever heard.

But I had blundered. I had said that Khassim was my husband. That went down fine with the Nigerians. They thought it funny – or had chosen today to think it funny. With the Niger police, however, it would make Khassim a marked man. And it was quite possible that the Nigerians might choose to communicate this funny story to their brothers on the other side of the border at Dan Issa. I had absolutely no idea whether they might be in phone contact but they were eternally zapping between the border-posts on motor-bikes.

"And dis man, dis *Alhaji* . . . " David was off again, this time reciting with great enthusiasm and graphic detail the frequency and methods of the *Alhaji*'s acquiring of venereal diseases. "Dese *Alhajis*, dey too like small boys! And dis thing – *dan tada* – "

A *dan tada* was a transvestite.

"David, can the Nigerians telephone from their side of the border to the customs at Dan Issa?" I ever so casually asked, my voice aquiver.

"Yes! Every day now! But dis *Alhaji* now, he catch one disease from one harlot in Sokoto. And his four wives – all – all – dey catch dis disease – and he dey call me and he dey smile, he dey laugh, and he dey say, 'David, you must take all my wives to de hospital now-now!' And I take the wives, with one small small wife – a *small* girl – *small* – nothing above, nothing below – she be straight now – no body at all and dis *Alhaji* he dey give her de disease . . . "

We drew up to the border-post. It felt like being driven in a tumbril to the guillotine, powerless.

"But he dey smile, he dey laugh . . . " David got out and slammed his door. Then he stuck his head back inside. "Buzu, *stay* here!" he said. "Come, madame!" He swaggered off up the path to the customs hut.

This was a much humbler setting than the sprawling Nigerian equivalent but the soldiers were much more formidable than their brothers across the border. They were dressed in a type of dark-green combat uniform that I found threatening and all seemed to be huge-boned muscular men. In one corner of the room sat three shabby young Tuareg men. Apparently detained for one reason or other. They looked at us and their fear was palpable. Christ.

Miraculously, the soldiers didn't question me beyond asking where I was going, in French. It seemed that entering under the auspices of *Université de Niamey* was going to be child's-play, as indeed it had been in September. They handed out forms to be filled.

There was no chair where I could sit or table other than the one where the officer sat. I went to the little window and wrote leaning on the windowsill, struggling with my French spelling. Then, as I riffled through my passport to find my re-entry visa, hands sweating, I heard, *"How is it you wrote three passengers here? Where is the third?"* behind my back. They were questioning David.

"He is in the car – he has no health," answered David.

Through the metal slats of the window I saw a soldier in black beret, gun slung over his shoulder, going down the path, with David strutting out ahead. I bent my head over my forms. When I looked again the soldier was leaning through the window of the taxi, questioning Khassim.

I scrawled in the last piece of information required and turned and handed the forms over to the man at the desk, with my passport.

"Shi ke nan – that's it," said the officer after he had scanned the forms.

I took my passport and smiled and thanked him and turned to go. The figure of the black-beret soldier filled the door, shutting out the sunlight.

"Baturiya," he said. "The person in the taxi, is he working for you?"

He stepped inside, loose-limbed, muscular, his military boots hitting the floor heavily. Had Khassim told him that? What had Khassim told him?

And then I saw David smilingly half-close an eye and twitch his lips.

"Yes," I said.

"He is guarding for you?"

"Yes."

"You must take him to the hospital quickly. Lest he die."

Afterwards, in Maradi, I gratefully handed over the sizeable sum of money David had slipped to the black-beret while they were at the taxi, and I embraced him like a brother when we said goodbye.

We spent the night in a little mud room in a hotel compound in Maradi.

Khassim had recovered his strength a little and we didn't go to the hospital, afraid of any further encounters with officialdom.

I watched over him a long time that night, swatting mosquitos away, Janis Ian running through my head – *Lay down in all your glory, This is a lover's lullaby* . . .

Then, in the morning, despite all, there was the joy of waking together. It was an overcast *harmattan* morning, dust thick in the air, obscuring the sun. It was quite cold.

I watched Khassim force himself weakly through *salla* in the compound, sitting for longer than was the norm at the end.

We lingered, making tea sitting on a mat inside the door because of the chill, while Minha played in the sand outside in her bead necklace, woven bracelets and leather charms, like any Buzu child.

Yet, pathetic as it was, this was it. This was my dream. I thought again of Maru and the simple little house with the rain-tank attached and the sunflowers – or perhaps they were just daisies – at each side of the path to the door. *"So simply and precisely did he translate his dreams into reality"*.

And I swore I would do it and in the same heartbeat despaired. I was bound to my work and my culture. What could Khassim do with me without the lifeline of my job? What would buy my child medicine without that? And the food to save her from malnutrition? We'd be dead within a year without Nivaquine. However much he loved me I knew he could not support me – and Khadija.

What if we bought animals, set up a herd? For droughts to wipe them out and leave us destitute?

A sudden desperate fantasy took hold of me. What if he and I just took off into the desert, where there were no mosquitos and the water and air was as clean as they could be on God's earth? What if we hid from the world that was hounding him? Hid from the world of bureaucracy and the military?

I knew it was impossible. Two months would not pass, however deep we went, before reports of the strange *Takafart* got back to the nearest police-post. The military Landrover would come, I could see it even now, the dust that would rise from it, as it swept up brutally to take me away. Libyan spy. What else?

There was no way out. No solution but the job in Niamey. I could not become part of his world. He must become part of mine.

He left at nine o'clock, alone, having kissed us goodbye and arranged for the hotel boy to take us to the station. If he did not arrive in Niamey – but surely he must – if he did not arrive and if I had not heard from him I was to be at the hotel in Birnin Konni on the fourth Saturday after. He would come there, no matter what.

I wanted to protest, *"But why four Saturdays? Why so long? Why four?"*

But I knew why. In Africa the mills ground slowly, incredibly so . . . I could but hope they would grind sure.

The way he high-stepped it out of the compound, his limbs stiff with fever, head bowed, broke my heart. I watched him go, dumb with the pain of it, soul outraged. I felt a kind of bewilderment. How could this be possible? How could the universe slice us apart so cruelly again when we were one organism?

He was going from my hands and could easily die. I could lose him finally.

Death seemed my servant on the road, till we were near and saw you waiting:

When you smiled, and in sorrowful envy he outran me and took you apart:

Into his quietness.

So Lawrence lost his Arab boy.

Chapter Fourteen

I set off for Niamey like an automaton, going through the motions, drained of energy and will. To lift an arm was a conscious nightmare effort. Moving west while he moved east – it was like rending a limb off.

A little drama on the way served as a distraction. We picked up an American at Madaoua. He was chewing on a sheet of peppered dry meat, a tall thin bearded young man, Peace Corps no doubt. He chatted cheerily in awkward French to the people near him up front. I was right at the back so I had no chance to talk to him – perhaps I didn't want to.

His ordeal began about forty kilometres on. He suddenly pushed his way out of his seat and almost fell over the driver's shoulder onto the steering wheel. We began to slow down. When we stopped he threw himself off the bus and made for the shelter of a clump of vegetation sparse enough to let us see him pull his pants down.

"Zawo!" Diarrhoea. They all began to throw the word around in good-humoured mockery.

He got back on the bus to gentle reprimands. He shouldn't have eaten the peppered dry meat in Madaoua.

"But it couldn't be that," he argued, very patient, annoyance veiled. "That was less than an hour ago. It must have been something I ate last night or this morning."

Grins and headshakes.

Ten kilometres down the road we had to stop again. This time he was luckier – there was a small rock there, so only a gaping young Wodaabe boy with his herd of long-horned cattle was treated to the spectacle.

On we went, the American pallid, sweat standing out on his skin.

His tension was tangible. I couldn't bear to look. The whole bus waited, in a light-hearted state of expectancy. We came to a scrap of a village, the American clutching at his belly as he went into spasms. I suffered with him.

The bus squealed to a stop. He threw himself off and raced for cover, startling the villagers who stared at the unexpected entertainment, the welcome spectacle of a Bature making a fool of himself. He reached a small bush and pulled up short. A couple of girls bounced to their feet from behind it.

Desperate now he changed direction and ran towards a hut.

The passengers craned their necks and grinned and laughed.

I suddenly felt savagely angry.

A man shooed the American away from the hut as though he were a rampaging cow.

The American was doubled over. He raced for the only shelter within reach, a slender palm tree. No shelter at all. So finally in what was only a pretence of shelter and privacy he hauled his shorts down and in full view of the bus and villagers released his thin stream of poison.

The laughter of the passengers filled me with despair. I

shouted: "For God, leave him alone! He's sick!" He was a comic figure to them, a creature not meriting courtesy. A thing of no feeling.

It was hopeless. No matter how far or how long you went, you'd never be more than a marionette to them. I hate these fucking people, I thought.

But to stop in the cool of the evening and find a semi-private dark place to relieve oneself, to let the fresh air dry the thin cotton chafing one's body, to sit on a wooden bench in the market in the benign warmth, all the cramped muscles relaxing, and eat peppered brochettes and fish and baguette and thick coffee sweetened with condensed milk in tall blunt glasses, and listen to the stir and laughter of the night market and see the myriad oil lamps in the little stalls and on the sides of trays, to drink in the smiles of the market women as they reached you your portion of rice in an enamel bowl. And to drink another hot sweet coffee and feel rescued by it, saved, returned to life.

That was heaven. That was joy. That was worth the pain, made sweet by it. It was joy earned. Earned hard. The body began to sing with relief and ease.

That was heaven.

And to reach Niamey. To draw painfully up to the police barrier, bodies screaming for relief, and see the well-lit places ahead. That was heaven. We approached the police as if they were angels guarding the gates. An order to take down the baggage from the top of the bus was a plunge into despair. Exhausted, we watched every last piece being untied, and unloaded. The last cruelty. Every last piece opened and scrutinised. And there was the fear for one's own few pieces. Anything could lead to hours of interrogation. Where are you coming from? Going to? Where are your papers? Where is your husband? Where is the father of your child? Why are you alone? Why do you have photographs of these Tuareg?

Goods were confiscated, bribes were paid, people marched off, faces blank, to interrogation in the office.

Dumb with exhaustion we climbed back in. There was a little more room in the back seat where I was. Someone must have been lacking papers.

But it was heaven complete to race through the well-lit streets, the familiar places, craving the joy of reaching home and bed and stretching out and drinking drinking drinking . . . *Lay down and know you're weary* . . .

They were good to me that time and took a route which allowed me to get off at Terminus at the entrance to the flats.

But my joy was confined. Under the dim electric light of civilisation in my flat I discovered that my thin cotton *zane* was soaked heavily in blood. They would not have seen in the dark. Wouldn't have smelt it in the powerful odour of sweat and dirt. But would have seen later if my seat in the bus was soaked. Or if they had spread out along the seat and sat on my place in their white cotton robes.

I was deeply shamed. As if I had betrayed their welcome.

I turned on my Janis Ian tape, lay down on my bed with Minha at last, and pitched into sleep.

Now I lay me down to sleep
Forever by your side . . .

The days passed in a fever. Khassim now had my home address so he would come here, directly, home. Every day, countless times, I went to the window and gazed up and down the street and over at Terminus, willing him to be there.

I was consumed by fear and tension and desire.

Every day at the university I summoned all my resources and put on a show. I'd given so much, not less than everything; I had made my choices and no one must pity me.

I made friends among the expatriates and gratefully accepted invitations to dinner where I talked about Minha's nomadic father who was still inexplicably on his way, but their iced drinks, their silverware, their air-conditioning and pricey African artifacts were a mockery and negation of him. He had fallen though a hole in the world. *I've fallen away from the sun . . .*

A week passed, another and he didn't come and there was no letter. I smiled and smiled, and put out energy for my students and all these new friends, never for a moment relieved of the terrible ache that possessed my heart, my belly, my brain, that grew into a physical tension pressing on my ribcage like a straitjacket and making me gasp for breath.

I had built myself into a trap – me, so wary of traps, always watching others build theirs so tightly around them and swearing I would never do the same. But now I had done it, and there was no one to release the poor animal. Unless, in blundering around, my foot stepped on a hidden spring and the whole thing flew open?

Then, I was through, rounding the corner into the

miraculous fourth week. *Saturday*. I could reach out and touch it.

Rejoicing, almost through. Rounding the corner into this blessed stretch of time, the blessed possibility of having him in my arms at any point, running through it swift and easy, day by day.

I had chosen to do *Romeo and Juliet* with them, to see what they would make of the whole notion of romantic love and knowing I could point them towards lively discussion on the hot issue of arranged marriages.

I stood in my class listening to emphatic voices pouring scorn on the jumble of errors and misdirections that lead to the tragedy in the end: "This Romeo is too too stupid. Why does he rush off like that, riding back to Verona at the risk of his life? He should have waited for Friar Lawrence to send a message!"

A laconic "*Bai da hakuri* – he has no patience," in a male voice, came from the back of the class.

One of my favourite students, a lively loud-spoken girl called Hawa, turned in her desk and, chopping the air with the edge of a raised flat hand in the direction of the offender, cried: "But he loved the girl now!"

"Yes!" came a loud female chorus.

"But what is his problem?" one of the boys asked. "He has no head! He just hears one useless rumour! He doesn't even ask his friend how she died! Nothing! He is a crazy boy, this Romeo! If he had patience he could have had everything!"

"*You! You!*" cried Hawa, arm and hand eloquent. "You do not know love, how it is! He cannot think because his heart is broken!"

179

The boys were all grinning at her unabashed vigour.

How long will it be unabashed, my Hawa, I thought? You'll marry a rich man and, as a modern educated woman with earning potential, you will state your conditions: no other wives. And he will agree and you will come into his parlour and then, down the road, he will buy another Mercedes and another wife and there will be sweet-damn-all you can do about it because he will have your children in the palm of his hand.

I wish you luck, Hawa.

"Does anybody think Juliet is to blame?" I asked. "Don't you think she was a bit hasty?"

But, male and female, their sympathy for Juliet and her brief and futile defiance of her father was absolute.

"Mrs Rutherford?" A small and graceful black hand was lifted. A dissenting hand?

"Yes, Ramatu?" I smiled encouragingly. She was a shy gentle soul, a thin pretty black-skinned girl, who rarely dared speak up in class.

She smiled and cast her eyes down. Then looked straight at me and began to speak, hands eloquent. "I think that Juliet should have had more patience. She should have gone to her father and begged him." Two hands joined and raised in graceful supplication. "She could have begged him to postpone the marriage and told him that she was sick. Or she could have said, 'Father, I am happy to marry Paris. But you know that when I become a married woman I will have many responsibilities. Please allow me to go and say goodbye to my girlfriends and stay with them for a while before I marry!' And then, later, when his mind had cooled and his heart had settled, he might not have forced her."

Murmurs of assent all round. Ramatu cast her long-lashed eyes down bashfully.

I tried the oldest joke in the book: "But, Ramatu, if she

had done that we would have had no story! There would have been no drama!"

I was ridiculously pleased when they seemed to get the point and laughed.

Of course, if I had wanted a really fun debate I should have done *The Taming of the Shrew*.

This time I'm going to win, I thought, as I set out for Konni. This time the miracle will happen. I'll make it happen. If I have to grapple with life and twist its arm.

I had paid the price. He had paid the price. We'd been to the end of the world and back. It was enough. I would do no further violence to my soul.

I could see my reflection in the window of the bus, a face full of new lines. Worn. I looked so worn. I felt so worn. Africa was killing me.

We met in an agony of relief and formality at the bus station in Konni. He had been waiting for four hours.

I stared up joyfully into the dark eyes crinkling at me through the slit in his *tagilmoust*. "Did you find *Capitaine* Sideka?"

"Yes."

"So, what is the news?"

"Only peace," he answered formally but his eyes smiled even more. "He will fix it."

"*Will*" fix it. Four weeks and he "*will*" fix it.

Sai hakuri.

He took Minha – all astonished glee to have found her Baba unexpectedly in this strange place – and we made straight for the small hotel.

I registered in my name only but there was no comment or complication. The hotel boy, Abdou, a long-limbed very black young Hausa, joked and laughed as he took us to a room off the first-floor balcony. What he thought of his ill-assorted guests he didn't betray.

The room had a green metal door and windows without mosquito netting, a concrete floor with a couple of the usual green-black-and-wine straw mats, two single beds with mosquito nets. At the back of the room was a bathroom with a yellowed toilet bowl and slightly grimy shower – the usual wad of hopefully-fresh straw provided as a sponge. But the sheets on the bed were clean and food could be ordered from the bar below. Abdou demonstrated everything, flushing the toilet with a flourish and showing me how to prop open the small metal bathroom window.

Khassim handed him out a more than generous *dash* in the confident and graceful way I could never emulate and Abdou took it between his two joined hands and, equally gracefully, went through the usual staccato series of bows and thank-you's. Encouraged by our *largesse*, he then offered to bring us food from the bar. So we ordered steak and baguette and salad and coffee and charcoal for making *shayi* and as soon as Abdou left we kissed and clung to each other and lay on the bed praying that Minha would tire and fall asleep. But she didn't and at last, in desperate arousal, we coupled briefly, fully dressed under the sheet while she played in the bathroom. As soon as I felt him in me I felt the first ripples of an orgasm and pushed his buttocks fiercely against me probing with my fingers between his thighs and his groin and in an instant he too began to come.

Then, while the waves of pleasure were still ebbing, Abdou was at the door with the food and Minha was back sucking on the straw sponge from the shower and I opened the door for Abdou with my body still quivering with joy.

The food was good. God bless the French, I thought.

And then, with the so-familiar movements and a smile on his face, Khassim made *shayi*.

And still I didn't ask him about Sideka, still I didn't press him for news. He played with Minha but otherwise we hardly spoke, back again in this annexe to the Wood between the Worlds.

When finally it was necessary he told me briefly, without any embellishment. Capitaine Sideka had been transferred to Zinder. Khassim had found no one in Maradi who would help to contact him – no one dared to be involved. He had to "lie down" with his fever for several days. Then it had ebbed and he had felt stronger. He had spent some further days trying to make contacts – the time for doing that was limited as he only dared move about at night. Then the fever had returned and a friend had carried him by camel to a Tuareg encampment in the bush. A few days later, by the grace of God, Sideka had paid a visit to Maradi and Khassim had managed to contact him. Sideka had driven him back to Zinder – openly in a military vehicle – casually pretending at security blocks that he was under arrest for petty theft. Then he had given him a *carte d'identité* from the "lost and found" office at army headquarters. Khassim had promised to say he had bought it on the black market if ever questioned.

"So, you see, the news is peace," said Khassim, smiling. "He will fix everything. No doubt. And quickly. *Surtout* because he himself is in some danger all the time I am using this false card."

It would work, said Khassim. He trusted Sideka.

He also told me he had been to see Khadija's people and he had divorced her.

We lay on the narrow bed in the hotel room that evening.

And he went inside me. And I held him as if he were the world's greatest treasure. We slept and woke and made love again. And slept. And the night drew on and we made love and slept. And every time we woke he entered me, again and again and again. And we slept and coupled again. And coupled again. And every time I think the tears flowed quietly down my face. And every time was a pact and a vow that nothing would ever take him from me. Never would the world tear him from me to dash his precious existence into a bloody mass. He woke and groaned and became erect again. And we made love. And then again. And every time I clung and cleaved and devoured him with my spirit. And still I was hungry. And would always be hungry. Heat and sleep and sweat swept us, tumbled us away into darkness. We still wore our pieces of cotton, the bed beneath us sodden. And the world let us alone. And I thought of my precious child and suddenly it seemed I would lose her, that she would be the sacrifice. And I could do nothing because nothing could take me out of his arms, ever, until the end of time. He woke and we coupled again. And every time I came I reached far into that other world, the one that sustained us, and I took him there with me, there where our oneness could not be logically denied, where we were truly one flesh. Dawn came and the cry for prayer and and we woke and coupled again and again. And made no talk, no quips, no comment, no laughter. And the morning passed and when we opened our eyes and he was erect again, we said nothing, we coupled and slept. And woke and coupled again.

And got up and prepared to go and turned at the door and made love again and yet again.

I went back to Niamey and waited.

Chapter Fifteen

The hot season came crushingly down on us. I could not sleep at night. The air-conditioner and the fridge laboured. We drank down the tepid water in the fridge by the bottle. We longed and hungered for rain and spent every afternoon wallowing in a stupor of sleep. That deep afternoon tumble into unconsciousness had its pleasure but the nights were utter torment. One night it was so hot that in despair I soaked my cotton *zane* with water in the bathroom and wrapped it around me and at last managed to sleep, eaten alive by mosquitos on the balcony.

I stood in front of my class, my soul crying inwardly, until to my horror my eyes began to swim with tears. I couldn't leave the room because they were doing a test. There was nothing I could do but stand there and try to fight my own body. I sat at the table and began to write any kind of nonsense so that, if they looked up, they would imagine I was in tears writing a letter home.

The jumble of frantic thoughts I was recording or the act of writing itself at length calmed me and the tears receded. I kept writing. I wrote: *I want to die.* Then: *I do think there is mettle in death, which commits some loving act upon her, she hath such a celerity in dying.* To the

Elizabethans "to die" also meant "to orgasm". I thought, I should have died back there in Konni. *The stroke of death is as a lover's pinch, Which hurts, and is desired.*

We were doing *Antony and Cleopatra* and, again, they were making a good hand of hacking through the tangle of language to get to Shakespeare's human heart. I had chickened out of doing *Othello* as a mature tragedy. In my fragile state I doubted I would be able to deal with it. Teaching it in Nigeria had been like walking on eggs. I had managed to do it without breaking any eggs, straining every nerve to demonstrate the complexities and they had loved the play and written some excellent essays on it – a few even astutely penetrating the onion layers Shakespeare had set up around the racial issue. So, shying away from *Othello*, I had thought of *Antony and Cleopatra* because it was running through my head so often in those dog days. It was an unconventional choice and that in itself was a reason for doing it, as an experiment. But I had my ulterior motives in wanting to see what they would make of Shakespeare's not-so-youthful lovers.

They were writing a paper now, these forty young people – mixed Hausa, Zarma and Fulani with not one Tuareg among them – whose very gestures of tension were eloquent and beautiful. I watched them for a while, seeing the little dark clouds of concentration and befuddlement dimming the normal brightness of their features, the tiny ruffles of unaccustomed frowns on clear lineless brows. They were as usual all dressed up to the nines, one maturer female student even wearing a satin cocktail dress in gold – and it looked wonderful on her.

In the main part of the paper I had simply asked them if they thought Antony was a fool and I was sure there would be a pronounced male-female divide on the verdict for that one.

Eternity was in our lips and eyes,
Bliss in our brows' bent, none our parts so poor
But was a race of heaven . . .

In this polygamous world, how could lines like that have any meaning? Or was there any hope that, at least in the ideal world of fantasy, the passion of individual soul to individual soul could signal across the barriers like an international code?

⚜⚜⚜⚜

I looked from the balcony in the early morning and he was sitting cross-legged under a tree outside, where he could keep watch on my window.

Alert, gazing.

Seeing me at once, he rose in one swift movement and a minute later was in my arms. We moved at once, speechlessly, to the bedroom and when we were one again he told me.

Sideka had brought him to Niamey in an army vehicle, Sideka could only stay for a week, Sideka would make some important contacts in Niamey, but unless a miracle happened it was unlikely he would be able to wrap everything up so quickly. Khassim would probably have to return to Zinder with him at the end of the week.

I heard it like a death sentence. And so, within half an hour of his blessed arrival, I was weeping in his arms.

We grabbed at the time given us but now my happiness was poisoned with desperation and I muddied the waters with it every hour of every day.

Then, to my intense joy, the end of the week came and he found he couldn't bear to leave. He would risk staying for another few weeks. The army jeep returned to Zinder without him.

But almost at once I began to feel a sense of unease. I worried about him. It was tough on him. He had to stay inside all day every day, only going out after dark to walk the streeets. But that wasn't the problem.

I found myself focusing on a trivial matter: the fact that I now had to cook. I had never cooked. Minha's father had always cooked for me or Husaini had or one of the others. They had all learned coarse cooking in Nigeria. At other points in my career I had employed a succession of cooks and house-boys. But Khassim was not in the "house-boy" category.

I knew how to do it, of course. That wasn't the problem. The problem was that now I had to "do" Khadija. And I was uneasy in the role. Was her rice-and-beans better than mine? When I sat with him in my soft black Tuareg robes, hair neatly plaited, my heavy silver earrings weighing down my earlobes, Tuareg blue bracelets and beads glowing, I felt I was acting out an impersonation of her and I didn't like it. This was irrational as far as the clothes were concerned – I had worn that gear for years, especially at home – it was second nature to me. That was why I focused on the cooking as a cause of my unease.

There were other changes, some of them wonderful touching things. He began to call me "*Tantouti*" – "my woman" – instead of the long-familiar "madame". One day when he was eating, on the mat on the balcony, he sat me down with him and put his spoon in my hand and from that day on we ate from the same bowl, sharing a spoon, if he didn't have guests. This disconcerted me. I had never seen it done between a man and a woman. What of the great menstruation horror? The fear of spoiling magic charms acquired at some cost down the years? I didn't understand and, at sea and unwilling to expose my ignorance, I didn't question him about it.

But I couldn't relax and take what he was giving me with any confidence. I became tense and increasingly passive.

My newly acquired expatriate friends got me worried about the flat, saying it was a ridiculous place to expect a nomad to live. Of course, I had never intended to stay there. But it was free university accommodation and while Khassim was still at risk, while there still was the chance we would end up paying a hefty bribe to sort things out, we needed to be careful about money. As soon as I had any breathing-space at all, we'd be back out under the stars. But, in fact, he never said he didn't like the flat and Minha's father had lived cheerfully with me in everything from a mud village hut to our university bungalow. The flat wasn't the problem.

He began to go out just as the sun set to say the *magariba* prayers with a couple of night-watchmen at a house down the road from the flats. He would then come back just after dark and we would have sex and eat and later again he would go out and walk and walk and walk around the dark streets of Niamey.

One night, on his return, he looked a bit distraught. I asked him why. He was silent and then he said, "You know, when I walk I worry about my children – about whether they have food – *surtout* about my poor cripple. And I feel it in my heart." And he placed a graceful hand over his heart as if he felt a physical pain.

That filled me with alarm but not surprise. That was clear, that he must fret about the children. In truth, even I felt fettered by guilt, particularly about Yakubu who had been my responsibility for so long.

There were other changes, more disquieting. He always came back just after dark, after the *magariba* prayers, to make love. Or to fuck me, I began to feel. I began to keep Minha awake in the late afternoons so that she would be asleep when he came. And he began with increasing frequency to turn me over on my belly and enter from behind and I had the same problem as before. I was too greedy for every coupling, to let it go without orgasm and I needed to be active and get my legs around him, get the pressure on my clitoris. Up-ended, passive, without that stimulus it couldn't work. I remembered me and Jonathan and the much-maligned missionary position. It was less funny now and I seethed quietly with resentment.

He articulated his pleasure once again, sensing my unease.

"You know," he whispered, "I feel sweetness like this. I like the feel of your buttocks against me."

I remembered Rhisa and his crude differentiation of sex between sweethearts and married sex. Did this mean at last that I was married, this graduation to rear entry? Had I been promoted?

Yet every night at the fall of darkness when he went out to pray with the watchmen, I cooked and took off my underwear and put on my soft black robes and lay down on the bed and waited. On my belly.

It was like a ritual. As if now, when we had freedom

and security and leisure, at that time every day we still had to re-enact our intense, fully-dressed couplings in the Wood between the Worlds. Like people under a spell.

My sense of unease grew and I couldn't really identify the source. I didn't want to admit the obvious: that it emanated from him.

One evening we made love and from the start I knew something was strange. There was a strange astringent sensation, a squeaky consistency as he moved in me. He fucked so violently and somehow entered so deep that there was an unpleasant bruising sensation. He seemed well pleased when he finished and even asked me if it had been sweet. I lied and said yes and knew I had been right. He had put something on his penis.

Later I searched. I opened his fringed leather bag and found a small bottle of pharmacy-thick blue glass with an inky substance in it tied securely in a handkerchief. My guess was that it was simple water and ink, such as a *mallam* uses to make Islamic magic, writing the holy words on a wooden writing-block and then washing them off. On the other hand, it might be a market "medicine" for God knows what purpose. African women were forever buying stuff to make the vagina tight and dry. It might have a been a sex aid of that sort. Did he think he still had to impress me with his prowess? Or did he not give a damn what I felt and had just done it for his own pleasure? Whatever, I felt outraged when I found it. Then I remembered my shenanigans with the diaphragm and held my peace. But the resentment at his deception took root. I was also afraid. I took the bottle and threw it away. He did come and ask me if I had seen it and the spark of anger in his eye made me lie. I said I hadn't seen it and we faced each other across a fence of lies.

I was lying on the bed one evening, miserable because my period was starting, with a hand thrust inside my black *zane* pressing my belly because I had a slight cramp. I heard Khassim come in and my heart beat faster. I still hated telling him I had a period.

He appeared at the door and, sensing at once there was something wrong, he sat beside me and stroked my hair. Gently he leaned over me and asked me: "What is it, my woman?"

"Oh," and I quailed to tell him. "Nothing. It's my period." I forced the words out.

His silence was such that I turned my head and looked at him. He had a strange expression on his face. He laid a hand tenderly on my stomach. "Oh, only that bastard thing. I thought it might be a little child," he said with utter gentleness and regret.

My soul shifted in surprise and dismay. A child! He wanted a child.

After all my heroic efforts with the fucking diaphragm. He wanted a child.

You bastard, I thought. How could you deny me and now, after it all, make me feel I've failed?

He had understood nothing. Was that what the ink-medicine was for? Was he trying to impregnate me? Why had that not even occurred to me?

"How could I be pregnant?" The words were thick in my throat.

He lay down behind me and put his arms around me and caressed my breasts and whispered, "How can you not be! You have drawn such *aman* from me – so much!" Using the most basic of Tamajeq words – the word for "water".

My spark of anger guttered out in bitter regret.

How could we have been at such cross-purposes?

I lay there trying to plumb the depths of this disaster.

In the Wood between the Worlds we spoke in whispers afraid to shatter the surface of the water. We had taken the plunge, as one must, and come up through the pool into a menacing world where realities battered us. Then I remembered that there were many pools in that wood and that it was vital to cut the turf with a knife to mark the one that led to your own world – lest you forget the way back.

And it seemed to me that we were still talking in whispers.

He still stayed and I began to hope that he would simply stay forever. That it might be possible to live like this, ignoring the risk.

When my period was over I didn't use the diaphragm again. And to make assurance doubly sure, I went and bought a thermometer, set up a chart of pencil lines in an old copybook and began surreptitiously to record my early-morning temperature, slipping out of bed to do it in the bathroom, worried that the result would be inaccurate because you were supposed to do it first thing after waking before any movement. I would make sure he stayed until after my ovulation, come hell or high water. The days passed. I reached what should have been the mid-point in my cycle, when the temperature is supposed to rise a few degrees, but it didn't budge. My pencil line continued in a straight line with a few zig-zags like the *route nationale*. I figured I was in for a very late period.

In a further attempt to do something to break the strange passivity that gripped me, I asked him about

Khadija's people. But not about her. "Have you told them about me? Khadija's people?"

"No, I haven't told them."

"But why? If you've divorced her?"

He hesitated. "They must not know about you. If they do they will hold me for money. They will think I can get money from you. So they will refuse to keep my children and feed them. I cannot tell them. Not yet. Not until we are well settled."

Yet all these disturbances were undercurrents and could not quell my joy in his sheer physical presence, in sleeping beside him, in feeling him reach for me in the night. Whatever my mental unease, my body was bursting with happiness.

Then, one day, while Minha was still at playschool, I looked out the front window and saw a colleague of mine, an Englishman named Colin, turning into the Terminus entrance on foot. Colin was a fanatical swimmer and I knew he was heading for the pool to do his laps. He was a good-looking guy in his late thirties, blonde, tanned, with piercing blue eyes and the hard body of an athlethe without a pinch of the fat some swimmers develop. Khassim was happily entertaining a friend on the balcony and I suddenly wanted to speak English – more precisely, to talk about Khassim in English. So I went downstairs and crossed the road to the Terminus hotel, just as I was, "with my hands hanging to me" as we would say at home in Ireland. I accosted Colin, who was already lapping, and we got into one of our sillier joky conversations – Colin had a quirky wit – about the state of play in our respective lives. Colin lapped intermittently and I sat on the side of the pool. I stayed longer than I had intended – Colin got out and had a Coke with me and then, fatal mistake, I waited while he dressed in T-shirt and shorts and we walked out of the hotel together. Outside he waved a cheery goodbye and I crossed the road and briskly walked the few yards to the entrance to our block.

Just as I reached it, a Tuareg man coming up the street towards me drew level and saluted me by name. I stopped, puzzled, not recognising him. It turned out to be the usual – he had worked in Katsina some years before and had met me there. So I raised the warmth in my response up by a few notches to atone for the blankness of my first greeting. It was midday and the sun was doing its gruelling thing. I was bareheaded so I raised an arm to shield my eyes from the glare with my forearm and as I did so I noticed Khassim watching through the window of the flat, the side of the blind raised. When I thought about the moment afterwards I shied away from the truth, just glimpsing it from the corner of my eye, so to speak. The truth was, there was an instant – fleeting enough to make it easy to ignore afterwards – when I decided to flaunt a bit for Khassim's benefit. So I smiled harder and laughed louder and moved my hips more. And afterwards I also realised that no doubt my bare head and the white nakedness of the underside of the arm I had raised had added fuel to fire.

I glanced at the window again and something about Khassim's stance alarmed me. For a flash I saw him as a vulture, hunched, menacing, eyeing the carrion.

When I went inside he was standing in just that pose in the centre of the room. I stopped, uncertain, and stood facing him. And to my utter dismay he began to berate me.

"Where have you come from? What were you doing in that hotel? Tell me!"

I was silent, shocked. Khassim, angry with me?

"And what kind of a man am I to let my woman go to a hotel with some *kato* . . . " using the Hausa word for a big muscular man, in utter contempt. He had seen me with Colin.

I know I flushed. "He's my work-friend!"

"Were you working there in the hotel? What kind of work was that?"

"I was talking to him about work!" Long-established and deep-seated alarm bells were ringing. This was a line I wouldn't cross. He had to let me relate to other expatriates as I pleased.

"And what kind of woman are you? How is it all your friends are men? How is it you can't have a woman friend like any other woman?"

I couldn't begin to answer this one.

I was puzzled by a faint false tone in his voice. Afterwards I realised it was something like the tone you adopt when scolding a child and that if I had said any small placatory thing at that point everything might have been saved. But not me. When pressed, I would always confront, never placate.

I said, "Don't think you can forbid me my friends!"

"It's like that, is it?" His voice deepened, growing thick in his throat. "I must watch you come down the street swinging your bottom like a whore and laugh with a man in front of the house with your mouth open wide!"

My hurt was absolute. I was outraged, more than the moment ravaged by his venomous interpretation. The nausea I always felt when accused of unfaithfulness gripped me.

"Indeed," he said, his voice shaking. "You have had enough of me!"

Tears sprang to my eyes. "How can you say that to me? How can you call me a whore? I who waited for you so long, and thought of nothing but you? I who drank trouble travelling back and forth to Nigeria looking for you? I am tired of you? I don't want you? How can you say this?" Because he's sorry he came. Because he wants to be back with her. Because he wants to have an excuse to reject me.

He was visibly shaking. "I think you are repenting that you waited for me!"

"It is you who have repented!"

"I, I have repented?" The long finger he brought to his breast was trembling. "I, I who left my children scattered in the bush – like chickens – to be with you? I have repented?"

Like chickens in the bush.

I hated him. He had destroyed me. If I could have slit my throat efficiently there in front of him I would have got my knife and done it. To demonstrate to him how he had destroyed me with his words. But I didn't know how to slit a throat. He knew how and had done it. Maybe he would do it for me.

We stayed staring at each other, eyes livid.

I would walk out. I would go to Colin. I would like to do that to him. I would love to fuck Colin for him.

No, I would appeal to Denis to help me negotiate in the African way. Denis would know how to stand proxy for the father or brother an African woman would turn to in need. He would come and demonstrate to Khassim how cruel he had been.

But I couldn't walk out of my own house, I would rather

die than fuck another man and I couldn't shame him in front of Denis.

I turned and walked into the bedroom and threw myself on the bed. I could cry. And cry I did, great noisy rending sobs that said, *"How could you be so cruel, don't you see how helpless and weak I am, don't you see how you have destroyed me?"* I got up and went and threw up in the loo. Then I went back and cried some more. *Don't you see how sensitive and passionate I am, unlike you – don't you see that I may die of the grief you have caused me, don't you see how I love you and how faithful I am and that I may well take out my knife and slit my throat if you don't come and make it better?*

And he came and lay down and put his arms around me and wiped my tears with his fingers and patted my chest comfortingly with the flat of his hand in the Tuareg way and I turned in his arms and clung to him and in an instant we had coupled and we made love frantically like two drowning swimmers desperately striking out towards the shore, trying to rescue something that had, that day, been irrevocably lost.

I missed Jonathan. I needed his balancing energy and intelligence, his tea and sympathy. I tried to imagine what he might say about the quarrel. I could almost hear his voice. He would say, shaking the head, raising the finger, *"No, Rutherford. Not that one! You can't take that from him!"* But, equally, he might say, *"But, Rutherford! How would you feel if he came flaunting along waving his prick at some gorgeous Tuareg woman before your eyes and a gorgeous expatriate for good measure?"* How would I feel? I would rend him limb from limb.

But the roots of my unease were now exposed. I felt it, now that the prize was at last almost in our hands, some disaster brooded. I felt it every minute and every hour. Somewhere in the maze a monster lurked.

I was worried about money. The local salary I was getting wasn't great and I figured we needed to pour a bit of money into the Sideka affair. That might well be the snag. Wheels here never turned without being thickly greased by money. Also, in the back of my head, I could see we were heading for a situation where I would be the main provider for Khadija and the children.

We discussed the Sideka part of it. Then he sold his sword. His grandfather's sword. He said he was keeping the money for his journey back to Zinder.

I was terribly disturbed by this. I said to myself, if he can sell his precious sword I can sell my camera. I advertised my camera at the American Rec Center and had a taker immediately. Then I bought Khassim a relatively cheap sword from a neighbouring watchman and gave it to him with the remainder of the money. The leatherwork on the sword was quite good, the bright red and clean ice-green which said cheap and modern, instead of the dark weathered red that said antique. The blade of Khassim's old sword had edges worn back from use and the satiny blue sheen of Toledo steel – and could well have been an antique Toledo blade. This blade was bright silver with a faintly visible grain and I feared it was some really crude alloy but Khassim was pleased with it and said it was quite good quality. He swung it around the flat alarmingly and made chopping passes that scared the life out of me. He said he liked the weight.

And still he said nothing about going back to Zinder. I questioned him as to whether he really trusted Sideka. Was anything happening? Had he in fact done anything? Was it a question of money? He said that Sideka had done all the groundwork, that of necessity he had to move slowly and that we must have patience. Patience was everything.

But I could feel his tension increase and found him a few times sitting with his head bowed in his hands as if he feared it was about to split. I was so used to his customary dignity and serenity that this frightened me.

Then the day came when he sat down beside me on the bed and told me gently, the sweat standing out in the pores of his face, that he must go back and that he would be gone for "a bit of a long time". Sideka was back in Niamey and this might be his only chance of safe passage back to the east.

Sideka would be coming to Terminus early next morning to collect him. But would not come to the flat. We must avoid closing the circle between him and me.

There was a note of finality in this that terrified me. He wasn't saying, *But I might be back tomorrow or next week, God willing* . . .

I nodded dumbly.

Yes, where was the customary *in sha Allahu?* Why a straight statement of intention: "*I will be gone* . . . "

I asked, without looking in his face, "Why do you say 'a long time'?"

"My woman, I am not going back to Zinder directly. I must stay in Birnin Konni for a while."

This was it. This was it. There was a mad voice within me that rejoiced at being right, that was laughing its head off at being so right.

"Why?"

His breath came harshly. His voice when it came was strangled. "Khadija will give birth."

"What did you say?" My heart lurching.

"She will give birth this month."

Oh no God no.

I sat immobile while my life came crashing down.

"I must be there for the naming." He didn't look at me. When I stayed dumb by his side he continued rapidly. "You know I must be there to claim the child. And for Khadija – I cannot shame the poor thing in front of her kinsmen. And I have no kinsmen in that part of the country to stand in for me." He gave me a look of mute agony. "I must be there. *Surtout* because her people have always despised me."

I said nothing.

This was what I had been waiting for. Here was the poison at the source. All that time, all my agonies and he was fucking Khadija all the time.

"I must go now. I have already stayed too long. She must give birth in these days if she has not already done so. If the child is already born and the seven days have passed I will drink a great shame, myself and all my kinsmen. But, God willing, she has not yet delivered and I will be in time to name the child. But, after that, I must stay until Khadija gets her strength back – Madame, I could be separated from you for two months – "

I got up and raised my hand and struck him with my fist at the side of the face, on the cheekbone.

He rode the shock and then he said without changing his tone, as if we were having a normal conversation, "I will send for you if she doesn't give birth quickly, to come to Konni – "

I hit him again, hurting my fist, and cried out my anger as I did it. My rings with the raised rectangular decoration caught him on the cheekbone and he bled. He dabbed at the blood with his hand, getting it on the side of his *tagilmoust*, and ducked his head as if he were going to sneeze. He kept talking in the same unchanged even tone. "If she gives birth quickly and there is no problem I will be back by the end of this month but I fear she will not – "

I grabbed at his *tagilmoust* and tore it from his head and hauled at it so he had to take the strain off his neck by grabbing the cloth with both hands. "*Bastard! Bastard! Bastard!* You told me you weren't eating her! All I have suffered and you were eating her all the time – you *lied* to me – you *lied* – you *lied*!"

He grabbed one of my wrists. "No, I didn't lie to you. I was true to you. It happened when you were not there, when you had gone to Niamey and I was left in Zaria and couldn't pass the border. I was full of fear that you would reject me. And I was afraid she wouldn't leave for Konni if she didn't trust me – "

I stared my hate and fury and pulled away from him and walked out of the room, out of the flat and over to Terminus, just as I was, trailing in my black robes, livid with rage. I hoped to find Colin there. I had no money on me, even to sit and buy a Coke. I knew that if I saw him, I would force my emotion back into its shell with a little whimper, and laugh and try to look cheerful. Let's not embarrass anyone – any of these respectable people living their reasonable lives. They had done nothing to deserve me. Such was the dichotomy in my life, my hypocrisy no less than it had been in Nigeria. Jonathan, where are you? I could inflict my life on no one else. No one else could make it intelligible.

Then, I suddenly saw that I was not altogether to blame for my hypocrisy. I couldn't take my pain to anyone – except Jonathan – and have it treated with respect. Khassim wasn't from Birmingham or Ballydehob or Boston or Bath. That meant no one considered my pain real pain, valid pain. What did she expect, they thought, with these savages – she must be looking for it. Those are not *real* relationships, they thought – and it's not as if she's *married* after all . . . no man has actually put his *imprimatur* on the situation . . .

In any case, there was no one at all I knew there. Very few people. It was early. I stood, at the edge of the pool, looking in. It was a cloudy morning. There would be a rain-shower. The light was falling at such a slant I couldn't clearly see what was under the surface. People stared. At me in my grubby food-stained, dust-stained, milk-stained, sweat-stained, sperm-stained, around-the-house black wrapper. At whatever I couldn't conceal in my face.

There were black-and-white tiles around the upper part of the pool half above the water, half reflected in it in a broken pattern.

They reminded me of a childhood storybook with a diagram of a design of cubes in steps that shifted even as you stared, concave turning to convex before your eyes. It happened even easier when you looked away and back again –

Look once, look twice,
Look round about –
And in a thrice
What's In is Out.

I walked back to the flat, thinking I had calmed but the blood drummed in my ears as I climbed the stairs. I had to knock and he opened the door with a guarded look on his face.

I walked in and faced him. My voice began to speak though I hadn't told it what to say. I listened with a sense of surprise. This really wasn't what I should say, in fact. "Well, go then. Go now. I want you to go." Cold. Cruel as I could make it. "Go now. I want you to go now."

He turned away and sat and stayed silent a while, then said, "Madame, be patient. For the sake of God, forgive me."

"I said pack and go!"

He stayed silent.

I went into the kitchen and began to bash the kettle around, filling it, clattering it against the taps, slamming it onto the stove. I thought it childish of me but the cold thing in me wanted to do that and worse. A thin ridge of spite glittered like a knife edge in my brain. I lifted the kettle and smashed it against the kitchen wall.

You are wrecking your life.

I went back. "Well?"

"There is something else." Now he was colder, too.

Good. That was what I wanted. Hate felt good. Hate between us, that would be good. I wanted that and thought it could keep me energised until I died. I would hate well and long. It was enough for any life. A better, firmer, harder purpose that any other.

"What."

"Madame, I must have money for the naming."

Bastard. How dare he? I stood, hand on hip, and stared.

"You know I have nothing. I will be shamed before her kinsmen. They are already feeding my children. But after that, if I have not money to provide for the children, her kinsmen might tell me I must take her with me and support her. If that happens, madame, I might have to take her all the way to Agadez and leave her with my kinsmen there and leave enough money with them to feed her. And then I cannot divorce her. For yourself, for your own sake, you must help me."

"You cannot divorce her?"

He stayed silent, staring at the floor.

"You told me you had already divorced her."

He looked up, with a faint trace of surprise. "I divorced her. But of necessity I had to marry her again until after the child is born."

Oh, elementary. How stupid of me. Of course, yes.

I wouldn't let him touch me that night. He insisted on lying beside me but I lashed out at him every time he put a hand on me. Then towards morning I softened and wept and he wrapped himself around me and this time I couldn't say no. But as he moved in me my feeling metamorphosed again and the thought of him moving in Khadija gripped me by the throat and I pushed him from me in such a fenzy that he fell from the bed to the floor and when he rose to his knees and flicked on the light there was blood again on his face where I must have scratched him. I sat up screaming and screamed and screamed abuse at him and screamed until Minha came round-eyed to the door and I covered my mouth and muffled my cries. He grabbed my head and held it to his chest so my cries were muffled, holding out a hand and calling to her gently, "Minha, Minha, come here to Baba! Come!" But she gazed rigidly at us so I freed myself and went to her but she ran from me in terror. Khassim came past me and scooped her up swiftly and she clung to him. He took her to the balcony and I left them and went back in the bedroom and locked the door. Later in sudden terror that he might take her away I got up and went and found them sleeping together on the balcony, she in the crook of his arm.

He came in the morning and lay down with me and made love to me and I lay there and punished him by making no response and he couldn't come and frantically begged me and begged me and begged me to put my arms around him and hold him and I couldn't in pity resist his appeal so I put my arms around him loosely in a travesty of my normal embrace and as soon as he felt even that he burrowed into me and his throat began to vibrate with a rhythm and my arms responded of their own accord and held him more tightly and suddenly his frantic passion moved me and I knew I was going to come after all. But I stayed still and felt the growing sensation of my body betraying me. I held him and lay and gritted my teeth and made not a sound but my groin began to burn with heat and before he came I did, in a sharp violent spasm. He felt it and came pulsing into me.

My body was pleased and sang with triumph but I, that "I" in my brain, would not give in so easily. So I went and got the money for the naming ceremony and the transport money and came and threw it on the bed and said, coldly, "There is your money."

He stared at it dumbly as he sat there and when he

at long last reached and took it I hated and despised him.

Then he swiftly moved around the flat and gathered his things. I felt like taking the sword back from him. The thought shamed me. But I almost did it anyway. He looked out the window. Then moved and picked up his bag. Sideka must be outside at Terminus.

He made as if to come to me and then bethought himself and went back into the bedroom. I moved to where I could see what he was doing. He was taking two of the leather charms from round his neck. He hung them from the brass knob of the bedstead, staking his claim.

He came and kissed me as I stood there and I didn't respond so he drew me to the door with him. "My woman," he said gently. "I will come as soon as possible. Be patient. Trust me. I am your man. Wait for me. But if she doesn't give birth quickly I will send for you and you must come once more to Konni. Do you agree?"

I stared at him like dumb ice.

"My woman, tell me. I need to hear you tell me. Say that you will come."

He kissed me, gazing at my face with pain.

I stayed dumb.

"Sideka will leave if I don't go. He is there at Terminus. I must go." He took a step down the stairs and turned below me, his head level with mine.

"I cannot go until you say you are coming to Konni."

I stood.

"Madame, I cannot move until you tell me you will come."

I couldn't save myself. I was sinking and I couldn't save myself. There was the rope but I could not, would not take it.

Then I saw the tears running down his face.

I stared at him, feeling nothing but a kind of dumb curiosity. How strange! How could he get himself to cry like that when he felt nothing?

He made a sob of exasperation and dashed the tears away. He gazed once more and then turned and started down the stairs.

I said nothing but inside me a voice suddenly was insisting, call him, call him, call him.

He stopped and swung around and leant his head against the wall in despair, the tears coursing down his face again. Seeing him there so broken, against the wall, his hand on his sword-hilt, I was glad, I was very glad. It was really good to see him in pain.

And pity or love moved my heart and another voice came swiftly in behind and said another inch is too far, you'll lose him and I said, "I will come."

I watched from the window as he walked down the road, sword slung over his shoulder, wrist against the hilt. He didn't look back. The dark-green military jeep was waiting down past Terminus. When he reached it he lifted the sword with his right hand and climbed swiftly over the tailgate and into the back, without pausing to greet the occupants. It moved off immediately.

⚜⚜⚜

I went on with my life, stunned and fearful.

I had my period at its allotted time. My temperature hadn't risen at any point. I wasn't ovulating.

The day I realised that, I came back from work a bit too early to collect Minha and stood alone inside the door, listening to the silence.

And in the winter extra blankets for the cold,
Fix the heater getting old,
You are with her now I know
I live alone forever not together now

I went into the bedroom, physically ill with jealousy and loss and fear. I thought, nothing that I had done to Khadija exceeded what she had done to me.

I went in the bedroom and took out the photo she had given me of her smiling self in the western trousers.

I wanted to kill her.

I couldn't do that so I massacred the photograph.

I cannot remember now what I put on it. It must have been red biro. Paint? Nail varnish?

Was it blood? My blood? Did I cut myself and smear it on?

Was it menstrual blood? I don't know. I won't let myself know.

I remember only the colour, the red streaks. I remember the savaged photograph. Her smiling face obliterated in red. A great red core where her heart should be. A great red gash where her womb and genitals should be.

But it was cut, too. And what did I cut it with? A blade? A scissors? My Tuareg knife? What did I drive into her heart? Her womb?

I don't know.

I put the photograph in my cupboard, with my clothes.

Afterwards I went to the mirror and stared and

mouthed my hatred. But I soon stopped, shocked and appalled. A mask stared back at me, the face of a snake, puffy, blanched, venomous, eyes pale and reptilian under heavy lids.

I was shaken. It was the first time I had seen what hatred does to a human face.

"Look. Look. Look," I said to the mask. "Look what this is doing to you. Look what you've been giving yourself to. Look what you've been doing to yourself."

Chapter Sixteen

The following day I stumbled as I walked down the road to get a taxi. I hadn't tripped. My right leg had just gone from under me.

The rest of the day I felt a faint numbness in my right leg and hip, and a slight tingling sensation in my fingertips.

It stayed with me, that sensation – came and went. I went to the clinic. My blood pressure was sky-high. They put me on medication.

I kept on taking my temperature in the mornings, now doing it properly in bed on first awakening. It continued like the *route nationale*, heading due east over a flat plain, with just the occasional zig-zag. It passed the mid-cycle mark and didn't rise.

There wasn't any doubt: I wasn't ovulating. I believed it readily, thinking of the way I had used the diaphragm. Of course there had been something wrong. It hadn't really been possible to use a diaphragm properly with the frequency of our love-making.

So, all that time.

I went to an overweight French doctor at the gynae clinic. He jiggled my breasts smilingly as I sat on the examination table. That didn't take me by surprise because

I had heard of his many misdemeanours with the African women patients.

He looked at my home-made charts and said, flatly: "*Plat.*"

He gave me some hormonal stuff to kick-start my ovaries.

I was weary, weary. For the first time in my life it was an effort to speak Hausa. My mouth felt twisted from talking to foreigners. My throat in a knot. I began to seek out English-speaking friends just to relieve that strain a bit but then that heightened my anguish in the old way. I wanted no part of that kind of life any more.

My heart began to skip beats and flutter faintly and alarmingly. I began to get infections around my calves and ankles. Starting from mosquito bites, several developed into boils which were very painful, slow to come to a head and slow to heal when they finally burst. One developed into such a pothole I could put half a centimetre of my small finger into it. I seemed to be eternally limping now. I reckoned my immunity was shot.

But I hadn't reached the depths, not yet, not yet. I asked myself how I had survived so far. I asked myself if I had survived? Was I still there, all of me?

I could hear Jonathan's voice, Be thankful, you're still holding on in there . . .

I knew, too, that beyond Khassim was an emotional wasteland . . .

And there is nothing left remarkable
Beneath the visiting moon.

My birthday passed. I hadn't celebrated a birthday for years, living as I did with people who had no known birth dates. Colin lured me over to the Terminus with Minha for dinner on the patio with the little rock fountain. I gave it my very best shot and even decided to dress all in green – long-sleeved T-shirt with a plunge neck, green cotton wrapper and green headdress – instead of the eternal Tuareg blue, so that for this one night I broke away from the Tuareg aesthetic. I spent the evening in an agony of nerves at the thought that it was within the realm of possibility that Khassim could walk in. I did enjoy it nevertheless and Colin probably thought we had a great old time but it just heightened my loneliness. I was alone as long as no one could come into the space of my private agony and share it with me.

It never occurred to me to just crack up, break down, give up. I tended my boils and carried on limping. It was so ingrained in me to believe that energy and courage would bring life and triumph. Anything else was despicable.

I went with an American woman named Connie to visit a fortune-teller-cum-medicine-man – he told me I would live to be an old old woman but he said nothing intelligible about Khassim. He gave me various liquids to use in a variety of ways and told me to sacrifice a cock for a solution to my problems. I baulked at the cock bit. I didn't have enough faith to slaughter a poor bird for my purposes. None really.

I preferred to moon-gaze, willing him to come back. I should have asked the medicine-man whether there was a way to summon a living being to you. The Tuareg believed there was: you bury a charm or hang it on a tree.

I walked into the bedroom and stared at the charms he had left on the bedstead. Hanging on a tree.

"*Leaving my children like chickens in the bush to be with you . . .*"

Had Khadija hung her charms on some thorn-tree out there in the bush? Damn you, Khassim. Are the great silences holding you?

I might die of it, I thought, I might just die of it.

The third week the letter arrived – *Come to Konni*.

Sick at heart I started out.

It started before I ever left. I made a last-minute trip to the loo and felt a very faint but familiar sensation when I urinated – cystitis. Disaster. I stood in my kitchen and thought. I knew I should down about two litres of water on the spot but that was impossible with the bus trip ahead. Perhaps I had imagined it. I decided to ignore it as strenuously as I could. We had hardly left Niamey when it began to sting in earnest and could be no longer denied. I hung on, praying for halts and police-barricades. At every stop I abandoned Minha on our seat and shot out and scuttled into the darkness to pee, terrified the bus would move off with Minha in it. By the time we reached Birnin Gaouré I was asking the driver to make stops. I would crouch and force out an increasingly sparse trickle of burning urine. *Barley water, hot-water bottle, bread-soda, cranberry juice* – I ran through the traditional remedies in my head but none were available on the bus to Konni. Between Birnin Gaouré and Dosso I just hung on grimly, my lower belly gripped in the pain of either severe infection or muscular tension. Dosso was the end of the line for me.

As I staggered off the bus our driver thrust a bunch of cards in my hand. Cards of pills. I didn't even have time to thank him or ask him what the hell they were. He drove off shouting, "*Go to the campement!*"

Bloody stranded. I hired a boy to take us to the *campement* which turned out to be no more than a line of stalls, something like a motel. Mosquitos buzzed to greet us as we entered but I didn't care. There was a sink with running water. I paid off the boy, locked the door, tore my clothes off, tied a wrapper under my arms and began to drink gallons of water and shovel in handfuls of the pills which I had now identified as some form of antibiotic. The driver must have had syphilis or something. *Here's hoping*, I thought. Probably give myself diarrhoea or typhoid or cholera from the water. Then, suddenly desperate to pee, I realised there was only an outside loo. I locked Minha in the room and fled. With luck she wouldn't notice the door was locked before I got back. I got to the loo to find it was the French squat-down kind and the light didn't work. I could see a horrific night ahead. I ended up peeing outside on the sand. Back in the room, I found Minha had conked out on the floor so I put her on the bed and lay beside her keeping mosquito-guard. Malaria now is all we need, I thought, and remembered our malaria preventative. Christ. I failed to rouse Minha and ended up pouring spoonfuls of her liquid version messily into the corner of her mouth. Then I took my own tablets.

Great, I thought. Blood pressure tablets, anti-malarials, hormones, antibiotics. Might as well write the suicide note and be done with it.

Unarm, Eros. The long day's task is done
And we must sleep . . .
But I will be a bridegroom in my death, and run to it
As to a lover's bed.

215

Not as long as there was a lover's bed to run to.

What if he had thought I wasn't coming? Had disappeared back into the bush? How could I contact him?

Maybe he had left a message with Abdou, the hotel boy.

I spent a large part of the night rushing in and out to pee on the sand and didn't fall properly asleep until the goats began to cry at dawn and I heard a distant cry for prayer. Minha woke me eventually by pulling at my hair. The bad news was that it was already ten o'clock. The further bad news was that the pressure on my bladder was excruciating. The good news was that when I squatted awkwardly on the white ceramic foot-rests in the French loo to pee, several gallons of warm urine gushed out with hardly the faintest twinge.

We were unlucky with our bus. It had a slow puncture that had to be nursed along and this meant stops to pump it. The spare tire, we discovered, was under the mountain of baggage on the roof. This led to rows between the passengers who wanted to take down all the luggage and change the tire and those who couldn't face the delay. In any case, the driver and his touts had no intention of making the effort to change the tire and on we went at reduced speed, waiting for the blow-out that would kill us all.

We made it to Birnin Konni in one piece but it was late afternoon when at last I stumbled dazed and crippled from the bus. Minha had fallen into a deep sleep and I couldn't wake her and so had to carry her awkwardly almost over my shoulder, cursing myself for not having the buttocks to carry her on my back. *"No buttocks."* I called a boy to carry my bag but baulked at having to ask an African man to carry my child. I staggered on to the hotel, sick with a mixture of apprehension and expectation. We got there to find that it was Abdou's half day. A scrawny young fellow named Lawal with close-set eyes and a shaved head took us to a room. He had no news of Khassim. The room looked like the same one as before but may not have been. I slid Minha, still unconscious, onto the bed, practically shoved Lawal out and made for the bathroom. I sat on the loo, hardly daring to breathe, waiting for the sensation. A trace. Going, going, gone. I shovelled in another bunch of antibiotics and washed them down with tap water.

I was in the shower when the knock came.

I stepped out, shuddering with nerves. I called "*Ina zuwa!*" – I'm coming – in a voice that was steady to the ear, and wound my *zane* around my wet body.

I listened for a moment at the door and from the very sound of the movements outside I knew it was a Tuareg man.

I could hardly breathe as I opened the door.

The silhouette against the sunlight. A dark *tagilmoust* and the glint of eyes.

"Kate?"

It was Husaini.

The disappointment was bitter. I swallowed it down and embraced him.

"Husaini!" My time of reckoning had come. What to say of my desertion?

"*How* did you know I was *here*?"

He didn't answer but passed me smiling and quickly went to the bed and squatted to stroke Minha's head. "Is Minha well?"

"Very well! Who told you I was here?"

He grinned bashfully. "I had luck. I was at the bus station, coming from Zaria. And I met a certain person who was working in ABU before. He saw you leaving the station and when I asked the boys who carry loads they told me where you were."

And, in fact, it was wonderful to see him, to see the grin, the faint tremor of nervousness in the long-limbed movements, the voice with the slight crack in it, all so familiar to me.

"*Ikwan Alla!* By the will of God!" he said. "I've found you."

With a groan, he pulled off his *tagilmoust* and stretched his long length out on the mat, shoving the *tagilmoust* beneath his head as a pillow, wriggling his cheek into it with a sigh.

His hair was a blue-black kinky mass. He had recently loosened his plaits.

"What?" he said, cocking an eye at me.

"Nothing!"

He closed the eye and settled again, with another deep sigh.

That's it, I wondered? No questions? No where are you going? What are you doing? Did he just assume I was on my way to Zaria?

Uneasily, I started to dress.

"Kate?"

"Yes?"

He was sitting up again. I knew him so very well. He was exhausted and edgy. He needed either tobacco or tea. I could feel it from him.

"I feel a need for *shayi*," he said. "You don't have any?"

"Yes, I have some."

"Did you bring your *elbered*?" My teapot.

"Yes, but I don't have a brazier or coals."

"Do you want *shayi*?"

"OK."

"Let me find some charcoal for you." And he got to his feet again and wound his headdress back on in the careless fashion that looped the cloth loosely under the chin and left a circle of hair exposed on top of the head. Bunches of hair stuck out the top. Then, as he reached the door he looked back and said, "Don't run away."

And there was something truly pathetic about that. How could I have reduced him, of all people, to saying that to me?

I went quickly to the door and called after him. "Husaini! What news of Rhisa?"

"He is in Tchin Tabaraden."

"But is he well?"

"Very well!"

I went out on the balcony and called Lawal, the boy, and ordered some food from the restaurant – the same steak and bread and salad I had eaten with Khassim.

I got out my little *elbered* and went and filled it with water in the bathroom. Then I sat and thought, or felt rather than thought. Every instinct told me to hold on to Husaini. The sweet seduction of support and companionship. A lifeline. A gift from God. My means of finding Khassim if he had disappeared back into the bush.

But if Khassim did arrive now we would all be at stalemate.

Husaini came back twirling a brazier with the coals

already lit in it, a smile lighting his face. He picked the still-sleeping Minha up and, sitting cross-legged, laid her across his lap and started to make the *shayi*.

The food came, tasty as last time, and we ate.

I don't know how it was so easy to tell him. Maybe that was a measure of my desperation. I told him after we ate. Why I was there. And his face closed. He didn't ask any questions. He didn't say anything. Just kept on with the ritual motions of making tea.

"Can you help me?" I finally asked, with all the helpless appeal I could muster. "To look for him? He might be at Khadija's brother's camp. Do you know where that is? But I'm not sure . . . it is possible he has moved in closer to the town because of my coming. Can you help me? For the sake of God, Husaini. I'm begging you!" Beg. Think of Ramatu's Juliet begging her father. Raise your hands in supplication. Grovel nicely.

He was silent, tracing patterns on the mat with his finger.

I waited, praying silently.

He looked at me. He was going to speak.

Yes?

"Do you know why Rhisa hasn't come to Niamey looking for you?"

"No." What?

"Because he heard the news about you and Khassim."

"Who told him?"

"It was I who gave him the news. When I went home. Before the time you left Zaria."

"Before! You knew before? How did you know?"

He was fiddling with Minha's hair and not looking at

me. "Since the start I understood the thing that you were doing."

I stayed silent, in a chaos of feelings.

"Then I went to the garden at Bomo lake one night. I saw you together. I stood outside the fence."

"Did you tell anyone?" My voice shook. Khadija!

"I didn't tell. I didn't tell anyone. Until I saw Rhisa at home in Tchin Tabaraden. It was necessary to tell him."

I sat there in a kind of shame and said no more. The image of Husaini outside the fence watching us make love had a nightmare quality. So he had found the gap in our magic circle. How much had he seen? How long had he stayed? How often had he come? I thought of the snake-scarf in the grass in the picture Ronald had sent me. Another image pushed in from the fringes of my brain: the garden with the magic apple-tree at the end of the Narnia book – a black-and-white illustration with the witch-queen lurking behind the tree-trunk. Wasn't that what happened in that story? If you didn't move fast enough when you took the plunge through the pool in the Wood between the Worlds they caught at your heel and unwittingly you pulled them through to your new world.

Husiani had caught at my heel.

The thought of him watching. The thought of Rhisa hearing.

I felt like an adulteress.

Husaini was waiting for some response. I stared at him speechlessly.

What was he waiting for me to say? Had he asked me a question? I couldn't think.

Then he drew a breath and began to speak. "The thing that we will do, we will leave this place and go on to

Elbarka's place in the bush here very near to Konni. They will have news of Khassim . . ."

My heart leapt with sudden hope.

"Also, there is one man who comes to visit a girl there, Elbarka's sister, and he has a Land-Rover. No doubt but that we will find him there this very night and he will help us go to wherever Khassim is. No doubt he will be with Khadija's people."

"But . . . what if Khassim comes here to this hotel?"

"We will leave a message with the hotel boy. But, *en tout cas*, I'll find Khassim and tell him this very night."

That night found us in a leather tent under the stars, with chattering people and goats crying and cool milk from a huge wooden bowl.

The courting Land-Rover owner had turned up, sure enough, and Husaini had set out with him and Elbarka some time before.

Elbarka was a young man who had worked in Zaria. He said he knew me but I didn't recognise him. He was married to a teenage girl called Esalamat and they had a little baby, a tiny girl. I found it painful to look at the young mother. I was horrified to see her withered elongated breasts, so pathetic with her youthful face. That spoke of severe deprivation. Did these people have anything to eat? And here was I, drinking their milk — which I had to do as a courtesy.

I remembered another image from some years before, when I was deep into the desert plains: a handsome young woman sitting cross-legged, bare-breasted on a Tuareg bed, laughing, skin glowing gold in the light of the late afternoon sun that filtered through a mat erected as a windbreak at the side of the tent. She had a little naked baby on her lap and I could distinctly remember her casual pride and joy in him, her lively interest in me, her unselfconscious physical glory.

The contrast with Elbarka's wife was shocking. Tuareg society was fraying from the edges inwards.

We sat outside and I listened with pain and pleasure to the vigorous sounds of Tamajeq being spoken around me. The women played with Minha and joked with me. Esalamat took the single bracelet on her wrist and pressed it on me, telling me that if I gave her some money next day she would buy some plastic thread at the market and weave bracelets for Minha. "*Beautiful* bracelets," she cried, pulling a supple forefinger through her fisted palm in the usual emphatic gesture. Grateful for the excuse to offer some money, I pulled out a few thousand francs and gave them to her.

She took it without fuss, in the proud way they had, and in doing so noticed the bracelets on my arm. She exclaimed at the silver bracelet – Zainabu's bracelet – and then pointed to the three thin ones woven in traditional black, blue with touches of green and red. "Who made these for you?" she asked.

"Khadija." I didn't want to say "Khassim's woman".

"She is able to! Very well!"

I wasn't sure what she knew about the reason for my presence in Konni but, blood beginning to drum in my ears, I plucked up my courage and took the risk.

"Do you have news of her?"

"She is very well! She is staying in the bush. I don't see her. She is pregnant. She will give birth in these days in *sha Allahu*."

"Did Khassim not divorce her before?"

"They divorced." She turned aside and rummaged in a

223

tin trunk until she drew out a small leather wallet. Then she folded the notes I had given her into a small tight rectangle and tucked them inside. Then she said, "But they had to marry again when she made a stomach."

As the night grew more chill we moved inside and sat on one of their low beds – reed matting on a carved wooden framework which broke down into bundles of heavy decorated clubs when they wanted to move camp. At last I excused myself and settled down, with Minha in the crook of my arm. I didn't think I would be able to sleep, in this fever of tension, and I dreaded the long waiting but I desperately needed release from the effort of seeming cheerful. The girl lay beside me with her tiny baby inside her veil.

But I did sleep at some much later stage and woke in joy to hear the sound of the Land-Rover returning. The girl stirred beside me in the dark and raised herself slowly on an elbow. Men's voices. I shook with joy and nerves. Two men squatting at the tent-pole, silhouetted against the bright blue of the night sky.

For the space of a moment which I remembered later with horror, I mustered all my defences and pretences to conceal both my joy and my embarrassment at having to seek him out.

"Khassim?" I said, and for all my efforts my voice carried its wounds clearly.

"It's me," said Husaini.

And that was the precise moment that destroyed me.

The other figure moved crab-like into the tent. It was Elbarka. He moved over to the other bed and lay down at once with a groan of relief.

The girl on my left made no move to join him.

"Didn't you find him?" Bitter fear at my throat.

"We found him."

I stayed silent, waiting. *Husaini, you bastard!* Tell me quickly!

His silver rings glinted in the moonlight where he held the tent-pole. "We went to Khadija's place – away to the north – he was there."

"*To?*"

"He said he is not coming." He moved into the tent and sat by me on the bed, pulling off his sandals. "God, I'm tired," he groaned.

"He is not coming? Just that?"

"Yes. He told me to take you back to Niamey."

"*But he told me to come here!*" I could hear the tiny edge of hysteria in my voice.

"*Kai*, don't worry your head!" I could feel rather than see his smile in the darkness. "I will go back tomorrow and bring him here. If I have to tie him with a rope. Don't spoil your spirit – be patient. *Mai-Landrobel* will be gone to work but I will take a camel." *Mai-Landrobel* – "Land-Rover-owner".

Husaini lay down beside me on the right and, turning his back, settled to sleep. I laid my head where my forehead was just barely touching him, Minha between us. I could smell the heat off his body but even the comfort of his familiar presence did not bring sleep. I tossed and turned in an agony of bewilderment and impatience until the early hours when the dawn was just streaking the sky with rose and the sound of an engine revving up, coughing in the morning air, told me *Mai-Landrobel* had spent the night courting his girl.

I woke in bright sunlight to find the bed surrounded by a

bunch of naked little shaggy-haired kids squatting there all intently staring at me and Minha nowhere in sight.

"What kind of sleep is that, madame?" cried Esalamat laughingly as she ducked under the tent leather, Minha tied to her back. "The day is going!"

She shooed the children away and, poor little breasts dangling, handed Minha over to me.

I looked around. Her little baby was lying in a wickerwork cradle suspended between two tent poles and rocked by an old man who raised a hand to me and greeted me with a hearty, "*Ma tege d-etes?* How did you sleep?" – eyes crinkling at me through his veil. He spoke as though he were bravely communicating with a visitant from Mars. He followed this in heavily-accented Hausa with "Husaini went! Elbarka went!" with two emphatic waves of a hand as if I wouldn't understand the words. "In the morning!" Pointing eastwards through the tent roof presumably to the position of a rising sun. Then "*alam*" with the familiar imitation of a camel's movement, flat hand raised, thumb erect to be the camel's ear.

I spent the long long morning sick to the soul, smiling, racked wth nerves, body in a semblance of relaxation, in a misery of hope. Laughing. Concealing. Heart in throat.

So Husaini had known all along. I remembered his "*Bastard! To do this to you!*" the evening in Zaria I had cried in his arms. Which one of them had he meant after all – Khassim or Rhisa?

It was *azuhur*, around two o'clock, when I spotted the camels loping across the sand from the north. Two camels, not three. No passengers. I still hoped. They drew nearer and I could see the riders were Husaini and Elbarka. My heart sank. Husaini practically rode up on me and, before his camel even knelt, slid off laughing, almost into my arms. I was not in the mood for bravado.

"Did you find him?" I asked sharply.

"No," he said, abashed. "He had already left early this morning, riding a camel. He said he was going to the market in Konni. We waited but he did not return. We will go back in the Land-Rover this evening. We will go as soon as *Mai-Landrobel* comes."

"I will go with you."

"*Kai*, you don't have to come! We will bring him! Without doubt!"

"I will go."

"*To!*" Voice muffled and drained of expression, eyes deflected. I knew the reaction well.

"Was Khadija there?" Blandly. Don't watch their faces.

"Yes, we saw her," Elbarka butted in. "She was cooking a bit away from us. But she pulled her veil down over her face and refused to look at us."

I spent the afternoon running through scenarios in which I encountered Khadija at the camp, all of them violent.

The sun was setting, the men kneeling for the *magariba* prayers, when at last I heard the distant drone of the Land-Rover.

I sat, quivering with tension, joking quietly with Esalamat, while *Mai-Landrobel* joined in the prayers. The prolonged period they spent sitting in meditation after the prayers proper felt to me like a deliberate cruelty.

But when they rose, Husaini exchanged the briefest words with *Mai-Landrobel* and came directly to me. "Let's go," he said, without greeting or preamble, his face serene.

227

We raced over the white plains in the moonlight, thorn bushes and dry grass flicking against the sides of the car. Later the going got more tough and we swayed and lurched over uneven sand, bouncing over rises and wallowing in hollows. The wheels churned in deep sand and made my heart stop. I found myself praying. I didn't think. I willed the Land-Rover on.

When we stopped at last, my fears flooded in with the silence.

We left the Land-Rover at a fair distance from the camp and walked in the white moonlight, taking the distant sounds as our guide. My feet slipped and struggled on the sand. I had never learnt the trick of walking efficiently on sand as the Tuareg did. Husaini saw my difficulty and took Minha from my hip.

When we were close enough to hear a baby's thin cry my nerve failed. I turned away and sat down on the sand, helpless. Nothing on earth could make me walk in on Khadija. I visualised it, full of fear. I had no idea of what she might do, how she might behave but I feared humiliation. I feared that if I saw her I would do violence.

"I can't go. You go. Bring him here."

They went and the sounds of their quiet murmur faded in the clear night.

I began to amuse Minha, letting the sand run through my hands while my thoughts raced.

I had really blundered. I had no idea what stage his negotiations with Khadija's people had reached. Now they knew about me – no doubt Husaini had told them everything. If he hadn't, Elbarka, who knew them well, would have. Now they could put pressure on Khassim for money, as he had feared. Hold on to him so he wouldn't be free to come to Niamey. Refuse to feed the children. Refuse to let him take Yakubu.

I had hung myself.

My ears caught the slip-slap sound of feet in leather sandals. Husaini, Elbarka, two other men. Two other men not tall enough to be Khassim.

I rose.

Husaini picked Minha up and stood aside. He had never left me to stand alone before.

I confronted the men. Older men.

"*Salamu rhaleykum!*" Peace be with you. A formal greeting. But a hostile greeting.

Then, "You are looking for Khassim. He is gone."

"Where?"

"When he heard the Land-Rover in the distance he mounted a camel and rode into the bush."

"But why? Didn't he know it was us? Didn't you tell him it was Husaini who came looking for him today?"

"We told him."

"He knew it was us?"

"He knew. You had better go and leave him in peace."

This was nightmare.

"I refuse. Until I see him."

"Listen. The man has his family here. His woman and his children. Go away and leave them in peace!"

Fury gripped me.

"I have a right to know where he is! I have a marriage paper from Nigeria. He is my husband too!"

There was a silence. I heard an intake of breath from Husaini.

The older of the men stepped forward a little. "We don't know anything about this marriage," he said. "We have no news of it and we don't care about a worthless paper from Nigeria. We know he is married to our sister. Leave him alone."

Now I was frightened. But the humiliation was worse than any fear. Overriding fear and confusion came the need to keep face.

"I will *not* leave him! He is my husband! If he refuses to see me I will come back and he will pay! Tell him that."

"We will tell him."

There was nothing more to be said or done. I turned and snatched Minha from Husaini and walked off, leaving them all standing there.

I stopped walking after a few moments and found that we were alone. I turned in a circle and in that moment found myself lost. Husaini wasn't with me. He hadn't followed me. That was the most desolate fact of all.

I sat on the sand in utter wretchedness.

So here Khassim was, with Khadija. And here he had been all along. In that moment, I forgot about his letters from Zinder. I forgot about Sideka in his army jeep. Suddenly, in my head, he had never been to Zinder. He had never been with Sideka. He had been here with Khadija all the time. While I suffered and went crazy.

Bastard, bastard, bastard. I would kill him. What if I went back now and killed him? I thought of the knife in my bag and wondered if I could do it. Would I have the strength to plunge it in? I imagined it hitting futilely against his breastbone, his ribs or deflected by the cloth of his tunic. Giving him time to fell me with a blow. I thought of his blood spilling on the sand, black in the moonlight. And my little child screaming in fear. I couldn't do it. They could kill me here in the bush and no one would know. I looked around for a stone or a piece of wood that would break his head. I imagined myself beating Khadija's head to a pulp, the people in the camp screaming, holding me down, a knife to my throat. Then they would have to kill Minha too, I thought, forgetting in my wild pain that Husaini was her uncle and she would come to no harm.

No, I would go back to Birnin Konni and bring the police or the military for him. Yes. I growled aloud, startling myself. Minha stared at me and her face twisted into a wailing cry. I reached for her and she flapped her hands and pulled away from me.

Voices. My teeth were chattering. I ground them together to quiet them.

Husaini and Elbarka had appeared as if from the ground and were moving rapidly over the sand towards me.

I got up, possessed with a blind energy, and walked on like a fury before they reached me. Husaini drew level effortlessly and took Minha again. He kept pace with my raging rush until I felt my right leg give way. His hand shot out and he caught me by the elbow. And once again I felt that numbness down my hip, thigh and calf. I leant on Husaini and limped back to the car.

I lay down in utter misery to sleep beside Husaini. Sometime in the night I woke to find his arm about me. At once, in the waking, sick with despair, remembering. I knew he knew I was awake but I instinctively held my breath, playing dead. I stared into a darkness alive with tension. An arm slid under my head and I didn't move. I didn't think.

He made a braver movement and pulled me closer. I listened to the breathing of the other sleepers. It was even, sound, the darkness live with it. A hand on my bare breast, a thumb on the nipple. My breath caught and he must have heard it but still I didn't make any movement. Lips touching my cheek, an infinitesimal movement back and forth. An infinitesimal movement of the hips, to and fro against me. A stop, a waiting. A goat cried. I waited, staring into the blackness of my blind future. Minha stirred and gave a little whimper. Abruptly he sat up and I thought with relief that it was over. Then I felt from his movements that he was taking his *tagilmoust* off. I felt him spread it over us, enclosing me in its perfumed warmth and when he lay down again he was naked to the waist. I felt him push the *tagilmoust* down further with his toes, his thigh crossing mine as he did so, and my hand moved in some small protest against his bare chest. But with his nipple against my palm and the thud of his heartbeat beneath that, something shifted, and I made no further movement. I closed my eyes and stopped searching the darkness. I felt the sting of the tears slipping through the lids and down my cheeks, silently, silently, but I made no sound at all as he moved against me and no movement at all as the hand slid in gentle caresses over all the places in my body that belonged to Khassim. The silent tears kept coming as I heard the little gasp that caught in his throat and with that little cry I remembered that this was my brother, my son, and it seemed right to comfort him. And when he covered me with his body and pushed inside me I did not think of Khassim, nor did I pretend he was Khassim, and I held him and moved with him in little tight movements, helping him to do it without moving, sucking at him with my body where the other sleepers could not hear, burying his little sobs in the crook of my neck when he at last convulsed, holding him as fiercely as he held me, my body at the very last welcoming him with proper joy.

Chapter Seventeen

The following morning he took me formally aside and, voice muffled inside his veil, eyes deflected, told me that he had actually spoken to Khassim the previous night before he had ridden off into the bush. Khassim had said I should return to Niamey and wait for him to come.

I neither believed nor disbelieved what Husaini said. I stored it in that place where I stored facts that were fiction and fictions that were facts. Remembering the notion of "suspension of disbelief" used in literary criticism – or was this suspension of belief?

We went back to Niamey and I grieved. I didn't sleep with Husaini again. I locked my door the first night and every night. He seemed serene and often threw an arm about me in the old way and hugged me briefly when he saw I needed comfort.

I was no longer immune to him. When his laughing face drew close to mine there was a new edge of awareness for me, a sexual electricity in his touch. But that was irrelevant. He was irrelevant, while I ran the gamut of anger, humiliation, bewilderment and desire from day to day and hour to hour. I could not comprehend my loss.

I made myself teach.

I missed my car. None of this would have happened in this way, I thought, if I only had my bloody car! For the want of a fucking nail, indeed. It was true. With the Toyota I would have been up and down that road and had it all sorted out for better for worse long since. Spared myself all this agony. I limped through the sand and dust of Niamey on my weak leg, in my cheap rubber sandals, on my blood pressure tablets and fertility tablets, ground down by heat and exhaustion and despair.

A week after we arrived back from Konni, I met a Californian named Connie who was on the board of directors of the American Embassy Recreation Center. I told her how frustrated I was with teaching and she told me that the American Rec Center, which was primarily a restaurant, was looking for someone to take over as manager. It needed no particular qualifications – all the managers to date were amateurs. The salary was local, unfortunately, but just barely exceeded my university salary. I said I'd think about it.

A few days later, she pushed a note under my door. The Rec Center wanted to do a *mechoui*, a sheep barbecued Arab-style, for the community dinner the following Friday. Could I procure a Tuareg who could do it?

Yes. I was good at procuring Tuaregs.

Husaini and I collected the money from her and bought two sheep at the market. We took them home and stuck them out on the balcony with water and feed and, on the day, an American Embassy chauffeur came to collect us in a huge powerful Rangerover with suspension so soft and deep the rutted streets of Niamey seemed like cotton wool under its wheels. Suddenly we were princes, riding high above the plodding peasants. The psychological effect was extraordinary. We rode through the streets, sheep and all, and my heart lifted a little and I belonged for a moment to a world of power and play and anticipation. All things were possible and death could not touch us in our Rangerover. The Force was with us.

In the garden at the Centre, Husaini slaughtered the sheep with the requisite prayers and skewered them upright in the ground with sticks beside two open fires, to cook slowly. It didn't look as if it could possibly work and the Americans were in a bit of a dither over it, to say the least. But it did work beautifully as we knew it would and Husaini was quite the hero of the hour.

I fed Minha ice cream made on the premises with real strawberries and thought about our short trip in the Rangerover and the unreal feeling of power and play it had given me.

I could do with the lift.

I'd take the bloody job and get out of bloody teaching.

But that little high didn't last. I resigned at the university and signed on for the new job. I started to look for a house. But I was ill with grief to the point where I could feel no more and moved like a suffering automaton. Then, before I actually started at the Rec Center, I got a letter from Khassim with a Tanout postmark and a date I could not read. Telling me Khadija had given birth to a girl. Telling me Sideka had sent a message calling him back east – at last, a solution to our problem had been found. He would soon be in Niamey, God willing. On his way he would collect Yakubu in Birnin Konni and bring him with him. He was waiting now for Sideka to complete some papers for him.

Tanout. Some hundred and fifty kilometres north of Zinder. That was what? Six hundred kilometres east of Birnin Konni minimum. When was this posted? How could he be there? When had Khadija given birth? There just wasn't time. Or had this letter been sent weeks before, *before* I went to Konni? The date was an indecipherable spiderweb.

I was utterly confounded.

I picked up Minha and took a few things, walked straight out of the house, leaving Husaini making tea on the balcony with friends, and travelled the nine hundred kilometres to Zinder.

I remember nothing of the earlier part of the journey but my burning determination. I was alight with it and felt no weariness, no discomfort. I would find this *Capitaine* Sideka. I would find Khassim. I would find out what had happened in the bush at Konni.

That, or go mad with not knowing.

My demons were following me. On the last stretch to Maradi the bus broke down and we spent three hours sheltering under a makeshift tent, the tarpaulin from the bus roof spread between some dwarfish acacia trees. As we at last chugged off, the bus shuddering, a naked madman emerged from the bush, a few rags over his shoulders, his head twisted at a tortuous angle. Between his legs his short penis emerged from one great swollen-smooth ball. He stumbled, begging, in the wake of the bus as we tried to gather speed.

We slept in Maradi in misery, outdoors on benches in the bus station itself.

It was twenty-four hours after we had left Niamey and we were at last close to Zinder when I jerked awake to commotion and the sight of a speeding mini-bus a few inches from my eyes – I had a seat at the back next to the window. Our driver was racing another bus, refusing to be overtaken, along the narrow single-lane strip of tarmacadam. The passengers were thrilled and entertained by this, some few faces full of weary apprehension.

"He'll kill us," I said to the man beside me.

"Truly," he answered with a shrug.

We were going to die. I thought of the fifteen acquaintances of mine who had died on the roads in Nigeria in my eight years there. Now was my turn. Frozen in helplessness. Sweating with anger. The faces around me full of lively interest. A few beginning to shout: *Do you want to kill us?*

On the side of the other bus was the little metal ladder that they used to climb to the roof. I watched it sway two inches from the window of our bus. Watched for the tip, the touch that would send me and my poor precious child spinning into nothingness. When one of these fragile eggshells flipped everyone died. We drew ahead, we fell back. Our driver was cursing the other driver.

More of the passengers were shouting at our driver now. But no one made a move. As if we had no autonomy. We were passengers and not in control.

The ladder swayed towards my eyes, towards the touch that would flip us off the road, reduce us to a bundle of blood and snapped bones.

I thought, not of Khassim or Rhisa, but of my family at home in Ireland and the terrible wrong I was doing them.

But we were slowing. The other bus slipped ahead and slowed. There was a police barrier. We had reached Zinder and had not died.

Shaking with nerves, I stood in the army headquarters.

I had asked the Zarma soldiers at the main office for *Capitaine* Sideka. Hearing me speak in Hausa, they regarded me with a mixture of curiosity and suspicion.

They didn't even say whether Sideka was there or not there. They questioned me as to what I wanted, how I knew him, where I worked. They asked for my passport and visa. I told them I simply wanted to enquire after an Agadez man Sideka knew who had been in Zinder recently. I invented a name for this person.

Without imparting any information whatsoever, not even in their body language, they had put me in an office to wait, for what I did not know.

I stood in the middle of the floor, too nervous to sit, rehearsing what I would say, cursing the fact my French wasn't better.

A long time after a Tuareg officer appeared, in full traditional costume, my passport in his hand.

Sideka? Surely too old? Surely Sideka was an active young officer?

He was wearing a *tagilmoust* of the glittering metallic purple *ilesham*, and was trussed in layers of robes and tunics bound with leather belts and bandoliers. He carried himself in that awkward way they do when caged within rooms, the free stride fettered. The eyes in the fold of the headdress looked hostile in a way that only Tuareg eyes can look when they don't trust you. Eyes, movements, everything wary, shifty.

All my hope died a death as soon as I looked into those eyes and I knew I should not have come.

"You are looking for *Capitaine* Sideka?" He spoke Hausa to me, in that particular half-guttural, half-querulous Tuareg way that is unpleasant to the ear. "He is not here."

"Where can I find him?"

"What is it you want with him?"

"It's a secret matter." Wrong answer. But deliberately so. I needed to break down his reserve.

His eyes grew colder. "He has been posted to N'guigmi."

N'guigmi? On the far reaches to the east towards Lake Chad, the vast lake which was being swallowed up by the sun. I had once been there and I had never forgotten the vision of a line of women in bright cottons dancing in a conga-line in a mud landscape where others scratched in the earth for water. Praying and singing for rain. Like some medieval vision of hell.

This had to be a lie. Sideka had only recently been transferred from Maradi to Zinder. "I must speak to him," I said.

"You must tell me what you want."

"I wanted to ask him about my – a friend – someone *Capitaine* Sideka knows. A man from Aïr."

"What is his name?"

I couldn't avoid it. "Khassim ag Amodi."

"Khassim? Ag Amodi? I've never met him."

"Sideka has met him." I tried again, by dint of not

239

GAYE SHORTLAND

giving information, to convey the fact that there was more
to it all than met the eye.

"What is his *tawshit*?"

I blushed in shame and confusion and despair. He was
asking for Khassim's drum-group, the one vital piece of
information used between Tuaregs for identification. I
didn't know it. I didn't know this intimate and vital thing
about my beloved.

"I don't know."

He stared quite a long while, eyes quite indecipherable
over the glittering *ilesham*.

"Wait," he finally said. "I can call N'Guigmi." And, still
standing, he lifted the phone, using it with the faint
awkwardness of the desert-born man. I was still Nigerian
enough to find this casual use of phones amazing and the
suspicion flashed into my mind that he couldn't really be
phoning N'Guigmi, the ends of the known earth. He could
just as easily be phoning another office in Zinder – or the
office next door, for that matter.

When he got an answer he launched into French so
rapid and guttural that I could not understand it. Then
a few minutes' wait and he launched into muted
greetings in Tamajeq. A rapid exchange followed, only a
fraction of which I understood. I heard him describe me
and refer to Minha, heard him read my name and details
from the passport. Heard a lengthy exchange about
Khassim.

When he put down the phone he said with finality,
"No, he has never heard of Khassim ag Amodi."

I should, of course, have talked to this Sideka or
whoever was at the other end of the line myself. But it

240

would have served no real purpose. The barriers were up. What had I expected? What did they know of me? An anomaly, a red-haired white woman in Tuareg gear who couldn't even speak French, blundering about like a bull in a shop full of land-mines.

I talked, of course, and begged and insisted. I opened my mouth and spewed the whole story out and his wariness went up a few notches. Eventually I begged him to meet me outside the headquarters, perhaps in his home, and the hostility in his eyes rose a few notches more.

In the end, he all but walked out on me, firmly telling me to let the matter alone and go back to Niamey.

I went outside and sat on the ground beneath a palm tree and pulled Minha onto my lap. A little girl approached with groundnuts in little opened tomato-paste tins. I bought a few tins to keep Minha happy and while she ate them I stared at the sand and tried to take stock.

Sideka must indeed have helped Khassim or be still in the process. It was the only thing that made sense. If he had pulled strings for a wanted man, he would admit no knowledge of that. Better again to deny all knowledge of knowing him. I had been mad to try to approach him. The last thing he needed in a delicate political situation was an unbalanced *Takafart* shooting her mouth off. The man was literally and simply risking his life for Khassim. And I was a fool.

And for Khassim's sake, I now had to shut my mouth. What if he were in hiding? Staying with Sideka? Living under a new alias? What I was doing, had done, could be fatal to them both.

I could find the house of this Tuareg I had just spoken to and speak to him outside his official environment. The memory of the look in his eyes made me quail at that thought.

There was no point in going on to Tanout, where Khassin's letter had been posted. He might never have been there. Anyone could have posted the letter. Khassim was most probably somewhere in the bush between Tanout and Zinder.

I could go to N'Guigmi. Madness. Sideka probably wasn't even there. He might be back in Maradi. Wherever. Probably down the corridor in the building I had just left.

For all I knew, the man I had just spoken to might be Sideka himself.

For all I knew, he truly didn't know Khassim because Khassim had never been to see him.

For all I knew in that despairing moment, everything Khassim had ever told me about Sideka had been a fabrication.

I knew nothing any more.

Minha had cut her finger on the rusty edge of the little paste can. I put her finger to my mouth and sucked it clean.

I had shed the last drop of my life's blood on this effort.

Since the torch is out, lie down,

And stray no further.

I must go home.

The *harmattan* dust was thickening the air when I reached Birnin Konni. We were lucky – we found a bus that was almost full. We bought bread and sheets of dried meat and warm drinks and climbed in. Half an hour later we had reached the blessed blessed stage where the driver's touts were clambering around the roof, strapping and covering the luggage. I was already lapsing into a state of suspended animation, an inept chameleon trying to fade into the background, when a loud *"Sannu, Madame!"* hailed me from the door. It was Abdou, the black and long-limbed boy from the hotel, with an armful of baguettes and a basket of mangos. I came back to life with a thud of the heart that actually was a physical pain.

I left Minha curled up asleep on my seat and climbed out to exchange interminable Hausa greetings with him, memories stirring, cleaving to this last little contact with past pleasure.

But as I laughed with him it began to feel more like a step forward – or back – to normality. Here I was, joking with a friendly soul, just as if I were anyone.

If I had turned my head I could have seen the vultures in the shadow, closing in, confident of blood.

Abdou said casually, "You know your friend?"

"Who?"

"The tall Buzu."

"Which tall Buzu?"

"The Agadez man – Khassim."

"Khassim?" He had seen him!

"Yes. Khassim. He who stayed with you before at the hotel."

"So? You have seen him?"

"He came looking for you."

"When?"

"That last time when you came to the hotel."

And everything pivoted.

Look once, look twice . . .

"He came looking for me?"

"Yes."

"But *when*? *When* exactly?"

"The day before your coming. He came late in the evening on a big white camel. *To!* The next day was Saturday and I saw him again in the morning but then I got off work early and I didn't see him again. And I didn't see you when you came afterwards."

"I came Saturday in the afternoon!"

"Yes – you came – they told me. *To!* The next morning after that he came again. But you already had gone back to Niamey."

"I didn't go back! I went to the bush outside town!"

"*Ikwan Alla!* The will of God! We told him you had gone back."

"But I told the other hotel boy!"

Husaini had told him.

"Lawal? That useless bastard of a boy! He has no head! He told him you went back to Niamey! *Kai!* That Buzu is full of wanting you, Madame!" Shaking the head in wonder.

What else had Lawal told him? That I had been in the hotel with a Buzu. That I had gone off with him. Khassim wouldn't have known it was Husaini. He might have thought it was Rhisa and that I was taking him back to Niamey with me.

A chorus of cries, male and female, from the bus. We were ready to go.

"I don't understand. He knew I wasn't in the hotel! He knew the place where I was staying in the bush!"

"*Shiga, Madame! Enter!*" shouted the driver, leaning from his cab.

"No, no, he didn't know, madame! At all! He was looking for you. He said he told you to meet him there."

And did I know what relationship he had to Elbarka and his family? For all I knew there might be sworn enmity between them. More likely than not. For all I knew it might have been impossible for him to go to Elbarka's camp, even if he had known I was there.

I had been utterly stupid to leave the hotel. Why did I?

"*Madame! Enter! Let's go!*" shouted the touts in English, beating with the flat of their hands on the bodywork of the bus.

I saw Minha wake and kneel up on my seat, bewildered, looking around at the strange faces. I climbed in and squeezed my way through the press of bodies back to my place.

"*Abdou!*" I called then, frantic, signing at him to come to the window. He came around. "Did you see him, you yourself with your own eyes?"

"Yes! With my eyes!" He thrust a mango through the window signing that I should give it to Minha, and smiling hugely waved us off.

Our bus trundled and swayed over the potholed surface of the station and made that painful stop at the gate where papers had to be shown to the police and the heart beat in fear that something would be lacking and we would have to go back.

But in the space of the time it would take to say a rapid decade of the rosary the bus shuddered and creaked and groaned and we moved off. I had four hundred kilometres ahead of me to taste that rank thought lurking at the bottom of the barrel: Khassim had come to the hotel. But Khassim knew I wasn't there. He knew I was at Elbarka's place. He knew that because Husaini had told him.

Chapter Eighteen

*L*ook once, look twice,
Look round about –
And in a trice,
What's In is Out.

I arrived back in Niamey to find Husaini gone and
Elbarka in residence in a flat reduced to chaos. Charcoal
and ash and tobacco juice everywhere, indigo dye on all
surfaces including a thick layer in the shower. A disabled
frigo. Someone had taken a knife to the icebox and pierced
the metal.

Elbarka stood in the midst of it all, bare feet in pools of
water spilled on the living-room floor. His hair was
dripping onto his bare chest – he looked as if he were now
cleaner than he had ever been in his life before. "He went
to look for you," said he, nervy and abashed as well he
might be. "He was very worried when you stole yourself
away like that. *Very!* Until I thought a sickness would
catch him. Except that he knew you had gone back to
Konni. So he went to bring you home."

"Why did you not go with him and see your family?"
Dork. Instead of staying here to massacre my fridge.

"He told me I must stay here and wait for you and guard
the flat."

Great job, Elbarka.

Irritation about the *frigo* made me blunt and brave. "Elbarka, when you were in Konni, did you yourself speak to Khassim?"

A brief hesitation. "No, I didn't see him. I saw Khadija – I told you – "

"You mean you didn't see him at all?"

"No."

"Not the first night you went looking for him?"

"No."

"But you said you had and that he had refused to come!"

"No – he had gone to another camp to visit and Husaini went and spoke to him there."

"But what of the night you told me he had mounted a camel and ridden into the bush?"

"No, no, I did not speak to him."

"Why not?"

"He had already gone at the time we arrived."

"But Husaini said he spoke to him!"

A shrug. "Maybe he did. Maybe he followed him into the bush."

"Don't you know?"

"You see, I stayed in the camp greeting the people but Husaini entered into speech with those men who came and spoke to you – Khadija's kinsmen – and they went aside. Maybe he saw him then."

"So you never saw him with your eyes? You never heard what he said?"

"No! I told you! But Husaini told you what he said."

Husaini. And Khadija's kinsmen.

I shooed Elbarka back to Konni – with a money gift, of course.

Four mornings after I woke at dawn and lay there in the bed with Khassim's leather charms still hanging on the bedpost, riding out the wave of bitterness and bewilderment that now always hit me when I woke. *Perfidy.* I checked my temperature. Up. Still up. Too late. I got out of bed and shuffled off to the kitchen to make a cup of tea. My pins-and-needles sensation was still there. My fingers tingled as I waited for the kettle to boil. *I had been lied to but by whom?* Irish tea. Well, French tea. I hitched my Buzu *zane* more firmly over my breasts and went out to the balcony.

When I saw the Tuareg figure sitting at a little distance gazing at the balcony my heart stopped. He saw me at once and got to his feet in one fluid movement. And then I saw it was Husaini. A minute later I heard his *rat-tat* at my door. I stood for a long moment, thinking, then I drew a deep breath and opened it. He was drawn and travel-stained and his usual half-shy smile conveyed something between relief and apprehension. I felt myself smile – I couldn't help it. Then he laid the weighted handgrip of his whip against my neck in mock threat and said, laughing, "Worthless Infidel woman! I have drunk trouble looking for you! You and your child! Better I had stayed at home."

⚜⚜⚜⚜

We were moving from the flat to a house with a garden with yellow mimosa trees and a patio ablaze with purple bouganvillea where Husaini could spit his tobacco juice and dump his tea leaves directly in the dirt and where I wouldn't have to worry that the baby would toss itself off a balcony – when it was born – *in sha Allahu*.

I wended my way through my half-packed trunks and boxes and piles of clothing and stood by the window of the flat, watching, holding the slats of the bamboo blind apart. They emerged from the entrance below me as though I were giving birth to them – with some pain but a lot of love. They took the little turn left around the garden fence and set off down the street. She strutted out ahead of him, self-importance in the bounce of the little pig-tailed head. She wasn't a baby anymore. Hussaini had a hugely amused grin on his face as he followed her, keeping that loping swaying Tuareg stride in check, letting her lead him. It had been her idea.

"*Mama, yau na kai Baba zoo* – Mama, today I take Baba to the zoo."

I had let them go, full of all kinds of fears and trepidations: that she might toss herself into the hippopotamus pool, be mauled by the baboon, walk out under a mobylette. That they might be arrested by the police and deported to Tchin Tabaraden – just for being Touareg.

He had listened in ironic amusement while I cautioned them both at length.

I watched until they had disappeared from view. I remember it distinctly, the minute when the knotted end of Husaini's *tagilmoust* flicked out of sight because at that moment a sigh arose from the depths of my soul and left me and with it something was lost. I realised I must have been crying and wiped my eyes, because I could see the wet black streaks of tears and dust from the bamboo slats of the blind on the back of my hand. I remember going to wash my face.

⬧⬧⬧⬧⬧

I stayed many more years there in Niamey and lived out another life. But in retrospect it seems that, in a subterranean way, my loss of Khassim was the beginning of the end. I was, at some deep level, broken. There, on that level, I still lived somewhere in the nightmare wasteland between perfidy and desire. Khadija had won in the end. I wonder what she lost in the process? I ask this because I sometimes think I lost my soul.

Outside Niamey the sparse grass sang. The silence sang. The sands sang. The veil shimmered. Behind it was the truth.

Pieces of my story continued to fall about me, like leaves from a tree, What use picking them up? Piece them together till doomsday but you can't make a living tree. I let them fall haphazard on that area where I store those facts that are fiction and the fictions that are facts.

These fragments I have shored against my ruins.

Consider this:

"*Did you hear the news of your friend Jonathan?*"

"*No! What news?*'

"*They deported him. Sans valise – without suitcase!*"

"*Why?*"

"*They said he was plotting against the government. They locked him up for two nights and then they took him to the*

251

airport just like that, in the little shirt and shorts he was
wearing, and put him on a plane for London . . . "

Consider this:

Husaini met Khassim in Agadez the following year, in the
cold season. Khassim came to the house where he was staying
and stood outside, armed with sword and bulala, demanding to
see him.

When Husaini went outside Khassim said to him in anger,
"Well, Hussaini?"

"Well, Khassim?"

"What have got to say to me now?"

"Nothing but peace!"

"Is it true what I hear? That you are staying with madame
now?"

"It is true."

"Is it true that you have a child – a son?"

"It is true,"

"It is not possible. Your sister? The mother of your niece?"

"Even so, it is true."

"Is it possible that she could accept a worthless boy like
you?"

And Husaini held up his fist and said, "Do you see this ring?
Do you know it? It is her ring and you know it well."

And Khassim said, with his hand on his sword, "Bastard,
how long before you cheat her?"

Husaini answered: "With you she drank nothing but
trouble. But I – I will be true to her."

With that, Khassim stared at him as if he would go mad.
Then, he turned his back on him and went away.

Is that fact or fable?

I don't know.

Husaini told me the story. It is his fact.

And consider this:

"*Do you have news of Zainabou?*"

"*Sidi's woman?*"

"*Yes.*"

"*Ah . . . she died.*"

"*She died?*"

"*She died. She gave birth again, in the desert north of Agadez and she died. Her mother wept for three days and three nights. It is said that as she died she was calling your name, saying "If Madame Kate were here, she would save me."*"

That, I have grave reason to believe, is true.

In yet another life I had to leave it all behind and they became distanced – like characters in some particularly vivid movie I'd seen. I've hardly thought about them at all in recent years.

Khassim was right. The Tuareg did take up their swords – and guns – again. Here in Ireland hardly any news filters through. A friend in Paris sends me French news reports of massacres by government troops and Tuareg revolt in Niger. I glance at them, file them away rapidly and don't take them out again.

Sometimes I see the them on Sky – last year there was a documentary about the on-going guerrilla warfare. They are dying, squeezed into the palm of the Sahara in the fist of the modern state – the five fingers of Mali, Niger, Burkina, Algeria and Libya closing upon them. I did tape the documentary. That's up in the attic, too.

I've survived. I keep jumping in pools to get back to the

Wood between the Worlds but now I'm wearing the wrong magic ring and land each time in a splashy puddle.

And, as I said, I don't have dreams. Or at least I didn't, before I began this clearing process.

I tell myself it's done with. I've been to the moon and back. It's no part of my life any more. And then my young son puts a graceful hand over his heart or my daughter looks at me with her laughing almond eyes.

Note on orthography:

There is no established system of orthography for Tamajeq.

I have not attempted to observe any strict phonological system in my spelling of Tamajeq names and phrases, preferring to use equivalents likely to convey the correct sounds to an English-speaking reader.

NORTH AFRICA

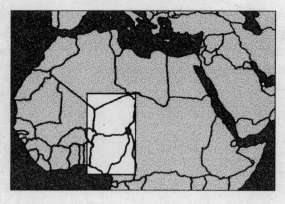

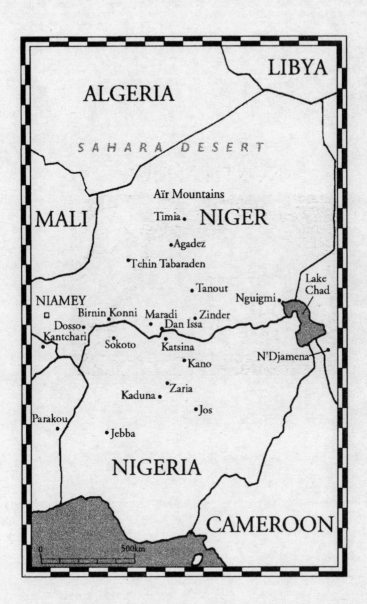